Death Rings a Bell

A Percy Peacock Mystery

By Cortland FitzSimmons

Originally published in 1942

Death Rings a Bell

© 2016 Resurrected Press
www.ResurrectedPress.com

Published by Resurrected Press

This classic book was handcrafted by Resurrected Press. Resurrected Press is dedicated to bringing high quality classic books back to the readers who enjoy them. These are not scanned versions of the originals, but, rather, quality checked and edited books meant to be enjoyed!

Please visit ResurrectedPress.com to view our entire catalogue, and like us on Facebook at Facebook.com/ResurrectedPress to stay updated!

ISBN 13: 978-1-943403-36-3

Printed in the United States of America

Other Books by Cortland FitzSimmons:

Sudden Silence
This—Is Murder!
Red Rhapsody
No Witness!
One Man's Poison

The Ethel Thomas Detective Story
The Whispering Window
The Moving Finger
Mystery at Hidden Harbor
The Evil Men Do

From the Arthur Martinson Series:
The Bainbridge Murder
The Manville Murders

From the Percy Peacock Series:
Tied For Muder
Death Rings a Bell

Other Resurrected Press Books in *The Chief Inspector Pointer Mystery* Series

Death of John Tait
Murder at the Nook
Mystery at the Rectory
Scarecrow
The Case of the Two Pearl Necklaces
The Charteris Mystery
The Eames-Erskine Case
The Footsteps that Stopped
The Clifford Affair
The Cluny Problem
The Craig Poisoning Mystery
The Net Around Joan Ingilby
The Tall House Mystery
The Wedding-Chest Mystery
The Westwood Mystery
Tragedy at Beechcroft

RESURRECTED PRESS CLASSIC MYSTERY CATALOGUE

Journeys into Mystery
Travel and Mystery in a More Elegant Time

The Edwardian Detectives
Literary Sleuths of the Edwardian Era

Gems of Mystery
Lost Jewels from a More Elegant Age

Anne Austin
One Drop of Blood
The Black Pigeon
Murder at Bridge

E. C. Bentley
Trent's Last Case: The Woman in Black

Ernest Bramah
Max Carrados Resurrected:
The Detective Stories of Max Carrados

Agatha Christie
The Secret Adversary
The Mysterious Affair at Styles

Octavus Roy Cohen
Midnight

Freeman Wills Croft
The Ponson Case
The Pit Prop Syndicate

J. S. Fletcher
The Herapath Property
The Rayner-Slade Amalgamation
The Chestermarke Instinct
The Paradise Mystery
Dead Men's Money
The Middle of Things
Ravensdene Court
Scarhaven Keep
The Orange-Yellow Diamond
The Middle Temple Murder
The Tallyrand Maxim
The Borough Treasurer
In the Mayor's Parlour
The Saftey Pin

R. Austin Freeman
The Mystery of 31 New Inn from the Dr. Thorndyke Series
John Thorndyke's Cases from the Dr. Thorndyke Series
The Red Thumb Mark from The Dr. Thorndyke Series
The Eye of Osiris from The Dr. Thorndyke Series
A Silent Witness from the Dr. John Thorndyke Series
The Cat's Eye from the Dr. John Thorndyke Series
Helen Vardon's Confession: A Dr. John Thorndyke Story
As a Thief in the Night: A Dr. John Thorndyke Story
Mr. Pottermack's Oversight: A Dr. John Thorndyke Story
Dr. Thorndyke Intervenes: A Dr. John Thorndyke Story
The Singing Bone: The Adventures of Dr. Thorndyke
The Stoneware Monkey: A Dr. John Thorndyke Story
The Great Portrait Mystery, and Other Stories: A Collection of Dr. John Thorndyke and Other Stories
The Penrose Mystery: A Dr. John Thorndyke Story

The Uttermost Farthing: A Savant's Vendetta

Arthur Griffiths
The Passenger From Calais
The Rome Express

Fergus Hume
The Mystery of a Hansom Cab
The Green Mummy
The Silent House
The Secret Passage

Edgar Jepson
The Loudwater Mystery

A. E. W. Mason
At the Villa Rose

A. A. Milne
The Red House Mystery

Baroness Emma Orczy
The Old Man in the Corner

Edgar Allan Poe
The Detective Stories of Edgar Allan Poe

Arthur J. Rees
The Hampstead Mystery
The Shrieking Pit
The Hand In The Dark
The Moon Rock
The Mystery of the Downs

Mary Roberts Rinehart
Sight Unseen and The Confession

Dorothy L. Sayers

Whose Body?

Sir William Magnay
The Hunt Ball Mystery

Mabel and Paul Thorne
The Sheridan Road Mystery

Louis Tracy
The Strange Case of Mortimer Fenley
The Albert Gate Mystery
The Bartlett Mystery
The Postmaster's Daughter
The House of Peril
The Sandling Case: What Would You Have Done?

Charles Edmonds Walk
The Paternoster Ruby

John R. Watson
The Mystery of the Downs
The Hampstead Mystery

Edgar Wallace
The Daffodil Mystery
The Crimson Circle

Carolyn Wells
Vicky Van
The Man Who Fell Through the Earth
In the Onyx Lobby
Raspberry Jam
The Clue
The Room with the Tassels
The Vanishing of Betty Varian
The Mystery Girl
The White Alley
The Curved Blades

Anybody but Anne
The Bride of a Moment
Faulkner's Folly
The Diamond Pin
The Gold Bag
The Mystery of the Sycamore
The Come Back

Raoul Whitfield
Death in a Bowl

And much more!
Visit ResurrectedPress.com
for our complete catalogue

LIKE us on Facebook for upcoming release announcements!

Facebook.com/ResurrectedPress

FOREWORD

Cortland Fitzsimmons was best known for a series of mystery novels involving sports and other forms of popular culture. It was his novel *70,000 Witnesses: a Football Mystery,* that brought his talents to the attention of Hollywood when the novel was made into a film. He subsequently moved to California where he became a screenwriter with over a dozen films to his credit including *Death on the Diamond: A Baseball Mystery* another novel of his that was made into a movie. He continued to write mysteries throughout the thirties and early forties, some of which involved professional ice hockey, a dance band, and a stage magician. These mysteries were well written, fast paced, and entertaining, and one suspects, at least after the success of *70,000 Witnesses,* that they were written with the potential for adapting them to film in mind.

The two novels featuring Percy Peacock, *Death Rings a Bell* and *Tied for Murder* were written late in his relatively short career. They feature as the unlikely detective a professor of psychology who also dabbles as a summer stock actor. Unlikely detectives were something of a trademark for Fitzsimmons, as he also wrote four novels featuring the seventy something Ethyl Thomas who was anything but a typical old lady in the vein of Agatha Christie's Miss Marple.

For *Death Rings a Bell* Fitzsimmons turned to a location that he had used several times before, a small seaside village along the upper East Coast. One of his first mysteries, *The Manville Murders,* was set on Long Island, and the Ethyl Thomas novel, *The Mystery at the Hidden Harbor,* takes place on an island just offshore. Such settings have long been popular with mystery writers because they provide a clearly delimited area with a small cast of characters who all are well known to each other and therefore provide plenty of opportunities for interaction.

The action in *Death Rings a Bell* occurs in the small Cape Cod village of Chatwich. Some of the characters including Percy Peacock are part of a summer stock theater company, the rest being local residents. Of particular interest to the story is Stryke Ryder, a young member of the company, whose mother, the daughter of the richest man in town had been disowned for marrying an actor, Stryker's father. The story begins with the question of whether Stryker will be reconciled with his grandfather, but things go awry when a woman is found murdered in the cupola of the town hall and the young man becomes the prime suspect.

Perhaps because of his work as a screenwriter, Fitzsimmons had an excellent grasp of pacing, and most of his later works move along at a rapid speed with few dull moments. The events in *Death Rings a Bell* take place over the span of little more than a day ending up with a climactic scene in the theater where Peacock reveals the murderer in a classic summing up of the case before all of the suspects. Along the way, there are plenty of red herrings and recriminations and several more murders making for a very entertaining read.

During the dozen or so years that mark his career, Cortland Fitzsimmons was both a successful author and screenwriter with over a dozen novels and as many movie scripts to his credit, including at least four film adaptations of his own novels. Yet today, he is relatively unknown It is therefore with great pleasure that Resurrected Press offers this new edition of *Death Rings a Bell*.

About the Author
Cortland Fitzsimmons was born in Brooklyn, New York (possibly Queens) on June 19, 1893 and died July 25, 1949 in Los Angeles, California. After attending New

York University and The City College of New York, he worked for some time as a salesman for several book distributors and publishers before turning to writing full time in 1934. Most of his works as a writer were mysteries, a number of which were based on sports themes such as *70,000 Witnesses: A Football Mystery*, *Crimson Ice: A Hockey Mystery*, and *Death on a Diamond: A Baseball Mystery*. A number of his novels were made into films and he moved to Los Angeles to work as a screenwriter. His last book was a cookbook that he co-wrote with his wife Muriel Simpson *You Can Cook If You Can Read*.

About the Cover

The Resurrected Press edition of *Death Rings a Bell* contains design elements from the original hardcover edition.

Greg Fowlkes
Editor-In-Chief
Resurrected Press
www.ResurrectedPress.com
Facebook.com/ResurrectedPress

CHAPTER ONE

MISS NELLIE PINE, who spent her days as fire lookout in the cupola of the Town Hall of Chatwich, was resplendent in a new gray skirt and a bright Roman-striped blouse as she trotted down Main Street as usual—she had never been known to walk in a leisurely fashion. Her movements carried with them a promise of things to come.

Percy Peacock, entrenched behind the honeysuckle on the Tuckers' front porch, looked at his watch. It was five minutes after twelve, but he knew that without looking. Nellie Pine was punctual. She left her roost at twelve sharp, sped down the six long winding flights of steps at the rear of the Town Hall and emerged on Main Street at 12:03 exactly. It took her two minutes to reach her own gate, whisk up her front walk, take the key from under the mat and disappear into her house. Percy knew that at 12:50 Miss Nellie would replace the key under the mat and start back to the cupola.

The screen door behind him opened and Mrs. Tucker, warm and moist from her kitchen, stepped out.

"The season's officially opened," she observed, looking toward Nellie Pine's house.

"What do you mean?" he asked.

"Miss Nellie. She's wearing her summer fair clothes and finery today. Puts 'em on early in June to be dressed for the summer folks who climb into the tower for the view. She was up to Boston last week to buy them. Kind of gaudy, ain't they?"

"But very effective. Is she always in a hurry, does she never move slowly?"

"Not Nellie. I wish there was more people like her. Abe, for instance. Did you see him go by side of the house?"

"No."

"Well I declare! I thought I saw him back to the barn a few minutes ago. Must of been Martin Chase goin' along the road. Folks often mistake them, at a distance. Not that I think they alike. I suppose it's the way they're set up." She peered down the street. "Dinner'll be ready soon as Abe comes from the mail."

"The noon mail is quite an institution, isn't it?"

"I've been married to Abe for a good many years and I've never known him to miss it unless he wasn't able to get up there." After another anxious glance along the street she said, "I've a mind to ask Nellie over for dinner, would if I thought it wouldn't bother her schedule."

As Mrs. Tucker considered the possibility of an invitation for Nellie there was a sharp sound of glass breaking, followed by a cry of fright.

"Land of Goshen! What was that?" Mrs. Tucker gasped.

"Came from Miss Nellie's," Percy said and jumped to his feet. He was off the porch and over the low picket fence in a moment. Mrs. Tucker followed more sedately.

They found Miss Nellie at the rear of the house peering angrily out of a shattered kitchen window.

"What happened?" Percy asked.

"We heard you cry out. Are you hurt," Mrs. Tucker queried.

"No, I'm not hurt and it's no wonder I screamed. A stray shot broke my window, that's what happened." She seemed to glower at Percy for a moment, then turned toward Mrs. Tucker. "It's just a miracle it didn't hit me. I turned for the dishtowel and in it came. Startled me some, it did." Her eyes were snapping sparks.

"Who would be shooting at this time of the day?" he asked.

"I don't know, but I'm certainly going to find out. Caleb Spring'll hear of this. Things have come a fine pass in this town when a body ain't safe her own kitchen."

"Anything I can do for you?" he asked.

"Not now, thanks," she replied.

Mrs. Tucker stood under the window. "Better come over and have dinner with us, Nellie. I'll have Abe put the window in for you after he eats."

"Cora Tucker, you know I couldn't go out and leave this mess. Thanks just the same," she added graciously. "I've his bed to make and all the things I have to do at lunch time. Excuse me." She vanished from the window as if withdrawn by some magic hand.

Percy was smiling as they returned to the porch to wait for Abe.

"The mail's late today," Mrs. Tucker said, as stretched her neck to look through the vines toward the house next door. He followed her gaze.

Abbie Glover, in a cotton house-dress and wide straw hat, was leaning her ample proportions on the Spring gate, talking rapidly and, it seemed, confidentially to Phoebe Spring, the wife of the Police Chief.

Mrs. Tucker seemed to have forgotten about stray bullet and the shattered window, but Percy continued to think about it, marveled a little at their calm acceptance of the supposition that it been a stray bullet. Suppose it had not been a stray? Suppose she had not turned for the dish-towel? He admitted that she would have been dead. He sighed. He was a fatalist about some things. Miss Nellie's number was not up, her time had not come, and by a fraction of a second and because of reaching for a dish-towel she was now probably making Stryke Ryder's bed and mumbling to herself in slowly cooling anger.

The episode bothered him. He began wondering if it had been a chance shot after all. If it were not, it meant an attempt at murder. He smiled. Who would possibly want to kill Miss Nellie Pine? It was a ridiculous idea. He turned and looked again at the two women at the Spring gate.

Mrs. Tucker saw his interest and said, "More than likely she's telling Phoebe Spring all about the Ryder boy. He's been up to see his grandfather at last."

"Has he?" Percy queried politely.

"Yes. Mrs. Verity saw him this morning. She called me to tell me about it. Everybody in town has been wondering if he'd go and when he'd go and what would happen when he did. I'd give a lot to know what Abbie Glover's telling Phoebe Spring, but I wouldn't ask either one of them, not if I never know."

"Miss Glover works for Silas Ryder, doesn't she?"

"Yes, she's done for him for twenty years." She wiped her face with the hem of her apron. "Funny about Nellie's window, isn't it? I've had a feelin' something was going to happen. I don't suppose a professor like you takes any account of such feelings."

"But I do. It's curious, now that you mention it, I've had a sense of waiting for something to hapen all day."

"Well, I never knew men folks had premonitions. I hope it isn't waitin' for your dinner that's botherin' you."

"No. It isn't that."

"And a good thing then. I'll bet that someone's told Abe about the Ryder boy and he hasn't sense enough to come home." She tried to see down the street. "He seems like a right nice boy, Stryke Ryder."

The remark was tentative, thrown at him conversationally for acceptance or denial, with a keep-the-ball-up technique.

"He is," he declared stoutly. "A very nice chap."

"Funny him coming here though," she mused.

"They sent for him."

"Did they? I hadn't heard that. Who sent for him?"

"Mr. Perine, the manager of the summer stock company."

"I wonder if he knew all about it."

"You've aroused my curiosity, Mrs. Tucker. All about what?"

"Land sakes, don't you know? No! Of course, you wouldn't. Here he comes now." She looked off toward a tall young man with corn-colored hair who was striding manfully across the street toward Nellie Pine's gate. "The spittin' image of his mother he is, same hair, same clear blue eyes, same erect way of carrying his head as if nothing was quite good enough."

"He's not like that, he's no snob," Percy declared.

"I ain't aimin' to say as he is. It's the way the Ryders has always been—proud and sure of themselves. She was."

"I presume you mean his mother."

"I do. As lovely a girl as I ever did see. She married an actor. That was twenty-two years ago this summer. Defied Old Silas, he wasn't so old then, but just as wilful, eloped she did, and Silas cut her off completely, disinherited her. I've heard it said that she had a hard time of it, poor soul, but she never came back, not her. She wouldn't crawl on her knees to her father, not if she starved to death. There's some as say she just about did starve. I guess the actin' business don't always let a man eat regular."

"So I've heard. So that's why all the village people are so curious about Stryke?"

"Naturally we've been wonderin'. The boy never has been here before. There was some as said he'd never go near his grandfather, but he did it this morning. He's been in town a week and more. I'll give him credit for taking his time. They can't say as how he rushed up there to try and get some of his grandfather's money."

"He wouldn't do that."

"If he's like his mother, he wouldn't. Miss Nellie says he's very nice and clean as a hound's tooth. Don't need no pickin' up after him."

Percy laughed. "I'll try to be a little neater, Mrs. Tucker."

She smiled. "I didn't mean it for you. I've been pickin' up after Tucker for thirty years and it just comes natural to me."

A big sport roadster slid to a grinding stop before the Spring gate and a voice shouted at the two gossiping women, "Has Silas started his nap yet, Abbie?"

"Eben Ryder, you know perfectly well it's past noon," Abbie retorted, with a note of annoyance in her voice.

Mrs. Tucker pretended to pull a few dead twigs from the vine as she cocked her ear to take in a that was being said by the group.

"Hello, Phoebe," Eben called. "You're still beautiful as ever."

"And you're still a lyin' fool, Eben Ryder." Phoebe retorted and laughed nervously.

Percy leaned forward. Eben Ryder was a handsome man, probably sixty and dressed in the best "Esquire" manner. He laughed, waved his glove hand. The car zoomed away with a roar.

"That's Silas Ryder's brother, never did amount to much, lives up Boston way. He's the father of Henry. You've seen Henry around paintin'. He's sulky. Always looks as if he was mad at something but I figure it's his stomach. Indigestion, if it's chronic, does things to people's faces. Show me a sour face and I'll show you a sour stomach. Henry does boats and sand dunes. They say they're right good." She looked after the vanishing car. "Eben must have heard about Stryke Ryder being here. Henry probably told him, although there's no love lost between that father and son. Henry's more serious. They say he'll get all the Ryder money, but I wonder if he will now that Stryke is here."

"Stryke's name shouldn't be Ryder," Percy said.

"No. It ought to be Merriweather, that was his father's name. We don't know why he's called Stryke Ryder. There's some as say she was never married, but I don't believe that. If she decided to call him a Ryder, she had a good reason for it. She probably changed his name after Merriweather deserted her."

"What did Miss Glover mean about it being past noon?"

"Silas has his lunch about 11:30 and then the house has to be quiet. He sends Abbie out every day rain or shine, and she don't dare go back home until after two. Here comes Abe now and a good thing. The fried clams won't be fit to eat." She hurried into the house.

Percy did not agree with her about the clams. He found them sweet, tender and delicious. "Stryke's been up to see the old man," Abe offered.

"We know all about it," Mrs. Tucker said. "Was you up there?"

"No, I didn't have time this morning."

"But you said—"

"I said I'd go if I had the time, and I didn't."

"We're buying this place from Silas Ryder," she explained to Percy.

"Yes," Abe agreed slowly. "That's why I asked you if you'd be willing to pay your board in advance. I've about got the money now and I want to see the old man and have it settled."

"I wish you had gone like you said you would," she said.

"There's no rush," he retorted angrily.

"I don't know as there is. I just feel you should have gone. He's an old man. What if he should die before we get things settled? I don't want to live anywhere else, Abe."

"He won't die," he mumbled over a forkful fried clams. "I'll go up there this evening."

Percy learned more about the Ryders duuring dinner. Heard that Stryke had been on his way to the Cape before they telegraphed for him, that Libby Powell had brought him to town and Nellie Pine's house.

"So that's how the romance started," he said

"If it is a romance. Why do you suppose he's coming here?" Mrs. Tucker queried thoughtfully.

"Well, if he wants to get on the right side of grandfather he'd better not take up with an actin' woman. It won't make no difference to Silas that Libby's a Chatwich girl. It's bad enough for the boy to be an actor without going and falling in love with one," Abe offered, as he shoved his chair away from the table.

The meals were good at the Tucker house, but eating was a job to do as part of the day's work. The gracious charm of loitering at the table had no place in the Tuckers' scheme of living. When food was eaten there were other things to be done and no time for nonsense.

Soon after 12:30 Percy was back on the Tucker porch. The life of the village had always intrigued him, but now he was doubly interested. So Stryke Rider's mother had been a Chatwich girl and he had been to see his grandfather that morning. And Stryke, an actor, was in love with Libby, an actress. Percy had rather suspected an affair between the darkly brooding Eve Knight, a member of the company, and Stryke, had heard about them in the group, but Stryke had no particular interest in Eve since his arrival in Chatwich.

Stryke came out of the Pine front door and went down the walk. Percy admitted that he was a handsome lad, just the type to turn any girl's head. He made a mental note to get in touch with his friend Peter Corbin, talent scout for one of the big studios back in Hollywood. He decided Stryke was good material to become a picture heart rave.

Percy found himself imitating Mrs. Tucker as forward to peer through the vines. Stryke Ryder and Eve Knight had met at the Tucker gate and he could hear every word they said.

"Have you finished your lunch already?" Eve asked.

"I'm not hungry today, Eve," Stryke replied.

"Come up to the Ryder House and have a cup of coffee with me," she invited.

"I couldn't, Eve. I've had all the Ryder I want for the present. I'm in a bad mood today."

"Today?" she repeated.

"All right, have it your way," he said tersely.

"What has happened to us, Stryke? Why can't we be the friends we were?"

"We can be friends, I guess," he said uncertainly.

"You haven't been civil to me since you came here. Why?" she demanded.

"I thought I had been." He seemed genuinely surprised.

"Well, you haven't. It's that—"

"Wait a minute," he cut in. "If you mean Libby Powell, you might as well know that I've asked her to marry me. I'm in love with her."

Percy saw Eve sway ever so slightly, as if she had been mortally wounded. He admired the way she caught control of herself and said, "Are you? Is it the real thing this time?"

"The real thing," he repeated.

She put out her hand. "Okay, Stryke. I hope you two will be very happy. Shake on it."

Slowly the boy took her hand. He seemed a little embarrassed. "Gosh," he said impulsively. "Thanks, Eve. She won't marry me now, but we're as good as engaged. It's white of you to take it like this. I didn't know how to tell you. I guess I was a little afraid."

Percy sat back. He didn't want to hear any more. It was too intimate and personal between them, but the street was quiet and their voices were clear and distinct.

"Why should you be afraid of me, Stryke?" Eve asked, and there seemed to be a sharp edge to her voice. "You didn't think I'd tell Libby about us, did you? You didn't think I'd try to hold you, not after this? Aren't you afraid of Libby, rather than me?"

Look, Eve. It was just this sort of thing I was afraid of. I feel like a heel, don't rub it in, will you? I think you're a swell girl, but I'm not in love with you. I'm sorry."

"That's fine, Stryke." She turned, went quickly to the Spring gate, up the path and into the house.

Percy felt sorry for her, realized as she stumbled just before she ran up the first step that she had been crying. He realized something else too as she vanished inside the house. Eve Knight was wearing a shirtwaist exactly like Miss Nellie's. At least it seemed to be a duplicate to him. It was a striped affair of gaudy colors and seemed much more becoming to Eve because of her dark coloring. He had heard stories of the feeling between women when they appeared at a party in identical dresses. He fell to wondering if the Roman-striped shirt waists would affect the rather odd friendship which had sprung up between the two women. They were so unlike. Eve was a cosmopolitan while Miss Nellie was the typical product of her environment. He wondered what they talked about during those hours when Eve climbed to the cupola. Some of the members of the company suggested that Eve was going native and was going to take Miss Nellie's job away from her. Whatever the reason for Eve's trips to the cupola, the two women were friends. He had often run up the steps to warn Eve that she was wanted for rehearsals.

He turned and watched Stryke moving slowly along Main Street toward the center of the village. He thought he knew what Stryke was feeling. The boy was young and handsome, had undoubtedly thought at one time that he was in love with Eve. Percy knew that phase of adolescence so well. He had fallen in love with an older woman himself--all boys do, or at least Percy believed that ninety-nine out of a hundred did.

Percy left the porch and followed Stryke down Main Street. He paused for a moment to listen to the chatter of some Portygees who came out of the chain store, and turned toward North Chatwich. He looked up and saw Martin Chase's feet on the windowsill of his law office over the barber shop. He saw Stryke standing at the entrance to the Town Hall, brooding and smoking his pipe. Some summer people drove up to the grocery store in a station wagon. Percy went into the drugstore to look over the magazines.

It was about 12:45 when Stryke came in, slid onto one of the stools at the fountain and ordered a chocolate malted milk and a deviled-egg sandwich.

Charlie Snow made some remark about the weather as he prepared the drink and put it in the mixer. Abbie Glover came in and hoisted her two hundred pounds to a stool and ordered a malted milk. If she saw Stryke she gave no sign of recognition.

Stryke was eating his sandwich when Eben Ryder breezed in. He wore a loud checkered coat, his throat was hidden by a silk muffler, and a soft rakish hat was pulled back just enough to show his white curly hair.

"Hiya, Charlie. You're good for sore eyes," he called and then spied Abbie. He walked over and gave her a pat on the back. "Hiya, Beautiful, aren't you afraid of getting fat?"

"You get along," she said.

Percy pretended to be absorbed in the magazine, but he was fascinated by the possibilities of the scene about to be played before him. Eben's hand still rested on Abbie's back.

"Get along," she said, and wiggled her shoulders to rid them of his hand.

Eben slid onto a stool at her side. "I had hoped to get here in time for lunch, but I couldn't make it."

"Too bad you didn't," she said. "There's clam pie up there that's never been touched. I wouldn't eat this noon, what with one thing a another." She cast a withering glance in Stryke's direction. "You can have it for your supper."

"I won't be here," Eben said. "Say, where's Henry today?"

"Said he was going to New Bedford to get some paint and things."

"Why, here he is now. Where have you been, son?" he called as the door opened.

"New Bedford." Henry clipped the words out He ordered a tonic and glanced down the count toward Stryke. "It's practically a family reunion, isn't it?"

Percy was conscious of Henry's sulky sourness, which Mrs. Tucker had described so well. Eben looked at his son with surprise.

Abbie sniffed. "They ain't met," she said. Henry called to Stryke. "This is my father, he's some sort of a relative of yours, uncle, I guess." Eben slid from the stool and moved toward Stryke. "You're Caroline's boy."

He extended his hand, but stood back as his eyes quickly appraised the handsome lad, who accepted his greeting.

"You're a Ryder, all right. I should have recognized you. You're the spittin' image of your grandfather at about the same time he had his ship. I remember him so well, tall, blond and handsome. I used to think he was a god."

"You've got over that," Abbie snorted.

"Seen the old man yet?" Eben asked Stryke, with a wink in Abbie's direction.

Stryke nodded.

"His bark is worse than his bite," Eben offered consolingly.

"His bite's bad enough," Abbie said.

"I'm glad you went to see him," Eben said and patted Stryke on the shoulder. "He's proud, but he's been very lonely. He missed your mother more than he'd admit."

Henry watched his father and Stryke with acid contempt.

"Henry is not a Ryder," Percy thought. "He's too dark, too surly-looking. This Eben and Stryke have the same coloring, they have personality."

"So you're an actor," Eben rambled on. "Well, well. I suppose you know all the good-looking girls." He gave Stryke a knowing jab in the ribs. "Say, I saw you talking to a dark girl a little while ago. Who is she? I'd like to meet her."

Stryke's low answer was lost in the commotion caused by the arrival of Sidney Stone, a house painter. He was white and cheery in his overalls and little peaked cap which accented his sharp nose and narrow eyes.

Percy knew about Sidney Stone. Mrs. Tucker had told him about Sidney and Miss Nellie. He took a good look at the man. Sidney was of medium build and rather slim. His little sharp eyes darted about the store, took in the group at the counter with evident satisfaction. A smile settled over his features. Mrs. Tucker said he was a gossip, could spread news, good or bad, faster than any ten women. "Sees a lot," she had said, "painting around the way he does, and likes to talk. I'll say this for Nellie, she probably knows more about what's going on in this town than anyone else, but she's no hand for talkin' about other people's business whereas Sidney tells all he knows. He still thinks Nellie will marry him some day, but I doubt it very much. Nellie likes to be independent."

Sidney moved up to the counter and then pretended to see Eben for the first time. "Hiya, Eben? Who you chasin' now? He laughed at that, looked about for companion smiles. Charlie tittered. "Oh, it's Abbie here. Been treatin' her, I see."

That brought a short hard cackle from Charlie.

"You see more than is good for you," Abbie retorted. "I pay my own way, askin' nothin' from nobody." As if to emphasize her independence, she slapped her money on the counter with a resounding click.

"What's that about your neck?" Eben asked and pointed to a thin leather strap which Sidney wore jauntily.

While Sidney lifted a pair of binoculars out of their case, Attorney Martin Chase and Clyde Perine, the the actor-manager, came into the store, followed by Abe Tucker. Abe peered about, spotted Percy, walked to him, and thrust a letter at him.

"Forgot to give it to you this noon. Too much talk."

"Thanks." Percy took a quick look at the envelope and said, "It's not important." He was too interested in the people in the store to stop to read a business letter. He dropped it into his pocket. Abe sensing his interest followed his gaze.

Martin Chase took a package of gum from the rack and threw down his nickel. Martin was the town lawyer, owned about everything in the village, including the drugstore, ran the Ryder House and seemed to be the man behind the theatrical venture. He was known as a silent man, rarely woke unless he was spoken to, never paused for idle conversation.

Perine bought a pack of cigarettes. Percy saw Eben's eyes roam over Perine in a searching way as if he were trying to recall a previous acquaintanceship, but Perine showed no recognition whatever.

Sidney Stone had the binoculars out of their case and was about to answer Eben's question when he saw Abe Tucker approach Martin Chase. He cocked an ear to listen. Abe's voice was clear as he asked, "You got those papers made up, Martin?"

"No," Martin replied tersely.

"But, he said—" Abe started to remonstrate.

"Things have changed."

"You mean to say he ain't going to sell me the place?" Abe's voice rose in anger.

"I don't know what he's going to do. I'm to see him later this afternoon," Martin replied.

Percy realized that Abe and Martin were the same shape and build, were probably related through some common ancestor.

"If I find this is some of your work I'll . . ." Abe did not finish his threat. He said forcibly, "I'll see him myself. He can't do this to me."

Abe's face was a puzzle to Percy. Martin shrugged and turned away. There was a second of complete silence in the store and then Eben's voice prodded at Sidney. "You haven't told us about the spyglasses," he said, as he winked at Charlie.

There was a snicker because of the word spy but the implication did not bother Sidney, who said proudly, "I'm painting the steeple of the church across from the Town Hall. While I'm up there I might as well have a look around the countryside and know what's going on. There's no point in giving the exclusive rights to Nellie Pine. She sees everything anyhow."

"How's the country look, or haven't you tried them out?" Eben asked.

"I went up a spell before noon today to test the boatswain's seat and the glasses too. The countryside's allright." He turned to Stryke. "I saw you too, dangling from the steeple," Stryke replied, "but I didn't know I was under inspection."

"You was," Sidney said smartly. "Nellie seen you too. We compared notes, we did. I waved and pointed and she nodded her head."

Abe, who had been standing like a man trying to make up his mind about a future course of action, turned and strode out of the shop. At the door he paused and asked, "What time you goin' up there? We might as well go together."

"I wouldn't recommend that," Martin said. "We've got business to discuss."

"So have I." The door slammed behind Abe.

Eben Ryder turned from the counter and approached Perine. "My name's Ryder, Eben Ryder. Seems to me I must have met you somewhere."

Perine in tweeds was a fattened echo of a matinee idol. He smiled professionally. "I've been of the theatre and the screen for many years. People often make such a mistake."

Abbie grunted. There was contempt in the sound not only for Perine and his profession but for all actors. She slid from her stool.

"Watch your calories, Abbie," Eben called after her and chuckled.

"And you mind your business instead of insultin' people," she threw back as she paused at the magazine stand next to Percy and looked rather wistfully at a copy of *Romantic Stories.*

Martin Chase, who had remained aloof, eyeing the group like an old owl, turned and left the store as Sidney replaced his binoculars in their leather case.

"Look out you don't get yourself into trouble with those things, Sidney. Remember what happened to Peeping Tom in Coventry," Eben warned.

"Huh!" Sidney scoffed.

Stryke Ryder left the counter and approached Perine, saying, "I'd like to talk to you."

"I've an errand I must do now," Perine evaded. "Later. Don't forget the rehearsal is called for 1:30." He moved to the door, stepped back with a sweeping bow as he gallantly held it for Abbie who waddled through, a copy of *Romantic Stories* under her arm, a chocolate bar in her hand.

"I'd like to know who he is," Eben said though fully, looking after Perine, who was crossing th street. "His face puzzles me."

"You'd be the same way about Barrymore," his son Henry sneered.

Eben shrugged, dug into his pocket and handed Stryke a card. "When you're in Boston, look me up. I'll show you the town."

"And he's the boy who can do it, too," Sidney chimed in. "Yes, sir, he was always one for the girls." He gave a dry hard laugh, looked across the street.

There was a flicker of color at the main entrance of the Town Hall, a flash of a Roman-striped blouse.

"Well, there goes Nellie Pine. It must be close to one o'clock and time to be gettin' back to work," Sidney remarked, with a verifying glance at the clock.

Stryke thanked Eben for his invitation and left the store. Eben and Henry had a few whispered words together, their eyes on Stryke's long slim figure as it crossed the street.

Percy moved away from the rack, paid for a magazine and went outside to stand in the warm sun.

CHAPTER TWO

SIDNEY STONE was known to have been Nellie Pine's perpetual beau for about twenty-five years. Sidney gossiped a great deal, drank a little, gambled some and smoked incessantly. Miss Nellie did not approve of his vices and so during the years had preferred the relative security of spinsterhood and her job to the doubtful blessings connected with being Mrs. Sidney Stone.

Sidney had been heard to say that when Nellie got so old she couldn't work he'd marry her an take proper care of her. That thought seemed to satisfy him; it did Nellie no harm and doubtly gave her some slight sense of old age companionship if not security.

Sidney left the drugstore, stopped a moment to chat with Percy, who had lit his pipe and was thinking about the opening act of the comedy drama he had witnessed in the store.

"All that talk in the store must have been interestin' to you," Sidney suggested as he picked at his teeth with the blunt end of a match.

"All people are interesting to me," Percy said.

"Just what do you teach, anyhow?" Sidney asked bluntly.

"That would be a long story, Mr. Stone."

"When I heard what you was I looked it up in a book and it said it was a science of the mind. What does that mean?"

Percy laughed. "Briefly, I'd say psychology was the study of our mental functions both conscious and subconscious which when in operation make us tick, make us what we are, make us do the things we do."

"Oh," Sidney said and sauntered across the road.

As he entered the churchyard from the front he saw Stryke Ryder come out of the side entrance of the Town Hall and cross to the churchyard.

"If you're looking for the Ryder plot, that's it over there in the corner behind those yews."

They weren't yews. It was a juniper hedge, but that made no difference to Sidney, who paused for Stryke to come abreast of him.

"How'd you make out with your grandfather?" he asked bluntly.

"What would be your guess?" Stryke countered.

"Well, I'd say the old man wouldn't give in none. He's powerful strong-minded. Funny your coming here, ain't it?"

"I suppose so," Stryke agreed.

"Been an actor long?"

"All my life," Stryke replied.

"Too bad your mother can't be buried here," Sidney said. "Seems as if she ought to be. All the Ryders that ever was, except those lost at sea, are buried in there."

"Some people are lost who never go to sea," Stryke answered and walked on.

Sidney was pondering that as he went into the church and started up stairs. From the bell gallery where he stepped out onto the first tier of light scaffolding, he saw Stryke. He climbed up the tiers until he reached his boatswain's seat from which he would paint the top of the tall spire. The pulleys sang as he tugged and pulled at the rope. He went up past the tops of the maples and looked down through a curtain of green leaves, saw Stryke standing in front of the tombstone of his grandmother Caroline Ryder.

Sidney went on up the tall steeple, unconscious of the quiet beauty beneath him. It was just the Cape, something he had known all his life, a familiar scene. A ribbon of road snaked through cranberry bogs between ponds. At the edge of pine wood stood the Ryder place, snuggling close to the earth, quiet and peaceful as a cat sleeping in the sun.

It was a clear day. Far away, following the hoot of the Cape the white shingle of shore along the bay was visible. Behind him the Port clung to the irregular shore, with white spires piercing the green mat of elms and maples. It was a good world, green gently swaying treetops. Underneath that protecting mantle people he had known all his life were moving about. He thought again of the scene in the drugstore and chuckled.

He looked about to see what people were doing, peered through the open places in the foliage. This was something that interested him, people. He was familiar with the scenery just as he was familiar with the great bulk of the building opposite him. Ryder's Folly was the local name for the Town Hall. It had been built by Silas Ryder's father as an investment. It was colossal for the Cape. The main floor housed a grocery and dry-goods store and in the rear several town offices, and the square stairwell. A T-shaped hall divided the building, separating the two stores one from the other and dividing commerce from official business.

The second floor was devoted to the theatre orchestra pit and stage and was completely equipped for modern productions. The third floor contained the balcony and the upper reaches of the stage.

The fourth floor was a combination of skating rink and dance hall. Above it was a floor set aside for bazaars, socials, etc.

The sixth floor was mainly attic, with trusses and joists, and storage space tucked between construction arches. Towering above the mass of the building was the cupola, reached by a circular staircase. It was in the tower room that Nellie had spent so many days of her life.

Sidney was thinking about the building as he jerked himself aloft, because he was thinking of the Ryders, of Stryke down there in the graveyard, Eben down from Boston and Henry back from New Bedford, of the two men whispering together in the drugstore, probably wondering, just as he was, about Stryke's meeting with his grandfather and what it would mean.

No one had known except perhaps Martin Chase, and he wouldn't tell what old Silas would do with his money, but it was generally believed that he would leave the bulk of the estate to young Henry, who was a sober-minded citizen, close with his money and not at all like his gay and debonair father.

It would make quite a difference to Eben and Henry if the old man suddenly decided to leave his money to young Stryke and him an actor, too. Well, funny things had been done by men like Silas.

Sidney admitted that Silas was smart. No one fooled the old man. He had captained his first ship when he was twenty, had sailed the seven seas, had made money and had been sharp and shrewd about his investments. He had been very smart to give Ryder's Folly to the town of Chatwich. There had been protests in town meeting, but Ryder had considerable taxes.

Sidney was pleased with the increased activity in the town. The company of actors provided food for talk. Percy Peacock, too, was an interesting subject of conversation and conjecture. Why should a man teach school for nine months of the year and then spend the remaining three as an actor? Peacock was the only person who could answer the question, and he had given no definite reason.

And then to top everything, Stryke Ryder had appeared as the young leading man of the company, and the whole village had waited to see what would happen when the boy and the grandfather met. Abbie Glover was probably the only person who knew, and if he waited he would undoubtedly find out, if not from her, then from Phoebe Spring. He could wait and he was determined to know.

He had almost reached the top of the spire and would soon be parallel with the cupola and could wave jauntily to Nellie, who would be sitting at her little table with the south shades drawn against the glare of the hot midday sun.

He looked over toward North Chatwich, where the small cottages of the Portygees gleamed white and bright in the glow of the sun. His eye followed the branch spur of the railroad which had for years provided train service to the offshore. It was abandoned now, and the rails were gray-black threads.

His eye followed the tracks, past the old town cemetery to a point just beyond the church, where they crossed the Webster Road a hundred feet or so behind the Town Hall and went through a cut in the knoll on Abe Tucker's pasture land.

He leaned forward and nearly lost his balance. Excitement filled him. Abe Tucker's cow, a vile-tempered beast, lay on her side just within the railroad cut. Her calf stood forlornly at her side. There could be no doubt of it. Abe Tucker's cow was as dead as she ever would be. Sidney tugged at the rope until he was even with the cupola, made himself fast and then waved his arms frantically to attract Nellie's attention. She could telephone Abe to let him know.

He couldn't see Miss Nellie. She was probably bending down, putting away or checking her old reports. He went up another foot and then looked.

It wasn't like Nellie Pine to be taking a nap in the middle of the day. He looked again, unable to understand it. Quickly he pulled his binoculars from their case. This would be a good one to hold over Nellie's head. Asleep while on duty. He chuckled to himself as he adjusted the focus. He looked for a long minute. His hands trembled. He looked again. Miss Nellie Pine was slumped over her work table. He could see the stripes of her gay blouse, but he could see more than that, for a dull stain covered her back and oozed out on the table beside her.

For one full minute he refused to believe the binoculars. He looked with his naked eyes, squinting against the glare of the sun on the white sides of the massive building. His teeth began to chatter. He had to use the glasses again. His hands trembled, his body shook. Nellie Pine was just as dead as Abe Tucker's cow, of that he was positive. He reached for the case, but his hands were so twitchy that the glasses slipped and dropped. They hit the steeple below him and caromed off into space.

He looked down, watching their flight, gasped and very nearly fell from his perch. He loosened the hitch and started to lower himself to the scaffolding. It couldn't be. In that fleeting glimpse below he thought he saw Nellie Pine run out of the side entrance of the Town Hall.

He rubbed his head, thinking he was suffering from a touch of the sun. Either the shock was making him imagine things, or he had seen Nellie's ghost, or . . . He went back up the steeple. The body still slumped over the table and yet he was sure he had seen Nellie dart out of the door below. He blinked. There was something new in the cupola now, misty curls of smoke moving up, filling the little room, clouding the windows like suddenly released fog.

Forgetting all caution, he let the rope slide through his hands and made the top scaffold. He couldn't let Nellie burn up there in that cupola, dead or alive; perhaps she had only been wounded.

In his confusion he knew that he had seen smoke, that there was a fire somewhere under Nellie, and things must happen fast. That massive old wood structure would burn like a tinderbox. The town must be alarmed.

He slid into the bell loft and rocked the great bell, pressed down hard, released the rocker bear and let it clang out to warn the village. He stood in the opening to shout the alarm, because he knew someone would want to know why the bell was ringing. He gripped a beam in cold terror as the bell rocked and clanged behind him. He had seen Nellie Pine's ghost running toward the firehouse which was behind the Town Hall. The ghost flittered just as Nellie did, with those same trotting steps. The next second the fire siren bellowed, joining its voice with that of the bell. Sidney swayed and clutched at the beam for safety and sanity too.

There could be no doubt about it. Nellie Pine had been a fire lookout for so many years, had been so conscientious about her work that even now in death her spirit had warned the community. Yes sir! That was exactly it. He had seen the ghost Nellie Pine as it hurried to turn in the alarm which even now was moaning and bellowing a dirge to Nellie and a warning to the village. A little more sure of himself, he cramped his leg around the side of the ladder and slid into the excitement.

CHAPTER THREE

VOLUNTEER firemen, summer people, natives and actors were milling about the entrance to the firehouse wherein was lodged Chatwich's pride and joy, a new fire-truck.

Stryke ran across from the churchyard. Percy ran down the side of the building along with others and stopped to ask Caleb Spring the whereabouts of the fire.

"Nobody seems to know," Caleb replied.

"I know," Sidney shouted as he ran up to them. "It's in the cupola of the Town Hall, that's where it is.

"Then where is Nellie?" Caleb called.

"Get the hose up into the building," Sidney shouted. "She's up in the tower. So is the fire."

Men ran with lengths of hose, stripping it from the truck, dragging it through the rear door and up the stairs. A coupling was made to the truck in preparation for the water signal. Other men equipped with chemical tanks dashed into the building and up the stairs.

Sidney had been directing men, telling them what to do and how to do it. He paused in front of Caleb and Percy.

"You wanted to know where Nellie was. She up there and she's dead. It was her ghost that turned in the alarm."

"You've got a touch of sun, Sidney," Caleb said, looking at him with kind, tolerant eyes.

"That's what I thought when I seen 'em both from up there on the steeple. Her body in the cuppola and her ghost down here turning in the alarm." The tolerant doubt in their eyes made him hurry on insistently. "I tell you she's up there. I'd just realized what had happened to her when I dropped my glasses and I looked down and

Nellie came whizzin' out of the side door, running like she does, and into the firehouse she went to sound the alarm. Give me an awful turn, but I guess Nellie in spirit would have to watch over the town's fires like she did in life." There was awe in his voice.

Excited men shouted and called. Hose snake into the building and wiggled up the steps, while the three men considered Sidney's story.

"Let me get this straight, Sidney," Caleb said gently. "You say Nellie's body is up there in the cupola and yet you saw her spirit go into the fir house and turn in the alarm."

"Yes, just like I told you. I know you think I'm crazy, but I ain't. When I looked across to make sure my eyes hadn't deceived me I saw the smoke filling the cupola, that's how I knew where the fire was."

"Then it wasn't an accident after all," Caleb said thoughtfully.

"Don't talk in riddles," Sidney snapped. "I tell you Nellie's in the tower dead and unless I'm greatly mistaken she was shot through the back by someone who sneaked up there, lifted the trapdoor and shot her without her knowing a thing about it. As Chief of the Chatwich police, Caleb, it's up to you to do something about it."

"My job for the moment is to stand here, keep people out of the way of the firefighters and preserve order," Caleb replied.

"What did you mean just now by saying it wasn't no accident?" Sidney demanded.

"Well, Nellie came into my office just about one o'clock and complained that there was shooting going on right here in the village. She said she was standing at the kitchen sink finishing up the dishes when a bullet came right through the window and would have killed her if she hadn't turned away at that particular moment for the dish-towel. She was powerful upset about it. I told her I'd look into it. I was sure it was nothing but an accident."

"They didn't miss the second time," Sidney said with conviction.

"Who'd want to murder Nellie Pine?" Caleb asked. "She don't have an enemy in the world."

"Someone's killed her and it warn't no friend," Sidney retorted.

"They're a long time calling for water," Percy said anxiously, looking up toward the top of the building.

"I'm going to see what's going on," Sidney said and darted into the building.

"Just a minute, Sidney," Caleb called. "I don't want you messing things up none. We'll all go."

Sidney went on ahead, his wiry little body taking the steps two at a time.

Caleb and Percy marched up together. "What do you make of what he said?" Caleb asked.

"He was doubtless mistaken," Percy replied "While I have heard many convincing stories about ghosts I do not credit their existence."

"But Sidney has known Nellie all his life. Don' seem like he would make a mistake."

"I am sure there will be some logical explanation," Percy insisted.

"Can your logic explain the bullet through her kitchen window and the one Sidney said went through her back?"

"Not unless Sidney fired them both," Percy replied.

Caleb stopped and looked at Percy. "That's what we call an idea, only it won't hold water. Sidney can't hit the broad side of a barn with a gun, never could."

"And he was in the drugstore when Miss Nellie went into the Town Hall at one o'clock," Percy answered.

"The whole thing plagues me," Caleb said thoughtfully, as their breath became shorter and their steps slower. "I don't see how she had time to get up there and then get down and turn on the alarm, even if she hadn't been shot. She wasn't out of my office more than five minutes before the siren sounded. I teased her about being late getting to her job."

"You're forgetting that ghosts move through time and space," Percy reminded him.

"And you don't believe Sidney's ghost story any more than I do," Caleb retorted.

"Do you know who turned in the alarm?"

"No. Nobody knew where the fire was until Sidney came panting up. Beats all, that it does. What do you think has happened, Mr. Peacock?"

"I wouldn't venture an opinion yet. I understand Mr. Stone has a reputation for talking."

Caleb looked at him with an appreciative gleam in his deep eyes. "He has, but no particular reputation for being a liar."

Above them excited voices shouted. Feet clattered and thumped on the hard floor.

"We've got it all," they heard a voice cry as they turned the last angle of the steps and their heads approached the sixth-floor level.

The air was thick with smoke and the acrid smell of the chemical tanks.

"Open that window over there," someone cried, "and clear this smoke."

Sidney stood at the foot of the circular ladder beside Stryke and was telling him the story of Nellie and her ghost. "The fire's all out," he called when he spied Caleb. "Now you can do something about Nellie."

"Yes. It was a pile of rubbish over there, old paper boxes and paper trimmings," one of the firefighters explained.

Stryke left his spot at the foot of the circular ladder and approached Caleb, holding out his hand. On his wrist just off the base of his thumb there was a dark red spot.

"I think Sidney is telling the truth," he said. "This just dropped on me from up there. It looks like blood."

"Of course I'm telling the truth," Sidney cried. "Why don't you do something about it, Caleb Spring?"

"Stand back, don't touch nothing," Caleb warned. He started up the iron staircase, his feet making a hollow sound on the treads. The men watched him approach the closed trapdoor.

"There's a stain here," he called down and pointed to the joint of the floor and trap. He took a handkerchief from his pocket and pushed against the door. A slanting beam of bright golden light cut through the still heavy air of the sixth floor. Holding the door gingerly, Caleb stopped on the top step and looked into the little room.

In the beam of the sunlight a widening spot of blood grew on the floor. The men looked at it soberly and then upward, waiting for Caleb. His feet moved carefully, feeling for the next step of the ladder. The trapdoor dropped into place, the beam of gold light was cut off and Caleb descended.

"Well, what did I tell you?" Sidney demanded.

"She's dead," Caleb said quietly.

"Are you sure?" Sidney demanded.

"I think so. I don't want to touch her till the doctor comes. One of you boys run down and call a doctor and then get the State Police over at South Yarmouth and tell them there's been a murder here." As several pairs of feet scuttled away, Caleb turned to Sidney. "Beats me, Sidney. You sure you didn't imagine you saw her down below?"

"Who turned in the alarm if she didn't?" Sidney demanded.

"I don't know. No one knew when we ran out. We were wondering why the bell was ringing."

"I did that to attract attention. I didn't want Nellie to burn up there, but I guess I needn't have worried. The thing that was Nellie ain't up there. I wonder where she is now? Maybe she's come back to haunt the place, to help us catch her murderer."

"Don't talk that way, Sidney. I'm willing to believe what you say because I've never known you to lie for the sake of lying, but I don't see how—"

"There's lots of things that happen that we don't understand. Ask the professor here," Sidney said.

"I don't deal in ghosts," Percy said quietly, and then he remembered his conversation with Mr. Tucker. They had both had a premonition of something that was going to happen. Could this be it?

"Well, I've heard plenty of stories about things that people don't understand, pictures falling, cups rattling, knockings, tappings, and soft footsteps in the night. Voices moaning in the wind, horses running over the moors. How do we know it couldn't happen?"

"We don't," Percy said.

"And would Nellie give up just because she was dead? No, you know she wouldn't, Caleb. She sounded that siren and she's likely right here now trying to give us a clue as to who killed her. Yes, sir, I bet Nellie's standing right here with us trying give us a message. What is it they say about blood coming from a corpse when the murderer goes near the body?"

Percy looked across and saw Stryke Ryder rubbing his hand on his trouser leg. He remembered the blood on Stryke's hand.

"Out, damned spot! Out I say!" Percy quote

Caleb and Sidney looked at him as if he had lost his reason, but Stryke, accustomed to taking cue, dropped his hand and flushed guiltily.

"Is there any truth in that story about the blood?" Sidney insisted.

"I wouldn't venture an opinion. Why not ask the doctor when he comes?" Percy suggested. "And the bullet in her kitchen wasn't an accident after all," Caleb said thoughtfully. "Seemed as if she knew it. I don't know as I've even seen Nellie as mad as she was. I thought it was because it broke her window."

The doctor came panting up the steps.

"She hasn't been touched," Caleb said. "Go right up. It's Nellie Pine."

Once again the shaft of sunlight filtered through the haze as the doctor disappeared.

"She's dead all right, Caleb, only it ain't Nellie Pine," the doctor announced when he came back.

"What?" they all cried.

"You mean the dead woman ain't Nellie? Then it's someone wearing her clothes!" Sidney shouted with evident relief.

"Makes me feel better. You didn't see a ghost after all, Sidney. You had my skin crawling there for a spell. Who is it, Doc?" Caleb asked.

"The victim is Eve Knight, the acting girl, and she's wearing a shirtwaist just like Miss Nellie's. I had to look at her face to be sure myself."

Eve Knight! Percy was shocked. Eve was one of their company. He understood the relief of Caleb and Sidney as they realized it was not Miss Nellie. His eyes sought Stryke. How would he feel?

"Then why didn't Nellie stay and tell the firemen where the fire was?" Sidney demanded.

"You'll have to ask Nellie that!" Caleb replied. "I've never been able to figure out what makes women do certain things."

"Are you sure she's dead?" Stryke asked, his face sobered and serious.

"Positive."

"Shouldn't we try to do something for her?' Stryke urged anxiously. "There might be some hope."

"There was no sign of a heartbeat, son. It's better not to move her until the police take over," the doctor advised. "Looks like murder. The bullet entered her back, and there's no gun up there that I could see."

Stryke's fine young eyes dimmed. He turned away.

"Will you handle the case or turn it over to the State Police?" the doctor asked Caleb.

"We aren't equipped for murder. The State Police'll have to do all the scientific work, like fingerprints, photographs and all that. Beats me. It was a natural mistake Sidney made."

"I wonder if the murderer made the same mistake?" Percy asked.

"I don't know as I know what you mean by that," Caleb remarked.

"I was wondering if the murderer meant to kill Eve Knight or if the bullet, like the one through her kitchen window, was meant for Miss Nellie."

"I don't know much about murderers," Caleb answered thoughtfully. "I know if I aimed to kill someone I'd make sure I got the right person right off. No sense of doing things twice."

"No, Percy agreed. "There isn't."

The first sound of the church bell through the building, made Percy and Stryke jump. It was followed by another and yet another dull "bong."

"Now what?" Percy asked. "Why the bell?"

"It's an old Chatwich custom, one we've had for a long time. At least ever since I can remember, Luke has tolled the bell for a death in the village. There's folks as says he looks forward to it, is right interested when he hears a body is sick."

The bell tolled on monotonously.

CHAPTER FOUR

PERCY'S ideas did not coincide exactly with those held by Caleb. He went thoughtfully down the long flight of steps, following the men who carried the hose. He left by the side door just as Sidney said Miss Nellie had done. He went to the firehouse and looked at the alarm button. Like Sidney, he was wondering why Nellie Pine did not wait to tell the firemen the location of the fire.

There was another question in his mind. Did Nellie Pine know that a dead woman was occupying her watchtower? If she did, why didn't she run into Caleb's office and tell him as soon as she had sounded the alarm? Who had started the fire? All interesting questions, and only one person could answer them: the briskly walking Nellie Pine.

Percy passed though the alley between the Town Hall and the post office building and out onto Main Street, which was more deserted than usual because most of the town was on the Webster Road talking to the firemen, speculating about the murder.

He glanced toward Caleb Spring's house as he passed by, but the curtains did not flutter as usual for even Phoebe Spring had gone "up street" to see what was going on. There was no sign of Mrs. Tucker, either, as he passed her house. Nellie Pine's gate was open. That was not like Miss Nellie. No matter how fast she traveled she always took time to close her gate. The mat on the doorstep was askew and the key was in the lock. He hoped he was in time to see her.

He pulled at the bell-knob, heard the old-fashioned bell jangle within, and waited. The house was strangely quiet, echoed hollowly as he rapped on the panels. After a reasonable wait he opened the door and called, "Miss Nellie!"

His voice rattled back at him. He felt uneasy. He looked up and down Main Street and stepped into the silent hall. He paused to listen, but there was no sound whatever. He jumped as the telephone shrilled through the house, sharp and insistent. For a moment he was tempted to answer it, then realized that would make it necessary to explain his presence there, and ignored it entirely as it rang and rang. He went into the sitting-room. It was neat, orderly and precise, with doilies under the lamps and antimacassars on the chairs.

He moved toward an open door. It was Miss Nellie's bedroom and it showed signs of disorder, of rapid flight. Dresser drawers were flung open, yawning in front of him. Her gaudy shirtwaist lay discarded on the bed. A pair of embroidered pink silk pants lay on the floor. He smiled at that proof of Nellie's femininity and went out into the kitchen. On the wall over a cabinet a bullet hole was a new scar on the clean white paint. The rear door was unhooked.

Percy went out into the yard, looked back at the shattered kitchen window. The doors of what had once been a woodshed were open. Nellie Pine's car was gone.

Percy walked back to Main Street, around the outside of the house. He had found the answers to his questions. Nellie Pine had seen the body in the watchtower and had fled because she was afraid for her life.

There was one other possibility that bothered him. He had heard gossip about Eve Knight and Sidney Stone, joshing gossip among members of the company. Eve had danced several times with Sidney at a church social a week or so before. She had walked with him one or two evenings, had ever gone to the movies with him down at the Port. It was the sort of thing Eve would do with a man like Sidney. She could never resist experimenting with men.

Percy considered all the things he knew about Miss Nellie Pine and wondered if she had heard of Sidney's recent flirtation with Eve. He had to admit that it was quite possible that a woman like Nellie would resent Sidney's interest in another woman Even though she had not wanted him herself, it might be that she considered him her property and would not look kindly upon a rival.

If those suppositions were true, then Nellie might have fired the shot at her kitchen window herself. That would be a rather neat way of avoiding suspicion. Now if Nellie knew that Eve had an outfit similar to her own, she would wait for the day when Eve decided to wear it. All that part of his theory worked beautifully, but he was unable to know how Nellie had lured Eve to her watchtower at this particular time. Perhaps Nellie had telephoned Eve to meet her there. He was willing to grant that as a possibility. Then Nellie shot Eve, lit a fire on the sixth floor and turned in the alarm.

If she were the killer, her actions had followed a well considered pattern. She had established the fact with Caleb that someone had shot at her, then later a woman dressed like her was found dead in her chair in the tower. It would seem logical for her to disappear. When she came out of hiding, she would say she was afraid for her life, that two attempts had failed, that she was taking no chances. It would be a very clever murder, defense and alibi.

He had reached the Town Hall by the time he had figured out this possible plan of campaign. It was good, it was logical and reasonable, but he didn't believe a single word of it. Miss Nellie Pine was not that type of murderer. She might kill in sudden rage, but she would never plan a crime. She had vanished, and he was convinced that she had gone away because she honestly believed her life to be in danger. Why should it be in danger? If she knew some dangerous fact, why didn't she tell Caleb?

He went up the long flight of steps slowly, pondering the problem of Eve Knight's murder. On the theatre floor he became part of a great throng of people. He recognized Abe and Mrs. Tucker, Phoebe Spring and Abbie Glover in a corner, their heads together, tongues wagging; Eben and Henry Ryder talking to some of the men; Clyde Perine the company manager, his face pale and worn, bemoaning the fact that he had lost an excellent actress; Libby Powell, poised and lovely, telling him that everything would work out all right.

He heard Perine, half crying, say that he should never have come back to the awful town.

Percy worked his way toward the steps, but was stopped by a State Trooper, trim and efficient in his natty uniform.

"There's something I must tell Caleb Spring," Percy said.

"There are a lot of people here with things to tell him," the trooper replied. "They'll be down after a while and you'll all have a chance."

Libby Powell came up to him and asked if he had seen Stryke.

"He was upstairs," Percy replied. "He was in on the kill, so to speak."

Libby winced, her eyes clouded. She put a hand on his arm. "Why did you say that?"

"Just talk," he replied and wondered why she was so concerned.

He found her attractive. She was cool and fresh and clean. She was an excellent actress, had a fine sense of comedy, was a hard worker. He knew it had taken courage for her to return to Chatwich to act before critical townspeople who had known her all her life. He liked her, understood why Stryke had fallen in love with her.

"You'll get to play the part of Sarah in 'Hidebound' now," he said.

New shadows flickered across her eyes. "I suppose so," she agreed.

The thud of treading feet sounded above them. They moved back and waited for the men who were approaching. Caleb and the head trooper were first. Caleb's face was troubled as he looked out over the people milling about just outside the entrance to the theatre. The trooper was cool and efficient, all authority and strictly business. A bad man to cross, Percy thought, with some misgiving as he made a mental appraisal of the man. He was tall, wore his wide-brimmed hat with dash. His eyes were straight, direct and fearless; his mouth firm, his chin rugged.

Stryke and Sidney were just behind them, walking beside Martin Chase, who seemed to be studying the faces turned upward watching them.

Percy moved forward, stepped in front of Caleb and the trooper.

"I've discovered something I think you ought to know," Percy said, barely above a whisper. The trooper eyed him critically. Caleb introduced them. They started toward the door of the auditorium. A thin wisp of a woman with scraggly hair and a face like a ferret wormed through the crowd, slithered up to Caleb and said, "There's things you ought to know, Caleb Spring."

"Just a moment, Suzie. I'll talk to you right off. Don't go away."

"As if I would," she said craftily, "knowing what I do." She had a quart tin pail which she hugged to her bosom.

Caleb led the men into the auditorium. Black, the trooper, closed the door.

"Who's the Ophelia?" Percy asked.

"The who?" Caleb demanded.

"He means the nut with the pail," Black explained.

"Oh, that's Suzie Briggs, not quite right in the head. She's harmless. Now what have you discovered?"

"Nellie Pine has skipped," Percy announced.

"Are you sure?" Caleb demanded, really surprised.

Percy told his story.

"Why were you so interested?" Black demanded.

"I'm interested in people, what they do and why they do it," Percy replied.

"He's one of them psychology teachers," Caleb explained.

"And was this general interest in people your only reason for going down there?" Black demanded.

"No," Percy replied promptly.

"You're a little worried, maybe," Caleb suggested. He turned to Black. "You see the professor here spends his vacations being an actor and although he's a professor, according to what I've been hearing, he's just like any other man."

"Meaning what?" Black demanded.

"He means that I've seen quite a bit of Eve tonight," Percy answered.

"Quite a bit," Caleb agreed. "You two were seen down by my bog house the other night."

Percy knew he was blushing. "Good God, can't you move in this town without being seen?" he demanded.

"Evidently some people can," Black said crisply. I'll have to send out an alarm for this Nellie Pine. Perhaps we can stop her before she gets off the Cape. This is your show, Caleb, you'll want to get evidence. Do you have a stenographer who can take notes?"

"Not one good enough," Caleb admitted.

"I'll get one of my men. You go ahead and pick up what facts you can and get them recorded. I'll busy for a few minutes, then we can get together and sift the wheat from the chaff."

When the doors were opened the people outside pressed forward.

"Come in, any of you that wants to," Caleb invited. "Come down front and take seats." He led the van toward the stage.

He stopped before the footlights and faced them.

When they had settled into seats he said, "As you know, we've had a murder which in a way will affect all of us. We've always done things in this town in the open and

I intend to make this investigation an open affair. A State Trooper will be here in minute to take down everything you say. Now I want you to stick to the truth, we don't want to know what you think, we want to learn what you know or saw. And I ain't interested in any gossip or anything else that isn't connected directly with the murder of that poor girl up in the tower."

A trooper came in. Caleb waved him to a small table which Perine had been using during rehearsals.

"Are you ready?" Caleb asked.

"Yes, sir. Carter's my name." Carter flipped open his book, pulled a pen from his boot top and unscrewed the cap.

"We'll begin with the man who discovered the body," Caleb announced. "I want all of you to give your names, to tell what you do, and to talk up as Carter here can understand you. Sidney Stone, you have the floor."

Sidney gave his name, address and occupation. He told his story with great relish up to the moment when he thought Nellie Pine was dead.

Carter objected, asked for the name of the victim.

"I didn't know it was the actress, then," Sidney retorted with indignation. "I thought it was Nellie and so did everybody else, I guess. You see, I thougt she was asleep and I wanted to get her attention on account of Abe Tucker's cow."

"What about my cow?" Abe bellowed. "What's she got to do with this murder?"

"I don't know about that. She's dead down there in the cut and I wanted Nellie to see it so as she could telephone you."

"Dead!" Tucker cried. "There was nothing the matter with that cow!"

"There is now," Sidney assured him.

The crowd tittered as Abe sprang from his seat and hurried out of the room.

The trooper at the door stopped Abe, who bellowed, "Don't you try to stop me. I got a cow to worry about."

Black nodded to the trooper. Abe was allowed to leave.

CHAPTER FIVE

SIDNEY went on with his story, giving all the details, telling about the smoke, his ringing of the bell, Nellie's sounding of the alarm. He had just finished when Black came back, to hold a few minutes' whispered conversation with Caleb.

Black took over the investigation. "What time was it when you realized there was a dead woman in the tower?" he asked.

"I don't know exactly. I thought I saw Nellie going into the Town Hall a little before one. Now might have been the other girl, since Caleb tells me he talked to Nellie and she warn't up there at one o'clock same as she usually is. It might have been a quarter after one. I don't know."

Black looked out over his audience. "Is there anyone here who can definitely give us an idea of Eve Knight's actions just before the crime?" He waited. "Did any of you see her sometime before one?"

Phoebe Spring moved in her chair, finally stood up. "I did," she said.

"Tell us about it," Black ordered.

"I'm Phoebe Spring, but I guess everybody here knows that." She smiled nervously. "Well, it was about 12:30, I don't know exactly, but Caleb had finished his lunch and had gone out back. I was at the sink doing up the dishes, when Eve Knight and Stryke Ryder stopped at the Tucker front gate. It was quiet on the street at that time and as they moved toward my house I heard what they said." She went on and repeated the conversation which Percy too had overheard.

Percy found himself marveling at the accuracy of Phoebe's memory, down to the slightest inflection of voices. He looked over and saw Stryke's face grow extremely red. He saw Libby Powell reach for one of the boy's hands and press it reassuringly.

"He left in a huff," Phoebe stated. "When she came up the path, half running, I could see that she was crying. She rooms with us," she explained to Black. "I heard her in her room sobbing as though her heart would break. A little later I heard her in the hall and saw her go out, that must have been just before one o'clock."

"How was she dressed?"

"A shirtwaist and skirt. She looked enough like Nellie Pine to be Nellie except for her hair. She gave me a turn this morning when she went out because for a moment I thought Nellie Pine had come up to my front door, not that she ever does."

"Then you at least knew that the two women were dressed alike," he said.

"Why, yes," she said slowly. "I knew it but if you're trying to—"

"I'm not trying to do anything but establish facts," he said crisply. "When she left your house about one, did she go toward the Town Hall?"

"Yes."

"Did you happen to see Miss Pine start back to the Town Hall?"

"Yes. She came out soon after Eve Knight and trotted along the street. It was some time after that that I heard the siren blow."

"You didn't see Miss Knight again, Mrs. Spring?"

"No."

"Thank you, that will be all." As Phoebe sat down and began whispering to Abbie, who was sitting beside her, he asked, "Did anyone here see and recognize Miss Knight? I would like to fix the time of the murder as accurately as possible."

He was waiting for an answer when Abe Tucker stormed back into the room, his face red, his eyes dagger points of anger. He marched down front, faced Black and bellowed, "I want to know who murdered my cow!"

The group stirred in their seats, and some of th members of the company tittered.

"It's no laughing matter," Abe roared. "I'll have the law on somebody."

"Are you sure your cow has been murdered Caleb asked with a twinkle in his shrewd eyes.

"Shot right through the head she was and if that ain't murder, what is?" Abe demanded.

"We're investigating the death of a woman." Black said. "Your cow will have to wait."

"What's the law for if it don't protect citizens and their property?" Abe demanded. "Caleb, I want you to find out who killed my cow."

"We'll come to that," Caleb promised. "Sit down, if you want to stay. You're interrupting the proceedings."

"Don't you tell me what to do," Abe growled as he moved toward the empty seat beside his wife.

"When did you pasture your cow, Mr. Tucker?" Black asked.

"This morning, early."

"Are you a friend of Miss Nellie Pine?"

Abe was surprised. "Of course, why?"

"I ask the questions," Black reminded him. "Were you acquainted with Eve Knight?"

A dull flush covered Abe's face. "I knew her," he said sullenly.

"That ain't what I heard," Sidney whispered audibly.

The audience became alive. There were grins, snickers, nudges and the nodding of heads.

"Good Lord!" Percy thought. "Not Abe too! He certainly acts guilty."

Abe gave Sidney a hard calculating look. "You see and know too much," he said.

"Sit down, Mr. Tucker," Black said crisply.

Abe glowered, slapped Mrs. Tucker's hand away as it tugged at his coat, but under the hard blue stare of Black's eyes he wilted into his seat.

"Mr. Spring, will you tell us about Miss Pine?" Black invited.

Caleb told his story about Nellie's indignation because of the bullet which had nearly killed her in her kitchen.

"How long was she with you?"

"Maybe five minutes. No longer," Caleb estimated.

"Did Miss Pine mention Eve Knight?"

"No," Caleb replied stoutly.

"Have you any idea why Nellie Pine has run away?" Black asked.

"No. And if you mean do I think she did it and then skipped, the answer is no."

"Would Miss Nellie have had any reason to do it?" Black asked.

"I wouldn't know about that," Caleb admitted. "She might have been jealous," Abbie Glover suggested.

Black pounced upon that, asked Abbie to stand. She told him what the whole town had known, that Sidney Stone had been "carrying on" with Eve Knight. She also explained the long dormant romance between Sidney and Nellie.

Sidney bounced to his feet. "That's just talk!" he shouted. "Old woman's gossip! Nellie Pine never hurt nothin' nor nobody in her whole life and every man, woman and child in this town knows it. And what's more," he was still shouting,

Eyes circled, pulled by the weight of common knowledge toward Percy, who looked straight ahead and hoped that he was not blushing.

"Who, for instance?" Black demanded.

"That I ain't telling. Just leave Nellie out of this." He sat down as abruptly as he had risen.

"I know," Suzie Briggs rose. Her tin bucket banged against the seat in front of her. "I know what Sidney means."

"What's your name?" Black asked.

"Suzie Briggs, and folks here think I'm crazy. I ain't. I'm just a little peculiar, my ma used to say. I heard something this morning. Can I tell it now, Caleb?"

"Go ahead, Suzie," Caleb said gently.

"Well, the wild strawberries are ripe and I wanted to get some, so I took my bucket this morning after my work was done and began picking. I went to the town park and was picking when they came along." She pointed at Stryke and Libby. "They didn't see me, couldn't see nothing or nobody but themselves. They sat down on an old log and didn't pay no attention to ticks or red ants or nothing. Just sat for a spell until he said, 'Will you marry me, Libby?'"

The crowd stirred and looked at Libby and Stryke. She held his hand tightly. Percy saw the pressure increase, but neither of them turned their heads.

"She said she wouldn't and he wanted to know why," Suzie went on. "She said it was because he was an actor, because Eve Knight made all the people in the company think that she owned him body and soul. He tried to stop her, but she said it would be foolish for them to think of getting married, because they were young and getting married would get in the way of their acting. He wouldn't listen to that talk and said they could be famous like a couple of people he mentioned. She said they lacked experience and a lot of other things." Suzie paused for a moment, looked across at the young lovers. "He kissed her then and she moved her hand over his hair. He took her hand and kissed it and said, 'That day when you picked me up on the road it was Stryke Ryder against the world. I don't want to be alone, Libby. I want you with me. Thanks for loving me.' He stood up and I crouched down because I didn't want them to see me. She looked up at him and her eyes were all shining and she said, 'Your grandfather won't like it, Stryke,' and he said, 'What do I care about my grandfather, Eve Knight or anybody? Nothing can come between us, can it?' She said 'No,' sort of low like.

"'I got to tell you about Eve Knight,' he said; 'we were lovers back in New York, but we quit. It was all over between us, before I came here.' She said sort of soft like, 'You thought so; she didn't.'"

Stryke jumped to his feet and demanded, "Do we have to listen to this?"

"You can leave the room or stay and deny her story later," Black said.

Suzie went on. "They talked about Eve Knight and some part she wanted to play. Libby said as how Eve Knight didn't like her because Stryke was in love with her, and that they didn't like sharing the leads in the plays they were going to do. Then he said that Eve could play the part in some play better than she could and Libby got real mad. He said they mustn't quarrel. She said he was taking sides against her. He said he would never do that. That he was going up to see his grandfather and that later he would take care of Eve, finish her off. That's what I wanted to tell you, Caleb. Seems like he must have meant to kill the poor girl all the time."

A gasp of surprise and shock rippled through the room. Libby bounded to her feet.

"How dare you say such things, Suzie Briggs?"

"Because they are true. I heard all you said." She smiled, quite pleased with herself.

Libby turned to Black. "I don't deny any of the things she says we said. We were two people with a problem, two people in love trying to see our way through the difficulties which life presents. It isn't fair to take our words, to have their meaning distorted. Phoebe Spring has told you of the conversation Stryke had with Eve at the gate. You must realize how honest he was with her. Can't we have this woman's story struck from the records of this case?"

"I'm afraid not, Miss Powell, but I assure you it will not become public property."

"It's public property now," she said bitterly and sank back into the chair.

Black turned to Stryke. "Do you deny the testimony just given?"

"I don't deny what we said, but I deny that woman's implications."

"Did you see Eve Knight after you left her at the Spring gate?"

"No."

"Where were you from that time until the body was discovered?"

"In the village."

"Where in the village?" Black insisted.

"Main Street. I used the telephone on the main floor of the Town Hall and then went over to the drugstore for a sandwich."

"That's right," Sidney agreed. "I saw him there. So did a lot of other people."

"And you're sure you didn't see Eve Knight again?"

"I was in the drugstore until Mr. Stone said it was nearly one. That was when he said he saw Miss Nellie go into the front entrance," Stryke replied.

"That's right," Sidney confirmed again.

"Then what did you do?" Black asked.

"I went back to the Town Hall and telephoned again."

"Why didn't you use the telephone in the drug-store?" Black asked.

"Because it is an open phone and I didn't want my conversation overheard."

"Did you see Miss Pine?"

"No."

"Are you sure you didn't see Eve Knight?"

"I told you I didn't see her."

"What did you do after you telephoned?"

"I went over into the graveyard."

"He's right," Sidney said. "I talked to him."

Stryke gave Sidney a look of sheer thanks.

"All right, Mr. Ryder. Sit down while I talk to Mr. Stone again."

Sidney popped to his feet, enjoying his importance.

"You say you talked to Mr. Ryder in the graveyard?"

"I did."

"Did you go there together?"

"No. He left the drugstore, like he says he did, before me."

"How much before?"

"Let me see," Sidney considered. "I recall Eben Ryder and his son looking after Stryke as he crossed the road. Then Mr. Peacock bought a magazine and went outside. When I went out Mr. Peacock was standing on the steps looking across the street. I asked him what he taught while he was a teacher we talked for a minute or two and then I went over to get started on my work. It was then that I stopped to talk to Stryke here. I showed him where the Ryder plot was located."

"Then there was a period of five minutes or more between the time that Stryke Ryder left the drug store and you talked to him near the church."

"That's right," Sidney agreed.

There was a whispered buzz in the audience at the implications of Black's questions sank home.

"How did Ryder act when you talked to him?'

"Sort of glum, like a person with something on his mind," Sidney replied after a thoughtful pause. "I told him all the Ryders were buried over there except the ones lost at sea and he said, 'Some people get lost who never go to sea."

"Was Ryder excited, short of breath, anything like that?" Black asked.

"He wasn't short of anything except information, as I recall it," Sidney replied quickly. "I seen him up to his grandfather's place this morning and I asked him how he got along with the old man, but he wouldn't tell me nothing."

"Humph," Abbie Glover snorted.

Stryke sat like an image, gazing straight ahead of him. Percy watched the boy, felt sorry for him. It was incredible that a lad like Stryke should have a charge of murder dangling over his head just because a few people had happened to hear some private conversation. Percy knew and he thought that Black must realize that there was no real motive as far as Stryke was concerned for Eve Knight's death. He felt certain that Suzie Briggs's story must help rather than hurt Stryke. He had frankly told Libby about Eve, had not spared himself in the telling. The only possible motive he could have would be to silence Eve, and he had eliminated that motive himself by his frankness.

Percy was startled from his reverie by hearing Black call his name. He rose slowly, gave his name and occupation and waited for Black's question.

"I've been given to understand you knew the victim rather well," Black began.

"I did. We were in the same company last summer in Maine."

"Do you know of anyone who might like to rid the world of Miss Knight's presence?"

"No."

"You have heard the testimony. Do you agree with the things Mr. Stone has said?"

"Yes."

"Would you mind telling us what you did from the time Stone talked to you until the fire alarm was sounded?"

That was a jolt to Percy, as he realized he had done exactly nothing but stand just outside the drugstore to bask in the sun.

"I just stood where Stone left me," he answered.

"Can you prove that?"

"I don't see how unless some one of these good people saw me and will verify my statement."

Black looked out over the people, but there was no offer of corroboration for Percy's story.

"We will have to let the fact stand without verification," Black said, "and believe that you stood just outside the drugstore."

"Thank you," Percy said.

"Were you in the drugstore when Stone said he saw Miss Pine?"

"I was."

"Did you see Miss Pine?"

"I thought I recognized her shirtwaist."

"Did you see Ryder cross the road toward the Town Hall?"

"I did."

"You didn't see two women wearing gay shirtwaists go into the entrance, did you?"

"No."

Black called Clyde Perine.

"Mr. Perine, as director of the theatrical company, you probably knew Miss Knight better than anyone else. Were her actions normal today?"

"Not for an actress."

"Explain that, please."

"You have probably gathered from the testimony given up to now that there was some feeling in the company over parts. Miss Powell has been most anxious to play the role of Sarah in 'Hidebound.' Eve Knight also wanted to play that part. There was some friction between the two girls. Libby Powell telephoned me this morning and said the honestly felt that Eve would do a better job with the part than she could. I was very pleased to hear that and told Eve that I had definitely settled on her for the role of Sarah. She did not seem pleased with the news; was quite indifferent."

"When did you tell her that?"

"I met her on the street, probably about ten minutes after twelve."

'Then you knew she was wearing a blouse similar to Nellie Pine's?"

"Why, yes," he admitted slowly. "They were alike, weren't they? I hadn't thought of that up to now."

"Did you see Miss Pine after you left the drug-store?"

"I saw Nellie," an unexpected voice spoke slowly. It was Martin Chase. All eyes turned in his direction.

"Where?" Black asked.

"Scuttling along Main Street just before one. I had been in the drugstore and went over to the post office. I saw her pass by."

"And you are sure it was Miss Pine?" Black insisted.

"Come to think of it, I couldn't be sure. I saw the flick of color and since I had seen Nellie earlier in the day I might have been mistaken. It might have been the other girl after all."

Black turned back to Perine. "Where were you at one o'clock?"

"I don't know. I was in this room at that table, however, when I heard the fire siren. I couldn't swear to the time of that either."

"What was the important business you had to do, so important that you couldn't stop to talk to me in the drugstore?" Stryke asked.

The question caused a stir in the room. Perine looked across at Stryke and recoiled as if he had received a blow.

Black and the group waited.

"It was a personal matter and has nothing to do with this investigation," Perine said slowly.

The crowd relaxed when neither Stryke nor Black pressed the question.

"When I asked about Eve Knight earlier in this investigation, you did not tell me that you had seen her," Black accused.

"I thought you meant just prior to her murder, before one," Perine declared.

"Did Miss Knight have any enemies?"

"Not to my knowledge."

"Thank you, Mr. Perine. The rest of you may go."

They rose, moved slowly toward the rear door, collected in little groups to talk in whispers.

"Now, how about my cow?" Abe Tucker demanded.

"Later," Black said sharply.

Percy walked down the room with Libby and Stryke. "Looks like we're the chief suspects, Stryke," he said.

"Because they are barking up the wrong tree," Stryke growled. "Why didn't Black go into the story of the bullet through Nellie Pine's window? Why don't they find her and get the answer to the riddle?"

Sidney had walked up behind them. "Because Nellie's no fool. If she saw that dead girl up there she more than likely figured the bullet was meant for her and Nellie never was one to take chances."

"You ought to know, Sidney," Martin Chase said as he went past them. "She was too smart to take a chance with you."

"Gettin' right talkative, ain't you?" Sidney flung after him.

Martin Chase passed on.

As they approached the door the group of townspeople moved to one side to let them pass through. They were in the hall when Stryke said, "Look here, Libby, they acted just now as if we had the plague or something. Until this thing is settled I think it would be smart to stay away from me."

"Don't talk that way, Stryke," Libby begged and took hold of his arm. There was patience and understanding in her eyes as she smiled up at him.

"I mean it." He shook himself free, ignoring the love in her eyes. He strode away to follow Sidney down the stairs.

Libby was biting her lips as she turned back to Percy. "It's a shame this had to happen to him just now."

"He's upset, naturally," Percy said. "A man doesn't like to have anything as intimate as his affairs reported in public, particularly when they are told to give the impression that he had kill an old sweetheart for a new one."

"It's ghastly," she said, "and so unnecessary."

"And rather unfathomable," Percy said thoughtfully. "It's a pretty problem."

"What's pretty about it?" she flared and walk away.

Percy watched her go. He was sorry for both them and a little concerned about himself. Like Stryke, he had no definite alibi for what must have been the actual time of the crime, nor had he seen Eve after the scene at the gate, but he couldn't prove that any more than Stryke could prove it. Also, he knew that more of the details of his little affair with Eve would come to light. Such things always cropped up unexpectedly. Perhaps this would mean the end of his teaching career. He visualized lurid headlines, "College Professor Moonlight Tryst With Victim." He knew he would make good copy. Reporters would love it. His University wouldn't, however. Nor would parents approve. Teachers were not supposed to be human, were not supposed to have normal feelings, or they had them, they were expected to live circumspect lives and must not be involved in an affair.

With an actress who allowed herself to be murdered. Who had seen them near the cranberry bog, and what were they doing there at that time of the night? Questions like that would be asked and answered by reporters.

Had either Mrs. Tucker or Mrs. Spring, who seemed to see and know everything that happened on Main Street, seen them meet several times on the back road? What was in Black's mind? He had never committed himself in any way. Was Black suspecting him or Stryke? What did Black think about Nellie Pine? Why did she run away? And where had she gone?

He wondered about the members of the company. Black had not talked to them at all with the exception of Perine, Libby, Stryke and himself.

What was the important business Perine had had to attend to when he left the drugstore? Why had he seemed so hurt when Stryke mentioned it? And why had Stryke recalled it? Had it been a desperate attempt on the boy's part to take attention away from himself?

Percy turned back into the room to talk to Black and Caleb.

CHAPTER SIX

STRYKE had rushed out of the the Hall with one idea in his mind, to get away from the curious eyes of people. He was a little frantic, animal-like in his desire for a place to hide. The churchyard seemed the very place. He crossed road, went past the steps of the church where Sidney's canvas and painting materials rested on ground, and sought sanctuary in the Ryder plot. It was shielded from public view and would him the sanctuary he needed.

He sat on an old white marble headstone and lit a cigarette. At the moment he was wishing that he had never seen Chatwich. He had always hated things that the name implied. As a boy he heard his mother's story, had heard of his grandfather's wealth, had resented the fact that his mother had had to struggle to give him a meager education. He thought of the days when they barely enough money for food, of the long spells between parts for her or himself, of their gratitude for what little work they could get.

All through those years he had had a child's resentment and hatred for the old man who refused to recognize his daughter, had hated him without understanding, without compromise.

When he had reached an age when he could have been of some help to her, his mother had died, had died making him promise to see his grandfather.

"Try to be his friend, Stryke," she had said. "He's old and he's proud. So are you proud, but you're young. I don't want you to make the mistake that we made. Promise me you will go and see him."

He had promised, and when it was all over he had started for Cape Cod. He had had no plans and very little money. He wanted to get the promised visit behind him.

Before he left New York he tried to enlist in the army. They found a slight heart defect, had given him several severe examinations, and finally dismissed him.

Stryke had felt badly about that, had questioned one of the doctors, who explained the case to him, had told him there was nothing to worry about, that he would be all right for years if he lived a normal life.

He had met Libby Powell on the Webster Road. He smiled at that memory. She had been driving a down-at-heel Ford. He had tried to thumb a ride, but she had clattered by. Even then, in that quick glance, he had realized how pretty she was, had called after her, "I don't bite!"

A quarter of a mile down the road she had had a blowout, had been struggling with the wheel trying to jack it up when he had caught up to her and had offered his help. She had refused. He had taken the jack from her hand and raised the wheel. He had stripped off his coat, had found the spare without air, had chided her about negligence, had discovered that the car belonged to her brother.

He had put on the spare and was ready for her to start on without him, when she had insisted, "Get in."

"No," he had said. "I told you I didn't help you to get a ride."

"Get in anyhow," she had ordered. "I thought you were a tramp."

"I am," he had said.

"But not the kind of a tramp I thought you were," she had smiled at him with friendship in her eyes.

"I'm going as far as Chatwich," he had said. "There's a job there I must do, then I'm going over to West Dennis to see if I can get a job. I'm an actor."

"Bad?" she had asked with a low laugh.

"Average."

"I live in Chatwich. I'm an actress, a member of a newly formed group called the Chatwich Players, and oddly enough we're looking for a young leading man. We're going to give the Playhouse a run for its money."

"I wouldn't want to work in Chatwich," he had said.

"Why not? There's nothing the matter with Chatwick."

"I'm sure of that for you, But there is for me," he said glumly.

"Then you've been to Chatwich before?"

"No. But I've heard about it all my life. I wouldn't feel comfortable there."

"But you said there was a job you wanted to do." she reminded him.

"There is, a man I must see, a job which I must do and then I'll forget Chatwich." He had hesitated. "Except for you."

She had laughed merrily. "You sound like an actor."

"I suppose you know everybody in Chatwich?" he had asked.

"Everybody," she had agreed. "And the town is all excited about this new theatre venture of ours."

"Oh," he had said shortly. He knew what was coming.

"It's a romantic story," she had continued. "Like something out of a book or a play. The daughter of the town's richest man fell in love with the star of the stock company. They eloped. Her father in his rage disinherited her just as they did in the old melodramas. She never came back. No one here knows what really happened to her." Her voice bad been warm and friendly, filled with genuine concern for the woman who had given up so much for love. "We've heard some stories and rumors but . . . Isn't it exciting that now after all these years the manager of the Chatwich Players has sent her son a telegram asking him to be our leading man? The whole village is waiting for Stryke Ryder come back."

He had been startled. He had received no telegram. He had smiled and had asked bitterly, "Was there to be a band?"

"No, of course not," she had said, aware, he had thought, of his bitterness.

"That's too bad. You see, I'm Stryke Ryder."

"Oh! I'm sorry," she had said quickly. "I didn't know."

"Of course you didn't. But you can see why I wouldn't want to stay in Chatwich."

She had nodded. "And to see your grandfather is the job you have to do?"

"Yes, before she died my mother—"

"Made you promise. Then you did get the telegram?"

"No. I've been traveling via the thumb route since yesterday afternoon. I spent part of the nig near Cohasset under a railroad culvert."

They had passed Big Pond and Pleasant La had mounted a slight rise and had had a view huge cranberry bogs hemmed in and patterned their small dykes.

"Why don't you take this job?" she had urged suddenly.

"Exactly what I've been thinking. I need a j badly and in these days summer stock seems to the jumping-off place for Hollywood."

"Then you'll do it?"

"I don't think so," he had said hesitantly. "Why did they send for me?"

"I don't know . . . neither does anyone else. Perine, he's the director, gave no explanation. Eve Knight is the only person who knows you."

A shadow had crossed his face. "Eve Knight, is she here?"

"Yes, we're sharing leads. She seemed very excited and pleased at your coming."

He had made no reply.

"You will stay, won't you? I'm Libby Powell. I'm in the company to keep local interest alive. I've done a few good road shows and have been looking forward to this experience."

"I don't know about staying. I'll feel strange in the village with everybody pointing at me and saying. 'That's Caroline Ryder's boy,' and asking, 'Why isn't his name Glutz or Smith or Brown? Why is he called Ryder? His mother married the man, didn't she?'"

Her laughter had rippled gayly. "For a person who has never lived in a small town you know the people."

"I've read a great deal and human nature is the same the world over. It's only the frame or setting that makes them seem different."

"Do you really care what people say?"

"No, it's not that, but I hate to be singled out for particular attention."

"Then you're really not an actor at heart."

"I don't like to be food for gossip. The towns people will be wondering about me, my grandfather, our contacts, what my grandfather will do, all that sort of thing."

"Are you afraid of him?"

"No."

"Then why not stay in town? You want a job, why should you let anything drive you away?"

"I won't." His jaw had squared, determination had filled his eyes. "Tell me something about the setup, my grandfather, things I ought to know."

"Your grandfather lives in the old house. Abbie Glover is his housekeeper, has been for years. She does for the old man and his nephew, Henry. Henry paints and is the son of your great-uncle Eben Ryder, who is something of a gay dog. At least that's what they say. He lives in Boston, comes down occasionally. There isn't much love lost between your grandfather and his brother Eben."

"Does anyone like my grandfather?"

"Probably not, in the way you mean. He's odd, that's the way we express it down here on the Cape. He has his luncheon at 11:30, naps from twelve to two, and the house must be absolutely quiet. Even Abbie has to leave. She comes down to the village every day and spends her time gossiping with Phoebe Spring, the wife of the chief of the local police. You'll soon get used to it. You're not really a foreigner, you know."

"A foreigner?"

Her laughter had sounded again. "Anyone on the Cape who is not a native is a foreigner. You come from Cape stock, so that does not apply to you. You'll like us when you get to know us."

"I like you already," he had said simply, without boldness or brashness and noticed that she was even prettier when she blushed.

"You'll have to have a place to stay. I'd invite you to our house, only—"

"Thank you, but—"

"I know," she had interrupted. "Nellie Pine's. She has a vacant room. You see, the village is fairly well filled now because of the players. Most of them room right at the Ryder House to be near the theatre, but it's full. You'll like Nellie, she's as neat as a pin, is away all day, and will let you do pretty much as you please. She won't serve meals, though. You'll have to eat at the Ryder House, the food is good Cape Cod."

"And do you think you can establish credit for me with Miss Nellie Pine?"

"I think so. If we hurry we can catch her before she leaves for work."

She had stepped on the gas and explained Nellie over the increasing roar of the motor.

"The local newspaper?" he had asked.

"No. Nellie is not a gossip. She may know everything we do, but she never talks about it. You'll like her. She's prim, she's an old maid, but she's nice."

They had turned the corner into Main Street, Chatwich, with a lurch.

"That's the Town Hall," she threw at him as they passed the enormous wooden building on the corner. "It is a compact village."

They had caught Nellie at her front gate. Nellie's face was long, a little on the gaunt side, but her eyes were friendly and gave only the slightest blink as Libby introduced Stryke and explained why they were there.

"Glad to have you," Miss Nellie had said after a moment's considered inspection. "Can't stop now. You'll find the key under the mat and fresh towels in the cupboard under the stairs. I'll fix your bed at noon time. There's plenty of hot water. You look as if you could do with a bath. Make yourself to home and if you want to sit in the parlor, lift the blinds. Libby, you take him in. It's the front bedroom just to the right of the door. Now I must hurry or I'll be late."

CHAPTER SEVEN

ALL that had happened over a week before. He had procrastinated about visiting his grandfather. He had grown accustomed to the curious speculative glances of the natives, had grown to like them, agreed with Libby that they meant no harm. He had become absorbed in his work, had fallen in love with Libby and had dreaded the visit he must make to his grandfather.

He had gone that morning after his conversation with Libby. His face colored anew as he remembered Suzie Briggs's factual recounting of their meeting. Life had been full of promise then.

He had walked up the road, had turned once to wave to Libby, had seen Suzie Briggs with her pail, but had thought nothing about her.

He had approached the Ryder house slowly. It was a nice house. His mother had been born in it, a long line of ancestors had lived there. From it had gone courageous men and women to sail the seven seas. His grandmother had sailed with old Silas, until her first child was old enough to go to school. He had recalled all the stories his mother had told him, for a moment relived the past with her.

He had liked the house, truly Cape Cod with its long sloping roof, bright red center chimney and friendly windows flanking the slightly recessed front door. A crimson rambler rioted over a trellis at the gate, a prelude to the flower-bordered walk, the beds filled with poppies, pinks, and tall spikes of dark blue larkspur. The gate latch had clicked behind him. The house seemed bound to the earth by flowers. A thin curl of smoke rose lazily from the kitchen chimney. He remembered stories of a side porch screened by honeysuckle. Somewhere

behind those vines, Abbie Glover was busy getting
dinner. Squaring his shoulders, he had approached the
front door, had lifted the old knocker and let it clatter
hollowly against the heavy wood.

For a moment he had hoped his knock would not be
heard. He had pressed his lips together and rattled it
again. He heard a clock strike 10:30.

"I hear you, I hear you, for gracious sakes!" he had
heard Abbie complaining from within.

The door opened slightly, just a crack, through which
she peered. "Oh, it's you!" she had said, as if she had
expected him.

"Will you tell Mr. Ryder that Stryke Ryder is calling?"
he had said, and had stepped just inside the door.

She had looked at him for a moment. She was plump
and round, but not jolly. Hers was a petulant face, lined
with disappointments and frustrations. Her eyes were
cold and unfriendly.

"Go in there. I'll tell him you've come. Hurry!" she had
commanded as he had moved out of her way so she could
close the door. "Letting flies in," she had mumbled. "And
me with a clam pie to put in the oven this minute. It's for
his dinner, you know," she had said accusingly.

So they had been expecting him, he had thought as he
went through the indicated door into the parlor.

The room had been stiff and cold, like a stage set,
spotlessly clean but lacking the warmth of actual living.
On the marble mantel two old vases held sheaves of
wheat, souvenirs of some long-forgotten funeral. A stuffed
owl glared at him from a glass cage on a whatnot in the
corner. Under it on another shelf was a lacy bowl of milk
glass. A huge family Bible with a brass lamp stood on a
stand under the mantel. The chairs were stiff and formal,
rosewood frames covered with horsehair. The sofa, too,
looked prickly and uninviting. He had looked again at the
Bible and had wondered if his name had been written
into the family records. Probably not. He had turned to
the old organ, closed and silent, and pictured his mother

sitting there when she was a girl playing hymns from the tattered hymnal resting squarely on the top. It had made him shiver. In that room time had stood still, nothing had been changed, it was still the country parlor waiting for the minister's call or the necessity of a funeral. The ingrain carpet seemed to say, "Be careful how you walk on me. I've been here for many years." Stepping gingerly, he had gone to the window and stood in the warmth of the sun.

"Well!" a voice brittle and querulous had demanded from the door.

Stryke had swung around. So that was his grandfather, the last of a line of ship captains, traders who had sailed the seven seas. He was as tall as Stryke and he had been blond. His eyes were the same deep blue, faded a little with age and subjected to a slight squint. He had stood with his feet braced against the floor as though it were the heaving deck of a ship. His hair billowed about on his head, full, heavy, unruly, like Stryke's. His face was wrinkled, his mouth clamped shut in a tight line.

"I'll look like that some day," Stryke had thought, "only I hope I won't be so stern, so severe."

"I repeat, young man, what do you want?" Silas had said testily.

"Nothing," Stryke had replied. "Mother asked me to call on you, made me promise I'd do it; that was just before she died."

"You took your time about it," Silas had accused.

"It hasn't been easy for me to come. I'm doing it because she wished it."

"Wanted you to get some of my money, I suppose," he had grumbled.

She had warned Stryke about him, had told him to curb his temper, had begged him to swallow his pride. He had remembered that as he said, "She hoped we could be friends. I think she was sorry—"

"Oh, she was, was she, that contrary, stubborn—"

"Don't call her names," Stryke had warned.

"I'll call her anything I like," Silas had declared.

"Not to me you won't."

Silas had stared at him unbelievingly, his eyes had sparked, had become suddenly bright.

"We're like a pair of kids," Stryke had thought.

"What about that shiftless father of yours?" Silas had asked.

"I never knew my father, know nothing about him, don't even know his name," Stryke had said coldly.

"What's that?" Silas had demanded. "So you've never met him?"

"No. I don't know what my name should have been."

"That name was no good. I marvel that your mother had the sense to abandon it. He married her for her money. I proved that to her," he had chuckled hollowly.

"You proved it?" Stryke had demanded.

"Yes. I bought him off, gave him money to desert you both. I thought that might bring her back to me." He had said that softly, more to himself than to Stryke.

"You should have known better," Stryke had said, hot contempt in his eyes.

"She didn't come, but she sent you. This is her way of admitting that she was wrong. That's why she sent you to me. She was smart."

"She believed that people should live like human beings, not like wild animals. She asked me to be your friend. She must have forgotten how difficult that would be. I'd rather be friend with—"

"You'd rather have your rattle-brained actor friends, I suppose. Actors. Bah! A bad lot, all them. You came here to mock me. Well, I won't have it. I'll have you run out of town, all of you! You're like your father, tarred with the same stick. We don't want actors in Chatwich, we won't have 'em. Out you go, all of you."

"You leave the Chatwich Players alone," Stryke had warned. "They're a group of decent people trying to make a living, they will do you no harm, will hurt no one. If you want to get me out of town I'll go, but you leave the others alone."

"So you're the self-sacrificing, virtuous type, eh?"

"No. It's a feeling you wouldn't understand. I couldn't see a whole group of people lose the work because of me. I'll go if you'll leave them alone."

"When are you going?" the old man had demanded.

"Right now." He moved toward the door. "I leave town, but I warn you, if you bother the others, you'll regret it, I'll see to that."

"Hah!" the old man had sneered. "No guts!"

"Do you want me to fight you?" Stryke had demanded.

"I don't care what you do."

Stryke had yanked at the door. Silas had cackled, but the rumpling sound in his throat had choked to silence as the bulk of Abbie Glover had sprawled into the room. It was obvious that she had been pressed against the door listening, that Stryke's quick yank had thrown her off balance.

She was on her knees. "It's time for your pill. I came to tell you," she had declared as she heaved her weight upward.

"So you've been listening again, you wall-eyed keyhole plug. You can pack your things and clear out. I've warned you enough. Get out!"

"Don't you talk like that to me, Silas Ryder, just because you—"

"Shut up!" he had shouted. "Git!"

"I won't git." She had stood defiant. "There's laws to take care of people like me, who've outlived their usefulness to men, and don't you forget it."

"Mutiny, eh! Well, I'll take care of that. Just try, and see what happens to you. Take a month's pay when you go, and don't come back."

Abbie had glowered at Stryke, had said accusingly, "This is all your fault."

Stryke had fled, slamming the door behind him.

He had walked for a long time, thinking about that conversation, angered anew because of the old man's irascible reception. He had kept his promise, he had offered his grandfather friendship and had met with a rebuff, had been ordered out of the town. He had promised to go, but he had changed his mind. He would not go! He'd stay and fight He had gone back to the house some time after 11:30, probably close to noon, determined to defy the old man, but the house had been closed and silent. He had knocked, but no one had answered. Then he had remembered the quarrel between Abbie and Silas.

He had gone back to the village thinking about his determination to stay, wondering how his decision might affect the others. Had worried about it. He had tried to reach Libby by telephone to talk it over with her. She had been out. There was no one in the theatre. He had wanted to tell Perine to ask his advice, but Perine had been too busy to talk to him in the drugstore. He had returned to the Town Hall and had called Libby again, but she was not at home. He had entered the graveyard and had talked to Sidney Stone and then Eve Knight had been found up there in the tower.

Now he was under a shadow. He wouldn't be able to leave town if he wanted to do so. Would old Silas try to run the company out of town? Would the actors hate him? They needed the work and the money.

Well, he had made up his mind. He wouldn't leave town if he could. He would fight the old man, the company should be willing to fight with him.

He ground his cigarette into the ivy leaves at his feet. He heard Sidney Stone come into the yard and putter with his paints and tackle, go into the church. He heard Sidney get ready, heard the first tug at the ropes, and the creek of a pulley.

The steady pull, pull of the ropes made the pulleys sing as Sidney went up and up along the line of the steeple. Stryke peered through the green of maple leaves, saw Sidney nearing the top of the spire.

Except for the song of Sidney's ropes the town seemed strangely quiet. He knew that just beyond his protecting screen of trees, however, most of the village was talking about what had just happened. He knew how the story would grow and grow with each recounting. He was sure that by now Suzie's story would be so twisted and distorted that people would be saying that he had told Libby he would kill Eve to get her out of the way.

He found himself hating people. Suddenly the air was torn and shattered by the most agonized cry Stryke had ever heard. It was filled with unbelievable horror and fear. The next moment something still shrieking hurtled through the lace of the tree tops and fell with a sickening, horrible thud just outside and beyond the hedge of cedars. The squash of the thud had stilled the screaming voice, but the air seemed to vibrate with the memory of its agony.

A bird fluttered in the hedge beside him. The slight noise sent a new shiver along his spine. He closed his eyes, pressed his lips together. He must go. He knew what was there but he must go. With slow, unhappy steps he went through the hedge and stopped. He closed his eyes and moved away from the sight of Sidney.

"Help!" he called. "Help!" and stumble blindly toward the fence.

In a few moments he was surrounded by silent gaping people who rushed forward to look and then turned away, their eyes filled with horror. Caleb Spring came and knelt beside Sidney. Percy Peacock and Black were there, too. Others came in after that, but Stryke didn't notice. He felt stunned, bewildered and just a little sick. It was so difficult to realize that a few minutes before Sidney had been alive, talking, joking.

"Who saw it happen?" Caleb asked.

Stryke told him what he knew, described what he had heard.

Then he heard Percy Peacock's measured, cultivated voice saying, "It wasn't an accident, Caleb. The rope was cut. Sidney Stone has been murdered, too."

CHAPTER EIGHT

THERE were people who said that Caleb Spring never laughed, but those people were unobservant. Caleb laughed with his eyes. They often sparkled with merriment, but they were cold, calculating and sober as he rose to his feet during the silence which followed Percy's bald statement.

"Who'd want to kill Sidney?" he asked bewildered.

"Who wanted to kill Eve Knight?" Black's voice echoed.

"If you'd use your head you might know the answer," Abe Tucker said accusingly. "The person who killed my cow don't want to be caught. He likely thinks that both Nellie and Sidney saw it done."

"Don't be a fool, Abe," Caleb said. "If Sidney knew who killed that cow of yours, he'd have said so upstairs when we was all talking."

"Well then, what other reason is there for killing Sidney?" Abe demanded.

"That's what we'll have to find out," Black replied, with a grim promise in his voice. "Tucker, you left the theatre while we were investigating the first murder, did you see anyone around here?"

"No," Abe denied stoutly. "I wasn't looking for anything but my cow."

Libby came running across the road, following more people. Stryke went to her, stopped her, turned her about. "Don't look," he warned. "It's Sidney. He fell. Peacock says he's been murdered."

"Oh!" she cried. "Oh! Poor Sidney!" She buried her face against Stryke and sobbed.

"I'll take a look at that rope," Caleb said.

The crowd parted as he moved closer to the church, where a rope lay sprawled on the grass.

"Yes, sir! It was cut all right," Caleb confirmed after a careful inspection of the end. "Cut halfway through." He let the rope ends fall from his finger and turned to Black.

"He ought to be covered," Abbie Glover said nervously. "It don't seem right for him to be layin' there like that, what with the flies and all, an' his eyes—" Her voice trailed away.

Percy and Black went over to the mute pile of Sidney's equipment, brought a piece of canvas and covered his body, thus breaking the morbid fascination which had held the people together in tight little circle.

"What made you think of looking at the rope?' Black asked Percy.

"Force of habit, I suppose," Percy replied. "In my work I'm always thinking of cause and effect. My first reaction was horror. Then I wondered how and why it happened. I could see that the rope had been broken. I looked at it."

"It was new rope," Caleb said. "He bought it at the hardware store the other day. I was there when he bought it."

"The doctor will be here in a few minutes," announced Charlie Snow, the clerk at the drugstore.

"We'll stay here," Caleb said. "Stryke, I allow as we'll want to talk to you, and you too, Professor. Now you others ought to move along."

He looked at them steadily for a long moment until a very old man came through the throng. "Hello, Luke. You're busy today," Caleb said with grim humor.

Luke did not bother to reply. He walked across the open space and into the church. The bell began its mournful toll, and Percy felt a shiver run down his spine as it stopped all conversation.

A pair of State Troopers began to urge the crowd back until they were forced over the low fence to the road's edge. The churchyard was cleared except for the white splotch on the ivy. Caleb and Black moved toward the steps, followed by Stryke, Percy and Libby. The voice of the bell died away. Luke ambled out, looking neither to the right nor the left as he passed the troopers.

Caleb sat down and looked up at Percy. "How do you account for it, Professor?" he asked.

"I don't," Percy replied.

"I thought you psychologist fellows knew why folks did such things," Caleb said thoughtfully. "Two murders within a couple of hours, and they don't either one of them make sense. Why?"

"If I knew what the conditions were I might be able to tell you something about why Sidney was murdered," Percy said thoughtfully. "But if I knew that, you and Black would know as much as I do. My interest lies in the study of mental life, of behavior under certain conditions. The only obvious fact which we all know is that the murderer was afraid of Sidney." He looked over toward the white canvas. "We'll never know what Sidney knew, now."

"Know anything about this, Stryke?" Caleb asked.

"No," Stryke answered. "I came over here to be alone. I thought I could get away from people for a little while. I heard him getting ready to go up. I was thinking about my own problems. Then I heard him scream."

"I guess the whole town heard it," Caleb said. "It must have been a terrific nerve shock," Percy said to Stryke.

"It was. I knew what was happening and how helpless I was to prevent his death. I couldn't move for a moment."

"Too bad you didn't run out. You might have seen the murderer," Black suggested.

"The rope was cut some time ago," Caleb said. He pointed to the frayed ends on the green. "It was cut well up toward the end by someone who knew just what to do. You see there would be a strain on that rope all the while Sidney was pulling himself up, but he wouldn't notice it until he was almost to the top of the steeple, if he noticed it then. Whoever cut the rope calculated that it wouldn't break until Sidney was pretty high in the air. And it didn't. It could have been cut any time after the fire siren sounded and no one would be the wiser."

"Did you see anyone when you came over here?" Black asked.

"Or right after he fell?" Black insisted.

"There was no one near when I ran out. I called for help and then everybody came running."

Martin Chase came over the fence and stopped before Caleb. "They tell me it was Sidney. Is he dead?"

"Awful dead," Caleb replied.

"What happened?"

"Cut rope."

"Why?"

"That's what we're wondering," Caleb said. Martin Chase looked over at the canvas, shook his head and turned away.

"That's the end of a long feud," Caleb said, looking after the lawyer as he moved through the crowd and vanished down the street.

"What kind of a feud?" Black asked.

"A combination—land, mortgages and Nellie Pine. They were rivals for Nellie's favor, which didn't set so well with Martin. Later Sidney done him out of a few parcels of land. Sidney's one of the few people in this town to cross Martin when he had his mind set on something."

Percy had been moving about, pacing in front of the steps, snapping off small pieces of a twig he had picked up from the ground.

"What's bothering you, Professor?" Black asked.

"The same thing that's on your mind. Who and why?"

"Any ideas?" Black asked hopefully.

"Plenty, but they don't fit into a logical pattern," Percy replied thoughtfully.

"Suppose you tell us about them," Black suggested.

"Yes," Caleb agreed.

Slowly, carefully, Percy told them of his earlier suspicions of Miss Nellie, of how he had supplied her with motive, opportunity and alibi. He saw doubt and resentment come alive in Caleb's eyes. "I didn't believe it either," he said and smiled at Caleb's relief.

"You must believe something," Black suggested.

"At the moment I'm suspecting Martin Chase," Percy announced bluntly.

"Martin!" Caleb gasped in shocked surprise.

"Why not? This is no ordinary murder. Two apparently harmless people have been killed. With two town people? Why? There is something behind these murders, something we can't possibly know at the moment."

"But why Martin?" Caleb insisted.

"Because it seems quite probable to me that the murderer was in the group when we found Sidney. The village has been full of people since the siren sounded at one o'clock. If anyone crossed over here to tamper with Sidney's ropes he would have been particularly careful to cover his actions. This murderer is taking no risks, I'm sure of that. I have a feeling that he waited in the church until after the body fell and then mingled with the crowd. In the excitement he would not have been conspicuous. Martin Chase did exactly that."

Caleb shook his head in unbelief.

"You yourself supplied me with the idea of a motive," Percy said.

Caleb looked up bewildered by the statement.

"The men have been rivals over land, mortgages and Nellie Pine. How do we know what happened last night or this morning to bring this rivalry to a head. Martin Chase knew these people, knew their habits. He would know how to strike effectively. He walked up here a few minutes ago, came casually. Where did he come from? Who told him it was Sidney? He was probably in the church all this time." Percy paused for emphasis.

Caleb rose and entered the church. He was gone for some time. "The back door's open sure enough. I wonder why. It's supposed to be kept locked," he said when he returned.

"Sidney probably," Stryke suggested.

"Weren't no need for Sidney to be back there," Caleb insisted. "I think the murderer used the back door."

"Who keeps the keys?" Black asked.

"The minister has a set and Martin Chase keeps an extra set in his office. He's a deacon," he admitted with some reluctance.

"I'll check about the keys," Black promised. "Now while we're waiting for the doctor, suppose you tell me something about Stone. Anything that comes to your mind," Black suggested to Caleb.

"When you've known a man all your life it don't seem as if there's much to tell about him," Caleb said after a moment's thought.

"Did he always live here?" Black asked.

"Except for a few years when he went off, roaming around. It was right after Nellie definitely broke their engagement because of a drunken party. He'd have probably gone anyhow. Roaming is in the blood around here," he added thoughtfully. "Most of the young fellows go off. In the old days it was whaling or to the Banks."

"Did you try it?" Stryke asked.

"Yes. Sailoring. But it wasn't what it used to be, wasn't like the stories I heard my father and grandfather tell about the Banks. That was different. Exciting, and some sense to it, but tramp steamers . . . I didn't mean to talk about myself—you asked me about Sidney."

"Did he go sailoring too?" Black asked.

"No, not as far as I know. He never talked much about what he did himself. He was more interested in what other people did. I've gathered from bits dropped here and there that he sort of traveled around the country some."

"And he went away when Miss Nellie broke the engagement?" Stryke asked.

"Yes. It happened a week before their wedding was to take place. There was a Portygee girl mixed up in it over to Teaticket. That was a long way from home in those days, but news traveled fast, even without radios and such inventions. Nellie heard about it and called off the wedding. It made quite a stir in the village at the time. I reckon Nellie's still got her wedding dress tucked away somewheres in her attic right now."

"How long has he been back in the village?" Black asked.

"Oh, ten or twelve years. I wouldn't know for sure, but it's been a long time. It was when his father died. They located him and he came home and stayed. Lemme see. It was in '29 along with the depression 'cause he said he had been cleaned out in the stock market."

"Was his affair with Nellie renewed on his return?"

"I wouldn't say that, but they were friendly enough. He hung around Nellie, divided her time with Martin Chase, but I think Nellie had grown man shy. I've seen 'em to movies and things like that, but I wouldn't say they were having an affair of any sort."

"So Martin and Stone divided Nellie's time between them," Black remarked.

"Now, look here, Black. I don't believe Martin Chase had a thing to do with this," Caleb defended stoutly. "I only mentioned the fact because it was the truth."

"The truth is what we are after," Black reminded him. "Chase and Stone were rivals. We've established that fact. Chase had access to keys to the church. We can't ignore these things, Caleb, no matter how much we like a person."

"It isn't a question of liking Martin Chase. I didn't say I did or didn't, that has nothing to do with it. I don't believe he killed them and you're not going to talk me out of that conviction, either one of you."

"Do you suspect someone?" Black demanded.

"No, not yet." Caleb's eyes were gleaming.

"From your observations which of the men seemed to have an edge on Nellie's time and affections?" Black asked.

"That would be hard to say," Caleb replied after consideration. "I guess maybe it was Sidney. I'm basing my statement on observation and not because I know anything definite. It was the way she acted toward Sidney, sort of standoffish."

"But they were friends," Black insisted.

"Yes. As a matter of fact, there was considerable rivalry between Nellie and Sidney. You know Nellie sees about all that goes on in the village and while she never has been one to gossip, there ain't anybody in town can dispute her statements, and nobody ever tried until Sidney came back and took up painting."

"If Nellie didn't talk, I fail to understand what you mean," Black said.

"Well, sometimes in conversation someone would say such and such a thing happened on this day or that. If it was anything that happened in the village Nellie would know. Sidney knew quite a bit, too. I guess house-painters and steeple-jacks see and know more than just normal folks who stay on the ground."

"That ought to give us something," Percy said.

"What?" Black asked.

"Sidney saw something."

"The binoculars!" Stryke exclaimed and jumped to his feet. He was excited. "He had them in the drugstore, took them out to show us."

Charlie Snow came across the yard and approached the men at the steps. He heard Stryke's statement. "He sure did," he confirmed. "Say, ain't the doc come yet?"

"What happened in the drugstore?" Black asked. "Anything that might have a bearing on that?" He pointed toward the canvas.

"I wouldn't know about that," Charlie Snow said, "but I can tell you what happened."

At a nod from Black he went on: "Eben Ryder was in. You know what a one he is for joshin' folks, Caleb. Well, Eben and Sidney had a little interchange of wit. Sidney said he got the glasses to compete with Miss Nellie. I think he said he had seen you, Stryke."

"That's right, he did."

"Sure he did," Charlie emphasized the point "because you said you seen him dangling from the top of the tower, said something about not knowing you was under inspection."

"Yes," Stryke agreed uncomfortably.

"Was there any other conversation about the glasses?" Black asked.

"Nothing special. There was a lot of talk among the customers."

"Then Stryke and Sidney were not alone."

"Lord, no, the place was filled for that time of the day. I was afraid I wasn't going to get out of lunch at all. Let me see, there was Eben Ryder and his son Henry, Abbie Glover, Sidney, Stryke, the professor, Abe Tucker, and the Perine fellow and someone else . . . oh, yes, Martin Chase came in for a pack of cigarettes. I think that was all, but I don't just remember."

At the mention of Martin's name Percy saw Black's lips clamp shut.

"Did all those people hear the conversation about the glasses?" Caleb asked.

"I don't see how they could help it," Charlie declared. "I did, and I was busy."

"Did you say Abe Tucker was in the store?" Black asked.

"Did they argue about anything?"

"Nope. Weren't no arguments, just friendly joshing," Charlie declared.

"What's on your mind now?" Caleb asked.

"There seemed to be some bad feeling between Tucker and Sidney in the theatre," Black replied.

"Natural enough," Caleb declared. "After all Sidney intimated as how Abe had been stepping out with Eve Knight right in front of Cora Tucker. That's enough to roil any man."

Black nodded agreement.

The doctor and the coroner arrived at the same time. When their examinations were finished, Black moved his little group over to the theatre for further questioning.

CHAPTER NINE

"WE'RE waiting for the second-act curtain," Percy whispered to Stryke as they sat the theatre before Black's arrival. Libby gave him a worried smile.

Caleb came and sat down beside Percy. He leaned across and spoke in a low voice to Stryke. "It looks like you might have a little trouble, son."

Libby gasped, "Why?"

"Rumors, talk. There's a couple of new witnesses. Black's bringing 'em all in. Folks is up and they talk. Everybody's worried about Nellie."

"You've got to do something to help Stryke, Caleb," Libby said sharply.

"I'll do what I can," Caleb promised, "but people are afraid that Miss Nellie has been done in."

"But they can't think that Stryke . . ." She didn't go on, just slid back into her seat, absorbed in her thoughts.

"While the folks was waiting down there, they talked among themselves and they've talked under suspicion, Stryke. Phoebe and Abbie to me. I had to tell Black about it. It's got nothing to do with what I think, myself; just my line of duty."

"There's nothing like tragedy to get people excited and show the stuff they are made of," Percy said.

"I dunno about that," Caleb replied.

"You're an extraordinary man, Caleb, most extraordinary, turning things over to the troopers this way."

"There's nothing so remarkable about that as I can see. I can deal with drunken Portygees on Saturday nights and during the cranberry-picking season, and the petty violations that come up in the summer months, but this is out of my line."

"Which is an indication of your character. You have a respect for murder, which makes me think that some time in your life you have had the desire to kill," Percy said.

A slow flush burnished the dark tan of Caleb's face and leathery neck.

Everyone, at some time or another, thinks for a moment that they could or would commit murder, Stryke thought. I've felt it, felt it this morning at my grandfather's, when he was saying things about my mother. Caleb has probably felt that way about that wife of his and her gossiping with women like Abbie Glover. She was gossiping today. They were talking about me. Now the whole town is talking. Caleb says they suspect me. Why should they?

"Don't worry, Stryke," Percy interrupted the boy's thoughts. "You don't look like a murderer."

"Except in my case, do people look like murderers?" Caleb asked, a twinkle in his eyes.

"A disarming statement," Percy replied. "Very disarming. I'll use it against you, if necessary."

"Won't ever be necessary," Caleb replied.

"That's what makes you a remarkable man," Percy said.

They both mean Phoebe, Stryke thought. But they'll never put their thoughts into actual word or in any concrete form. They understand each other.

There was a further commotion at the door Phoebe and Abbie came in. Phoebe's eyes were smoldering points of hatred as she turned them on Caleb for a full moment. Abbie sat beside her and their whispering began as usual.

Black faced the audience.

"The curtain is going up," Percy said and leaned forward.

"You are here because you have voiced opinion about these double murders," Black began. "If you have things to say, if there is anything you know this is the time and place to talk. We want to catch the murderer; you should want to help us. We are men trying to do our duty, and you, as good citizens, should help us all you can."

"Why don't you listen to reason, then?" Abbie Tucker rose to his feet. "You're looking for a motive for these here murders, and I told Caleb when these people were killed. They know who killed my cow, that's why they were killed."

"Mr. Tucker thinks this is a triple murder," Black said, and his eyes were smiling.

"And that's what it is," Abe insisted. "And it ain't no laughing matter neither."

"Have you any idea how long the cow has been dead?" Black asked.

"Now, how would I know that?" Abe demanded annoyed. "I'm just trying to supply you with a motive."

"And I have tried to impress upon you, Mr. Tucker, that Stone did not know who killed your cow, he merely realized it was dead. If either Stone or Miss Pine had seen the execution of your cow, they would have spread the news at once, wouldn't they?"

"Yes, I reckon they would," Abe agreed. Stryke rose to his feet. "The cow must have been killed between twelve and one," he said slowly.

"Why?" Abe demanded. "The cow couldn't have seen nothin', and if she did she couldn't talk, leastways I never heard her say nothin'."

"Thanks for eliminating the cow as a witness," Black said.

'I ain't eliminatin' her. I'm still saying she had something to do with the murders," Abe insisted.

Black turned to Stryke. "Why are you sure that the cow was killed after twelve?"

"Because I went through the cut just about noon and she was there, alive."

"Did she run after you?" Abe asked.

"Yes, she did," Stryke admitted.

"What were you doing in the cut?" Black asked.

"I was going back to the house. I had walked down the Webster Road and took the cut to avoid the village." He sat down.

Abbie bounced to her feet. "I want to go home," she announced. She turned toward Caleb and said, "Caleb Spring, you had no right to drag me into this, knowing that I have work to do, that I can't get nothing done between the hours of twelve and two, and me with a big wash on the line and not a soul to take it in for me before the dampness sets in."

Stryke wondered about that. Had she made peace with old Silas? Then he saw a sudden look of realization come into Abbie's face, an expression which seemed to say that nothing mattered, not even the clothes she had just mentioned.

"If you didn't talk so much, Abbie, you wouldn't be in trouble now," Caleb said quietly.

"Trouble!" she shrilled. "Trouble! I'm in no trouble, Caleb Spring, and don't you stand there and say I am, even if you are Chief of the Police and have no respect for your own wife. Just because you drag her into such things is no reason—"

"That will be all, Mrs. Glover, for the moment," Black's voice cut across her tirade, broke it in midair to leave it suspended in space forever.

Surprised, she glowered at him, started to speak.

"Unless you keep quiet I'll have you removed in the custody of an officer."

For a moment Abbie seemed ready to defy Black. Had he continued to look at her, she would have had the courage to tell him what she thought of him. Instead, he turned away to refer to a list on the table, and in ignoring her robbed her of the courage to defy him.

When Black looked up from the list and said, "Now, Mrs. Glover—" her resentment flared anew.

"Miss Glover," she corrected.

"Natural mistake for him to have made," Percy whispered to Stryke. "She doesn't look like a person who has missed anything."

Stryke remembered her words to Silas, about outliving her usefulness, about laws to protect women like her. Had she been a common-law wife? Is that what Percy meant? He looked at Abbie Black went on.

"You and Mrs. Spring repeated some gossip to Mr. Spring. Where did you get your information?"

"From Mary Verity and young Delano Crowell."

"Is Mrs. Verity here?" Black asked.

Mary Verity stood up. "I'm Mary Verity."

"What do you know that might help us, Mrs. Verity?"

"Well, we was talking about these murders and I just happened to say that I saw the Ryder boy cross over to the church some time before Sidney went in to the churchyard. That was all."

"Did you see anyone else near the church?" he asked.

"No."

"Thank you. Delano Crowell!" Black called.

A young lad probably sixteen or seventeen, dressed in greasy, dirt-stained blue jeans rose to his feet.

"What have you to offer?" Black asked.

"The same as Mrs. Verity. I was under my car, which was parked alongside the church fence. I was fixing my brake rod when someone went by. I looked up and saw Ryder. He went into the yard along by the steps, stood for a minute alongside of Sidney's things and went up the steps to the church door."

"Did he go into the church?"

"I don't know that he did. I didn't see. I just saw him stop. I quit looking then."

Eyes pivoted in Stryke's direction.

Black looked out over his audience. "We have three mysteries . . . no, four," he corrected with a quick look at Abe. "They must be related. Eve Knight was murdered a little before one. Tucker's cow was killed some time between twelve and one. Miss Nellie Pine has disappeared. And Sidney Stone was killed right after the first meeting we had here in this room. There are some of you who think Miss Pine has met a similar fate." He turned to Caleb, "Do you think Nellie Pine is dead?"

"No, I don't," Caleb answered readily.

"When do you think you can locate her?" Black asked.

"That depends on where she's gone. She went home after she turned in the alarm. Mr. Peacock here can testify to that. She took her car. She may have gone some distance."

"Why are you so sure that she is not dead?"

"Well, Nellie was a person who had had a good many years of putting two and two together. She probably had some idea as to why the woman who was dressed like her was murdered. When she discovered the telephone line in the tower was cut she probably decided to clear out."

"What makes you feel sure that she saw the woman and knew the telephone wire had been cut?"

"Unless Nellie changed her habits right quickly she must have seen the dead woman," Caleb declared. "Nellie Pine is a smart woman. She knew it was easier to climb the ladder and telephone the fire alarm than to run down the stairs to the call box. Another thing I noticed, an old coat which she always kept in the tower for chilly days was near the rubbish that burned. It seems to me that when she couldn't use the telephone she took that old coat and tried to smother the fire. When she realized she couldn't, she ran down and then during the excitement, cut loose."

"Do you think Nellie Pine knows why Eve Knight was murdered?"

"I wouldn't venture to say that. We don't know why these two people were killed. We've been trying to find motives but they don't seem reasonable excuses for murder, not to me they don't. I'd say it was quite likely that Nellie decided the bullet was meant for her. If she thought that, she more than likely figured it was because of something she knew. It would seem to me that Sidney's death was for the same reason. The thing we've got to do is find the motive."

There was a concerted nodding of heads and whispered agreement with Caleb's expression of opinion. Black considered thoughtfully for a brief moment.

"We're getting nowhere here," he finally said. "This meeting is over. You may go back to your duties. I will expect all of you who have testified in these cases to remain in town."

Caleb walked up to Black and asked in a low voice, "Why didn't you question Martin Chase since you seem to agree with Peacock?"

"Because the flow of evidence is in young Ryder's direction. I'll work on Chase alone. See to it that he does not know of our suspicions," Black ordered.

"You're right smart, Black. Martin Chase is a powerful man on the Cape. You'd better be awful sure before you accuse him publicly," Caleb warned.

"Are you suggesting that I forget my duty for political reasons?" Black demanded.

"You know better than that. If I thought he did it I'd lock him up right now and damn the consequences. We're officers of the law and we have duties to perform. At the same time there is no point in making an enemy until you are sure you're right." Caleb turned away.

As the crowd moved out, Eben Ryder came forward, took Stryke's hand, told him he was sorry that suspicion had pointed toward him, that he believed none of it and to call on him if he needed any help: he had to get back to Boston at once.

CHAPTER TEN

EBEN hurried away. Stryke was looking after him, a little hungrily, Percy thought, as they resumed their way toward the exit.

"Oh, Ryder!" Black called.

They all turned and realized that Black had just finished a whispered consultation with Caleb.

Stryke turned and walked back. They followed at a discreet distance and heard Black say, "I'd like you to stay here with me."

Percy heard the quick intake of Libby's breath which sounded like a prelude to Stryke's quick demand, "You mean I'm under arrest?"

"No, I wouldn't put it that way," Black said "Let's say that there are a few points I'd like to discuss with you."

"Does it mean the same thing?" Stryke insisted.

"No. Call it protective custody, if you like," Black said easily.

"Why don't you arrest me and be done with it?" Stryke asked gloomily.

"Are you confessing?" Black asked.

"Like hell I am. I didn't kill either one of them and you ought to know it."

"Perhaps I do," Black replied easily. "I want to talk to you alone," he added for the benefit of Percy and Libby.

"Come on," she said and tugged at Percy's arm.

She ran down the steps and out through the main hall of the building. She paused for breath at the entrance and asked anxiously, "You don't think Black will arrest him, do you?"

"Not unless public opinion forces him to make such a move. He's as bewildered as the rest of us. Reporters will be coming in. They will pounce on this story, play it up big. The townspeople will talk, will have views of their own. It's a mystery, all right. You and I believe in Stryke, but his connection with the murders will make very interesting talk and more interesting reading."

She moved away from him, across the street. He looked up and saw Martin Chase's feet on the windowsill.

"Doesn't Chase ever move from that spot?" he asked.

"He can move fast enough when he wants to," she said. "I saw him down the street this noon and by the time I got to the post office, there he was with his feet on the windowsill. He's smart and just the man we need." The next moment her feet were running up the wooden steps to Chase's office.

As she burst into his office Martin removed his feet from the sill and eyed them speculatively. Without a hat, his gray hair and his wrinkles made him look older than Percy had thought him.

"If Stryke Ryder is arrested, will you act as his lawyer?" Libby demanded without preliminaries.

"Kind of rushing things a bit, aren't you, Libby?"

"I don't know. I want to be prepared. Stryke seems to be the number one suspect and I want to be able to act."

"I don't know," he said after thoughtful consideration. "His grandfather is my best customer."

"What difference does that make?"

"Well, the old man and the boy aren't exactly friends, are they?" he asked.

"I don't know."

"But you knew he was going up there this morning," he reminded her with a smile.

"But I don't know what happened. He's been in a mood ever since. Will you be his lawyer or not?"

"If he needs me, I guess you can count on me," he said slowly.

"Now that that's settled, I've a question I'd like to ask you about the church keys. Who had then today?" Percy asked.

"They always hang on that nail." Martin looked up, blinked and then rose deliberately and fingered an empty nail on the wall above his desk. "Funny, he said. "They were there. Someone has take them."

"Who?" Percy demanded.

"I don't know. I don't look at them unless someone wants to get into the church for one reason or another."

"There goes another good idea," Percy said. "There seem to be no direct lines leading to the culprit." Percy backed to turn around and upset a pair of riding boots. As he righted them against the wall he asked, "Where do you ride, Mr. Chase? I'd like to go with you some time."

"You can rent horses down at the Port," he said.

Libby laughed. "Martin on a horse. That's funny. Or have you gotten over being afraid of horses?" she asked.

Percy looked at Martin with new interest.

"Do you know why you are afraid of horses, Mr. Chase?"

No," Martin said slowly.

"Many people are, you know," Percy said easily.

"That doesn't help when people like Libby laugh at you," Martin replied.

"I didn't intend to be mean, Martin."

"I know. It seems silly for a man brought up in the country to be afraid of a horse, but I am. I bought those boots, tried to force myself to ride, but it was no use."

"No," Percy agreed. "You can't force a thing like that. It has to be cured."

"In the meantime, I'll sell you the boots, if they fit," Martin suggested.

Percy laughed. "I have boots. I might take you up on the trees, however. They're extra long. How much do you want for them?"

"I wouldn't sell them. My grandfather made them. I guess they're antiques now."

"And they could be jacked onto the window ledge from a chair to give a good alibi," Per thought.

Libby was restless and turned away from the men. "I may not be back for the rest of the afternoon," she said. "If anything happens about Stryke, take charge."

"Where will you be if I want to get in touch with you?"

"I don't know." She turned and walked out the office.

"And where are we going?" Percy asked before they started down the stairs.

She gave him a quick, rather grateful look. "I'll find Miss Nellie, if that is possible."

"We'll take my car," Percy said. "People don't know it."

Libby laughed scornfully. "Everybody in town knows your California license plates. Every time you pass they say, 'There goes that professor fellow. What is he anyhow, a professor playing actin' or an actor tryin' to be a teacher?'"

"We'll take it just the same," he said.

They walked through the drive to the Tucker barn, which was on the next street. It had the warm sweet smell of cows and the more pungent odor of horses. Libby paused at the main door while Percy went to the shed for his car.

As she sat beside him she said, "A man standing in the cow's manger could have taken a pot shot at Nellie Pine's kitchen window without a chance in the world of being seen."

"It's an idea, Libby. We'll have Black trace the course of the bullet. They can tell from which angle it was fired." He swung toward Cross Street. "Tucker have any grudge against Miss Nellie?"

"Heavens, no! What made you think of that?"

"Was the mail early or late today?"

"It was a little late, but not much. Tucker was there when I was," she replied.

"Did you see Stryke?"

"No. I expected to. I wanted to know what happened up at his grandfather's."

"Has he told you?"

"No. There's something on his mind, Percy. He's not himself."

"Just the possibility of being arrested for a double murder is enough to make a man preoccupied."

"I don't mean that," she insisted. As he slowed down for a cross street, she said, "Keep going, and turn right at the next dirt road. That will take us up past the old cemetery and we can hit the Webster Road above the village. You won't mind few scratches on your car, will you?"

Percy made no reply. The road was old and sandy and not very wide. He heaved a sigh of satisfaction when they hit the Webster Road. She laughed. "Turn right at the next dirt road. I'm trying to keep out of sight."

"You're doing all right," he said as he made the turn.

Libby leaned forward and looked ahead. "There are fairly new tire marks here. We may be on the right track."

"Do you think Miss Nellie might have gone that way?"

"If she's at her cabin, yes," she answered "Shucks," she said in a few moments, "the tracks are gone. There hasn't been anything over dirt this road for a week. Must have been someone going to the Ryders'."

"Isn't there a better way to get to the Ryders'" he asked.

"The street from the village stops just a little beyond the Ryder House. Anyone coming from Webster could come in on this road, snake through the pine grove and come out at the rear of the Ryder place. There was a cart road in there at one time."

"Think we'd better turn back and look somewhere else for Miss Nellie?" he asked.

"No. This is a short cut. I hope the road is all right."

They bumped and jogged over stones and ruts, went up a slight grade and were rewarded with a glimpse of a long pond.

"Is her cottage on this lake?"

"No. It's beyond this, on a little pond but very lovely. Nellie's had the cottage for years. It was her father's. He'd come up here in the winter for geese."

"A hunting lodge?" he queried.

"No. It was a shack before Nellie fixed it over."

"Does Miss Nellie shoot geese?" he asked.

"Certainly not. Take the next turn at the right. We'll be there in a few minutes."

Before they reached the turn Percy jerked the wheel suddenly and headed for trees at the edge of the road.

"What on earth!" Libby exclaimed.

"There's a car coming along the road. It will pass us in a minute."

"Do you suppose that the murderer—?" she gasped.

"I had some such idea. Duck down just in case there should be fireworks."

"What about your danger?" she demanded with tenseness.

"I'll have to trust my luck. It's always been good. Get down! Here it comes."

A car nosed around the clump of shrubs. Percy laughed. Libby bobbed up.

It was Caleb. "So you had the same idea. Well, she ain't there," he said.

"Oh, Caleb!" Libby cried. "Where do you suppose she has gone?"

"I don't know now. I had a feeling I'd find her here. She may be somewhere in the village. I'll have to look. I won't be easy until I find her. You can turn round up at the cabin or go back on the other road though this one is shorter." Caleb's car slipped away through the trees.

A short distance beyond the bend she told him to stop about fifty feet from a small cottage whose porch had a clear view of a small tree-bordered pond. "That's the cottage," she said.

"Let's take a look," he was out of the car and holding the door for her.

"Caleb has nice new tires," he said and pointed along the road where a double set of tire marks showed clearly in the dirt. He moved forward several feet. He pointed ahead. "See anything?" he asked.

"Tire marks," she replied.

"How many?"

"Just one."

"And over there about twenty feet?" he demanded.

"Why there are a double set there," she exclaimed.

"Right! Caleb's and some others." He moved away, his eyes on the soft mat of pine needles. "A car turned in here off the road, stopped right here. Why?"

She ran ahead of him toward the cabin and on tiptoes reached her fingers along a beam. "I don't see how you could tell," she said as she handed him the key. "I wouldn't have noticed. How did you happen to?"

"I was brought up in the West. Spent a lot of time in the woods when I was a boy."

"An Indian pathfinder?" she asked.

"No. There weren't many Indians left when I was a youngster but my grandmother often had to run to the stockade when an alarm was sounded. I picked up a few things from an old buck."

She had put the key in the lock and opened the door. "Nellie must have been here," she said, "though it is not like her to leave the curtains open."

"She was in a hurry. Look!" He pointed to the cupboard door, which was standing open.

"She came here for food. That cupboard is always full of canned goods, beans, corned beef, canned milk and that sort of thing," she exclaimed. "Where do you think she has gone?" he asked. "I can't imagine."

"Maybe we can trail her." She turned, surprised. "I saw tire marks just ahead of mine when we turned right onto this road. If you'll drive the car and drive slowly I'll try to follow those marks. It rained last night and the ground is just damp enough to show the prints. I saw some deer marks as we came in too."

"We can try it," she said eagerly. "Let's go before someone else thinks of this place."

"Caleb came up that road," he said as they passed a fork.

They followed the odd tire marks around the pond and through some scrub pine and thick underbrush for what seemed miles. They crossed a wider road and went on deeper into wooded country. There were boulders in the road and rounded stones scattered through the trees.

"This is glacial-moraine country," he said once "Do you know where we are?"

"Not exactly, but in general. How's the trail?"

"Still there."

The trees grew taller and the undergrowth danker. The road was covered with leaves and twigs and the trail was not as easy to follow. He told her to stop, and got out to examine the road.

"We've missed her. She turned off somewhere, I'll go back. Can you back up? Go slowly. Wait few minutes to give me a start."

He found the spot where the car they had been following had turned into the woods. It had beer a road once, but was so seldom used that it had been very easy to miss. Libby jumped out and stood beside him. She pointed to a split board nailed to one of the trees.

"This is funny," she said. "This leads to a hunting cabin. My brothers brought their decoy geese here. It would be just like Nellie to think of this place. No one ever comes here except in the hunting season." She went ahead of him along the path.

"I'm very excited," he said. "I feel that we are on the verge of discovering the reason for the murders."

He stopped and peered into the brush at the side of the track.

"What's the matter?" she asked.

"Miss Nellie's car." He strode away from her, parted some branches and pointed.

Nestled in a covering of low shrubs the car was well hidden from the makeshift road leading to the lodge. "Thank God we are in time," she said. "I've been afraid of what we might find."

"Unless someone came on foot, we are the first," he assured her.

"We must get away before someone as clever as you follows our trail," she said and started toward the building, calling as she went.

There was no answer from the cabin. They went on, up the steps to the door. The curtains were tightly drawn, the woodland silence smothered everything. Libby banged at the door with a closed fist and cried, "Nellie! It's Libby Powell! We must talk to you. We trailed you from the cottage. You must come out! We need your help desperately."

There was silence for a long moment before they heard a slight movement inside hardly more than the slithering a rat might make as it scuttled over a rafter. The door opened slowly and Miss Nellie stood facing them, blinking her eyes against the light.

"Why did you have to follow me here?" she demanded impatiently. "I didn't suppose anyone would think of this place." She was surprised when she saw Percy.

"He found your trail," Libby explained.

"Well, now that you're here, come in."

They slipped inside. She closed and bolted the door behind them.

Libby told her all the things that had happened, of Stryke's danger, of the excitement in the village because of her disappearance.

"Do they think I ought to sit quietly and wait to be murdered?" she snapped.

"No. They are afraid you have been murdered," Percy explained. "They know about the shot through your window and about Eve in the cupola."

"That poor girl!" Miss Nellie's mood changed. Tears welled in her eyes. "She died for me."

"She died because the murderer thought she was you," Percy corrected her.

"Never-the-less she is dead," she retorted with a return to her crispness.

"Did you know she would be in the tower?" Percy asked.

"Now how would I know that?"

Percy shrugged. "Did you know she had a shirt-waist like yours?"

"Of course, I did. She showed me hers, wanted to give it to me when she realized how much I liked it. I wouldn't take it but said I'd buy one like it if she didn't mind. She said she thought it would be fun, that we'd put them on some day and walk down Main Street together and give people a chance to talk and figure things out." A pained smile flickered over her lips. "She had a sharp sense of humor, that girl."

"There are many questions we'd like to ask you but I don't think we ought to take the time now," Percy said. "We can talk as we go back."

Nellie's eyes were moist again. "Who did it?" she asked. "Who would want to kill me?" She knew from their blank faces that they had no ready answer. "And poor Sidney. Why?" Tears trickled down her thin cheeks. "I told him he'd talk too much one of these days, but he wouldn't listen to me. Sidney thought he knew it all. I guess he knew too much today. He must have seen something." She brushed the tears from her cheeks, her lips tightened.

"What do you know?" Percy asked.

"Nothing."

"What did you see this morning, Miss Pine?" he asked. "Think hard. Do you know who killed Abe Tucker's cow?"

"No. What about Abe Tucker's cow?"

Percy started to explain, but Libby interrupted him. "Can't you give us some clue to these awful murders," she begged.

"No. If I knew anything I wouldn't be here." She squared her shoulders, shook the last of the tears from her eyes. "Did you ever have someone murdered instead of yourself? Of course, you didn't. It's a queer feeling. That poor girl, just because she was wearing a shirtwaist like mine she had to die." She sighed. "It makes a body wonder about the ways of Providence. I've escaped death twice in one day."

"Your time has not come," Percy said bluntly, hoping to jerk her out of her philosophical mood. Her eyes snapped at him. "We hoped you could give us the answer to the riddle. Think hard and tell us what you saw this morning."

"I didn't see a thing." The words cracked out. "I had a splitting headache, had zigzags of light flashing across my eyes all the live-long morning. I didn't do any observing. It didn't worry me nont though on account of the rain last night. Things were pretty wet this morning and not much chance of a bad fire."

"If you know nothing and saw nothing, why'd you hide?" Libby demanded.

"Because someone figured just as you did that I knew something. They weren't going to ask first, though, if I had seen anything. They were taking no chances. No, sir. They proved that twice, so I lit out."

"We want you to go back with us," Percy said.

"And get killed for my trouble?" she asked.

"No. There is no question that you are in grave danger, but so is Stryke Ryder."

"How can I save him?"

"The very fact that you are alive will help him."

"How?"

"There is an undercurrent of talk in the village. It has been suggested that he has disposed of you too."

"How on earth could he?" Miss Nellie demanded. "That's ridiculous!"

"Of course it is," Percy agreed, "but people are not logical at a time like this."

"Folks talk too much. Help me pack up again, Libby," she said with grim determination.

Percy watched and admired the courage of the thin-lipped serious woman as she bundled her few possessions together, ready for departure.

CHAPTER ELEVEN

THEY made plans as they worked.

"Where would be the most unlikely place for you to hide in the village?" Percy asked.

Miss Nellie considered for a moment. "As far as the town is concerned, Caleb Spring's house. I haven't spoken to Phoebe Spring for twenty years."

"Then Phoebe Spring is going to have a second boarder," Percy said with a smile.

"Will you do it, Nellie?" Libby asked anxious

"It'll go against the grain, but I'll do anything to help a poor lad who is in trouble."

"Then we'd better get started," Percy suggest

They closed and locked the cabin and start for the road. It was very still off there miles from a village. A light wind soughed through the tops of the trees and rippled the surface of the pond. Their feet on the damp, moss-covered earth made snapping sounds as twigs broke under the progress.

Libby paused, put a hand on Percy's arm a whispered, "Listen."

They stood like three statues. The unmistakable purring of a car could be heard on the road byond the clearing.

The sound faded into silence. "They've stopped," Miss Nellie said.

"They've seen our car," Libby whispered.

"This will change our plans somewhat," Percy said tersely. "Whoever is out there may be on an innocent errand or it might be the person most concerned—the murderer. I was going to suggest that you leave your car here, Miss Nellie, and ride in with us. That would deepen the mystery of your disappearance as far as the world at large is concerned. Now I don't know. We'll be followed when we leave here and it won't be safe for you to ride with us. After we go I want you go get your car out of here. Find some place that can hide both yourself and your car until dark and then ride in somewhere near the village, leave your car and walk to the Spring house. I'll see Caleb in the meantime and prepare them for your coming. Remember, I don't want you to go to Caleb's until after dark and I don't want you to be seen. Agreed?"

"If we live that long," Nellie said as she dropped to the earth.

Percy and Libby followed suit, for they had beard the sharp ping of a bullet whistling through the trees. They were behind an old log. Two more bullets zinged over their heads.

"He means business," Libby said grimly.

"Do you think we ought to try to get back to the cabin?" Miss Nellie asked.

"No. I wish I had a gun," Percy breathed.

"Well, here's one. I don't know how good it is. I just brought it along for an emergency and it seems like this is it." She pulled a revolver out of the Boston bag she carried and handed it to Percy.

He took the gun, looked at it, leveled it over the log and pulled the trigger. It was an old gun and it made a loud report. They listened.

"Hit something," Percy grinned, showing his white teeth in a satisfied grin.

"Sounded like metal," Miss Nellie said.

"It was," he agreed. "I only hope it wasn't our car."

"It wasn't his," Libby said, as the roar of a motor sounded through the trees.

"That road we were on, does it go straight ahead or turn anywhere near here?" Percy asked as he bounded to his feet. "Quick!"

"It goes straight ahead for about a quarter of a mile and then there's a fork, one leads over toward the north and the right fork goes down to East Chatwich."

Percy dropped the gun. "Take care of yourselves and wait for me. I'll be back."

He leaped over the log and dashed through the trees, going in the general direction of the road. The crashing made by his progress was louder than the sound of the motor which was racing away.

Percy ran as fast as he could. He leaped low bushes, vaulted over dead tree trunks and boulders. His foot caught in some brambles. With a muttered curse he was on his feet and speeding toward the road. If he could make it, the riddle would be solved. He dashed through the last of the big trees and found the road, just as a car took the right fork of the road and vanished from sight.

Unhappily he made his way back to the two women still crouched behind the fallen tree. "Where's the nearest telephone?" he demanded.

"On the East Chatwich road, almost to the village. John Snow's place," Nellie said to Libby.

"You know what you're to do," Percy said. "Libby and I will get to the telephone. Remember—wait until dark before you come to the village."

"Hurry, or you'll be too late," Nellie called after them as they raced up the road.

"A great girl, Miss Nellie," he said as he reached for the key to turn on the ignition. The keys which he had left dangling in the lock were gone.

"Damn!" he cried as he leaped from the seat and to the front of the car to release the hood. He back in a moment, an extra key in his hand. "I'm glad I did that little key stunt," he said with satisfaction. "Our man thinks of everything."

"And is desperate," she agreed as they race down the road.

At the John Snow place Libby and Percy ran toward the house. The door was locked. While Percy pounded,

Libby looked under the mat and the flower pots until she found the key and opened the door.

"Nice of them to be so trusting," he said.

"A lot of people never even lock their doors", she replied.

He was jingling and banging away at the telephone, his face red with annoyance and anger. She took it from his hand and in a moment was speaking to the operator.

He took it and asked for Caleb Spring's office. They waited impatiently. There was no answer. He asked for Caleb's house. That line did not answer. He asked for Martin Chase's office, but that line did not respond.

"Give me the drugstore," he said in desperation. They waited, but received no response to the insistent ringing.

Libby took the receiver and asked for her own house.

"Mother," he heard her say.

"Where are you?" he heard an anxious voice demand through the receiver.

"Never mind. Get in touch with Caleb Spring. Tell him and the troopers to watch every car coming into the village. It's very important."

They put the key under the mat and raced for the car.

"It was rotten luck, those people being out. They might have seen that car as it raced by. Is the murderer going to get all the breaks?" Percy asked as they gathered speed.

"I know one he didn't get. He didn't know about Miss Nellie's revolver," she said.

"And I had to hit my own car when I fired. A bullet hole in his would have helped us a lot, but no such luck for us."

"You were lucky you didn't hit a tire," she reminded him.

"We'll never locate the car now. No point in killing ourselves at too reckless a speed."

"Does it make much difference what kills us?" she asked. "We're on the list now. He isn't going to be sure that we didn't spot him."

Percy looked his admiration. "He's pretty sure about that. The thing he doesn't know is what Miss Nellie might have told us."

They bumped across the railroad tracks of the spur and whizzed past the few houses at the east end of the village.

They were racing by the town park when it happened. A front tire blew out. The car swerved and lurched. Percy's hands went white as they gripped the wheel. There was one breath-taking minute when anything might have happened. He held her to the road and as her speed reduced, the chance of overturning was eliminated. White-faced and grim they leaped from the car.

"Bullet," he said tersely. "He thinks of everything. Want to run for it?"

"Why not?"

He took the side of the road from which the bullet had come, to protect her, and together they ran toward the village.

They cleared the thick wooded section of the park and were opposite the grandstand when Libby reduced her pace. Her face was flushed, her breath came in quick little puffs.

"We're not out of danger yet," he warned her.

"I saw a car going up the road, Eben Ryder's car. I thought he said he was going to Boston. Do you suppose . . ."

"But why should he?" Percy asked.

"Why should anyone? Suppose he parked up beyond the ball park and was waiting for us? I don't know what to think."

"I haven't seen a soul," Percy said. "Where are all the people? This end of the town is like a deserted village. I wonder what's up."

"It's too quiet here. I don't like it," she said thoughtfully. "What's that?"

They stopped to listen.

"Voices," he said.

"Angry voices. She began to trot again.

They passed the bank and the Ryder House, which like everything else seemed deserted.

When they reached Miss Nellie's house she ran across the street. The front door was open. He heard her call for Stryke. She came out, disappointment on her face.

The garbled sound of human voices was louder row. He had been listening while he waited. She heard it too.

"I'm worried about Stryke," she said. "Come on."

They were at the gate when they heard the first toll of the bell, long and slow as the others had been. She gripped his arm.

"I'm afraid, Percy. The bell! Another death!" Her voice trailed away, lost in the resonant moaning.

"Yes, and we can thank our lucky stars that bell is not tolling for us," he answered grimly.

CHAPTER TWELVE

WHEN Stryke saw Libby and Percy walk away from him at the Town Hall, he was fighting mad. A slow resentment had been taking shape and flared into words as he demanded, "Well, when do I go to jail?"

"Don't act that way," Caleb said kindly.

"What do you expect me to do?" Stryke retorted.

"We want a little cooperation," Black said quietly. "My men have been taking fingerprints, here and there. We are doing everything to catch the murderer and you can trust us to help an innocent man. Circumstances have conspired against you. You can help us to prove your innocence. We want your prints now. If you are innocent, I can imagine how you feel, but you must admit you have no alibis for the murder periods."

"Suppose I did kill Eve Knight, why on earth would I want to kill Sidney Stone? He told you everything he knew before he died."

"I wouldn't be too sure of that," Caleb said quietly.

"What do you mean by that?" Stryke demanded.

"I don't know what I mean. I'm sure puzzled," Caleb admitted.

They went down to Caleb's office, where Black's men took Stryke's fingerprints.

"I'm going back to the station with the photographs and the prints," Black explained. "I'm leaving two men on guard here, one at the cupola and one at the church. I'll be back later, after I've examined everything. My advice to you is to go home and sit tight until you hear from us. Avoid people and don't talk."

"I haven't a home now that Miss Nellie has vanished," Stryke reminded them.

"You go back there and wait. I'll take that responsibility. If we can't find other accommodations for you I'll get Cora Tucker to take care of Nellie's house until she gets back. Don't worry about that, just follow Black's instructions," Caleb ordered.

"And remember," Black cautioned, "don't talk."

"No, there's too much talk going on now," Caleb agreed.

They walked with him to the front entrance of building. Stryke recoiled as he heard various remarks from the crowd.

"There, that's the one."

"He don't seem to be under arrest."

"He ought to be." There was indignation in that voice.

"Isn't he handsome!"

Stryke blushed at that remark, coming from a young girl.

"A stiff upper lip, son," Caleb said. He gave Stryke a reassuring pat on the back.

Stryke squared his shoulders and with head up walked through the knot of people as if they did not exist.

Caleb was worried about Miss Nellie. He drove over to the telephone office to check with the operators to see if any calls had come in from Nellie's house shortly after one o'clock. Miss Nellie had made no calls, but he learned that Martin Chase had called Nellie between one and two but there had been no answer.

He did not like that information. He knew Percy and Black would pounce on it as further evidence to substantiate their suspicions of Martin.

He decided that if he were Nellie he would probably go to the woods. The most likely place would be her cabin.

When he met Percy and Libby near Nellie's cabin he had not been as blind as they supposed. He had realized that she had been there. He had also decided that she had gone on to hide. He remembered a little shack on the beach which would make a good hiding place. He felt confident that Nellie had gone there. He decided to keep his opinion to himself and returned to the village, which was in a direct line with the beach place.

He stopped at his ofice to check with the troopers to see if any word had come from Black. The troopers were worried because of the temper of the crowd which still milled about the Town Hall.

"I'll see what I can do with them," Caleb promised as he started down the long hall toward the front of the building.

He could see them milling about outside, could hear the mumbling of their voices before he reached the door. There were a lot of strangers in the group now, summer people, salesmen, Portygees and some men from the construction camp.

He looked over the crowd. "Why don't you folks go home? You women will have meals to cook, and Abbie, what was it you said about clothes on the line to be taken in before the evening dampness sets in?"

"I want to talk to you, Caleb Spring," Abbie said and stepped forward. "I want you to go home with me," she said.

"Don't tell me you're afraid, Abbie."

"It's my legal rights I'm thinking of, Caleb Spring." She explained about her quarrel with old Silas and her dismissal from his service. "Threw me out like an old shoe," she said.

"I don't know as I can help you," he said thoughtfully, his eyes on the crowd, which had scattered a little before the weight of his authority.

"You can help me if he won't let me in. I wouldn't stay in that house another night, not if you paid me. And Phoebe says I can stay with you for a little while."

Caleb winced before he said, "You've known the old man for a good many years, Abbie. You know his temper. How come you're taking exception this time?"

"I've had enough, that's why. Are you coming with me?"

"All right," he agreed. "Come round to the side, my car is parked there. I'll run you up and you can get your things."

As they drove up the road toward the Ryder place, Caleb remarked, "Your clothes look dry enough, Abbie. They're doing a right smart bit of flapping in the breeze."

"They'll have the ends frayed out of them. Not that I care now," she said bitterly. "I declare, Caleb, even the house seems to have turned against me. It don't look the same."

"Kind of letting your imagination run loose, ain't you?" he asked.

"Laugh if you want to, but the house seems to be different."

"Looks the same to me. I'll drive in near the kitchen door. Your room's in that ell, ain't it?"

"You know perfectly well it is, regardless of what people in this town have been saying." She wiped a tear from her eye.

"You shouldn't mind what people say, Abbie. You do a right smart bit of talking yourself."

"Don't you criticize me, Caleb Spring. Everybody in town knows that Phoebe . . ."

"Yes, I know, that Phoebe talks too much. I've been wondering whether it's going to be a good thing to have you in my house, right now."

"I can pay my way."

"I wasn't thinking of money." He pulled the car up close to the low kitchen porch.

"It'll make ruts in the grass," she said, as she slid out. "but I don't care now."

"Kind of bitter, ain't you, Abbie?"

"And why not? I've been put out of the only home I've known for years because of a murderous young whipper-snapper and denied refuge by an old friend for the same reason. It's cause to be bitter."

"But you shouldn't say such things about Stryke Ryder," he cautioned as he walked with her toward the kitchen door.

She turned the knob, but the door wouldn't open. "That's funny," she said. "No, it ain't, neither. Just as I thought, the old coot has locked me out."

"Where do you leave the key?" he asked, looking down at the old braided rug at the sill.

"It won't be there," she said as she put her fingers down behind an old sea chest which she had used for an extra supply of wood for the kitchen range. "It isn't. It's a good thing you came with me."

She marched around the house and banged the knocker on the front door. She jangled the bell, but the sounds echoed hollowly.

"If he thinks he's going to keep me from getting my things, he's mighty mistaken." She retraced her steps to the kitchen. "That window hasn't had a lock on it ever. Get in through there," she ordered.

"That would be unlawful entry," he warned.

"If you're going to stand on technicalities, I ain't." She tugged at the window and pushed it up. "Darnation, where's the stick? Here, hold it, unless you're afraid," she said scornfully as she prepared to swing one fat leg up and over the sill.

Caleb obliged while his eyes twinkled.

She threw the door open. "Come on in if you want to or stay out there, just as you please. I'll only be a few minutes."

He went into the kitchen, looked at a pie on the well-scrubbed kitchen table.

"Looks like a clam pie," he said.

"It is."

"You make the best clam pies on the Cape," he said.

"Help yourself."

"It ain't yours to give away now," he said with a gleam in his eyes.

"Humph," she retorted. "There's a knife in that drawer." She left him eyeing the pie.

Caleb found the knife and cut himself a good wedge of the pie. The crust was crisp and rich, the clam filling delicious. Between mouthfuls he cocked an ear to listen, expecting old Silas to come storming out at any moment. Except for the clatter in Abbie's room, the house was far too quiet.

The pie finished, he brushed his hands over the spotless sink and walked to the dining-room door. The old mahogany gleamed richly in the late afternoon glow. The silver on the sideboard shone brightly. It was a restful room, a pleasant place to dine, not like the kitchen table from which he ate his meals, unless Phoebe prepared for a "set" of company and used their more formal dining-room.

Caleb was thinking of the niceties of living which he did not have at home, as he called loudly, 'Silas!"

There was no answer, not even a stirring sound. "That's funny," Caleb muttered. "Are you in the sitting-room?" he called loudly.

The door was closed into the sitting-room. He waited, expecting some sound in answer. The house was breathlessly still. He could no longer hear Abbie stirring about. He waited.

A long howl came in answer. He knew what it was. Silas's old bird dog was howling under his window.

He thought of all the folklore and superstitions he had heard through the course of his life. A howling dog meant death, so did knockings on the wall, falling pictures, birds in a room. He looked through into the parlor and the old owl that had blinked at Stryke glared vacantly at him from its button eyes. Caleb shivered. The howling went on.

Abbie came bustling through the kitchen, asking, "What ails that dog? He's been up in the woods as usual. I saw him come down across the lot and went to the kitchen door to let him in. Unless he has caught a bird, he hasn't had a thing to eat all day. Where is he?"

"He seems to be under the sitting-room window."

"Funny he don't shout at him," she said.

"He isn't saying anything," Caleb said grimly. "I've called to Silas a couple of times, but he didn't answer. Was he all right when you left?"

"Of course he was. Ain't never been nothing the matter with him."

"Maybe he's gone out."

"He's just being contrary," she snapped.

She walked to the sitting-room door, opened it and said, "Silas Ryder, I'm . . ."

Words stuck in her throat. She turned wide, terrified eyes at Caleb. He saw the color drain from her face. She clutched at the door jamb for support. Her fingers stiffened, then became lifeless. Abbie Glover slid to the floor in a dead faint.

Over the bulk of her body Caleb saw Silas. He lay sprawled on the old sofa. A white handle gleamed from his chest. He had been stabbed with a whalebone knife.

Caleb shivered again. Silas Ryder, too, had been murdered.

CHAPTER THIRTEEN

FOR a moment Caleb was stunned. Then a quick realization came. He saw clearly the reasons for all that had happened since noon. The murder of Silas Ryder was the answer to the riddle, was the motive he and all the others had been seeking through both investigations.

"No wonder we couldn't find a likely motive," he said aloud.

He looked down at his feet where Abbie lay slumped. "Get yourself together," he said with impatience, but Abbie lay an inert mass. He breathed heavily and looked about for water. There was none nearer than the kitchen. "Just like a woman to faint at a time like this," he thought as he went out and came back with a quart measure brimful. He doused her with it, doused her with some satisfaction, and put the measure on the gleaming surface of a pie-crust table.

Abbie gasped, her eyes fluttered, opened, held the immortal question.

"Now don't say 'Where am I?'" he warned. "You're right where you were. You fainted. Get up! There's things I have to be doing."

Abbie looked at him. "I never done this before," she said. "Help me up."

He housed as she heaved. She spied the measure standing on the gleaming table. "That's no place to put a wet pan."

"You're all right now, complaining as usual," he said and went into the sitting-room for a nearer new of Silas.

He felt his face and hands while Abbie stood in the door, the quart measure held in front of her.

"Just as I thought. He's been dead for hours. Stone cold he is. When did you leave here?"

"About my usual time. I don't know exactly."

"Was he all right when you left?"

."Caleb Spring, are you intimating that I—?"

"I ain't intimating nothing. I asked you a question. Was he all right when you left here?"

"Of course he was. Told me to get out, that he didn't want anything to eat. And that after my making him that clam pie this morning, too."

"See anybody round about?"

"No."

Caleb grunted, crossed to the telephone and jingled the hook up and down. The line was dead, hadd been cut at the box, or rather had been pulled out, as a quick investigation showed.

"We've got to get back to the village," he said. "Maybe you'd better stay here with the body."

"I'm not staying here alone in this house with murderers all over the village, and you can't make me," she cried through tears.

"Then come on."

In the car she begged him to say nothing about her dismissal by Silas.

"I'll say no more than need be said," he promised her. "Black will do the questioning later. You'd better tell a straight story. Unless you're careful, you're going to be suspected. I'll let you off at our place. I suppose you might as well stay there as anywhere, but remember this: If you don't want to be talked about, don't do so much talking yourself. Promise not to tell Phoebe about this," he insisted as they stopped at his gate.

"I promise," she said glibly, almost eagerly.

Abbie was on her own again, with a chance to talk, to pour an astounding story into a warm, appreciative ear. Her promise to Caleb was forgotten before she reached the Spring porch.

"Well," she gasped as the screen door slammed behind her. She started for the wooden rocker at the window. Her voice was pitched in a low key as she sat down. "I ain't supposed to tell you this, Phoebe; Caleb made me promise, but I know you won't tell. Come here." Although there was no one to hear her, she whispered the words, "Silas has been murdered, too."

Phoebe took the news with stunned stoicism. "Really! Murdered?"

"Yes. Caleb and I found him. I fainted."

"And no wonder. What a shock. I'll fix you a cup of tea while you tell me about it." Phoebe put some pine sticks into the stove and pulled the kettle forward.

"It was awful, Phoebe."

Phoebe turned from the stove. "I can imagine. And Caleb made you promise not to tell me, did he?" she asked vindictively.

"Yes. You won't let on I told you, will you?"

"I won't breathe a word to a soul."

Over their tea they reviewed the case. Between them they decided that Stryke was the only person who had cause and could have killed all three victims.

"Caleb says it explains everything," Abbie suggested.

"Of course it does," Phoebe agreed.

In their excitement and lust for gossip and speculation they tossed ideas at one another. Stryke had gone to the house, had quarreled with the old man. Silas threatened to run the boy and the show troupe out of town. Stryke had returned to the house and had killed him. Then, because he was afraid, he had killed the Knight girl, thinking her to be Miss Nellie. But that wasn't enough. In the drugstore he learned about Sidney's glasses. A dead Sidney wouldn't be able to testify to the time. That was it, that was the reason for Sidney's death. How awful! How terrible! It wasn't safe with a man like that in town. And Nellie Pine? Where was she? Probably killed too. People ought to know about such things. Caleb or no Caleb, people had a right to hear the truth.

They tossed theories at one another until they reached a fever pitch of self-hypnotized conviction In the heat of their excitement Phoebe called several of her intimates and related the news to them. She neglected to say that she and Abbie had developed a theory about the murders. She gave the impression that she was telling facts. She told them Caleb said it explained everything. Her listeners, if they thought at all, knowing Caleb was Chief of Police, believed her. The story grew, gained authenticity in retelling.

Filled with importance, the two women left the house to spread the news. Mrs. Tucker was in the yard. Phoebe was so full of excitement that she called to Mrs. Tucker, spoke to her for the first time in five years and said, "Silas Ryder has been murdered. I guess now we know who has been at the bottom of all this. Stryke Ryder, of course!"

Mrs. Tucker was stunned both by the news and the implication. She went into the house and called her friend Mrs. Verity, the woman who had seen Stryke when he was at his grandfather's.

The news spread, increased in volume and credibility as it was retold by one excited person after another. The women told the men, the men told other men, and inside of twenty minutes three-quarters of the village population and all the strangers were again milling about the entrance to the Town Hall.

Caleb heard the uproar and went out to see what was going on. He was stunned and amazed. "What did I tell you?" he asked Abbie.

"You can't keep a thing like this quiet," she retorted.

"No, Caleb. This is once your secrecy won't work," Phoebe said vindictively.

"Where is the murderer?" a man's voice called to Caleb.

"That's what we'll have to find out."

"Huh. It's funny you don't know, when everybody else does," the man replied.

"It would help us quite a lot if you'd tell us, since you seem to be holding back information," Caleb replied.

"It's Stryke Ryder, that's who it is. Your own wife told us!" the man shrilled.

Caleb's eyes were full of murder as he turned them on the defiant and important Phoebe.

"You needn't scowl at me, Caleb Spring," she scoffed.

Martin Chase came across the road and joined the throng. "What has happened?" he asked.

"Stryke Ryder killed his grandfather and then killed these other people, that's what," Abbie said loudly.

"I don't believe it."

"Then who did?" fifty voices demanded.

"There's no point in getting hysterical. Caleb here is the law and will take care of everything," Martin said.

"Caleb says he don't know who did it," someone jeered.

Eben Ryder's car pulled into the curb near the post office. He ran up to see what was happening.

"Stryke Ryder killed your brother," they shouted at him.

"What's this, Caleb?" Eben demanded, working his way close to him.

"The town's been putting two and two together and they are a little excited. Silas has been murdered and they've jumped to conclusions," Caleb explained.

"Where's Henry?" Eben said.

"I don't know," Caleb replied, and looked at Eben's white and sober face.

Clyde Perine, the director of the players, came through the crowd.

"Try and keep these people quiet if you can," Caleb said, to Eben and Chase. "Talk to them, do anything. I'll be gone for a few minutes."

Perine shoved his way through the people, who craned their necks to see where Caleb had gone. Perine became annoyed at the jostling he received. He shook himself free and stepped beside Eben.

"What is the excitement?"

"Silas Ryder, my brother, has been murdered too. You wouldn't know anything about it, would you?"

Perine recoiled. "Me?"

"Why not? I know who you are now," Eben answered accusingly.

Perine turned quickly, walked away.

Caleb went back to the office to discuss the situation with the trooper on guard there.

"Break up the crowd," the trooper advised.

"They ain't the breaking kind. I'm their friend. Suppose you go out and talk to them. They're all around by the front door. See if you can get them to move and go home."

The trooper was back in ten minutes. "I'd better call Black. I couldn't do much with them. They're as excited as hell. Why don't you go out there and talk to them?"

Caleb went back, looked for Eben, Chase and other citizens upon whom he could rely. They had gone, as all sensible people would, and had left the milling crowd.

"Look here, you folks," Caleb said to a tight knot talking excitedly together. "Most of you are strangers and don't rightly belong here, anyhow. Why don't you go home?"

"Because we don't want to," a man replied insolently.

"And we ain't agoin' neither," another voice took up the defiance. "We've as much right as you or anybody else to stay here. Why don't you do something, or are you waiting for more murder to happen right under your nose?"

His companions laughed jeeringly.

Caleb appealed to some of the women who flittered from group to group, begged them to home and forget the whole thing.

"Forget it," a woman shrilled, "and maybe murdered in our beds tonight! No, sir, we're safe here where there is folks to protect us if you won't."

There was general approval of her hysteria.

Caleb didn't like it at all. The crowd was too excited, too unreasonable. He knew them for what they were, the town riffraff who had been drawn to the village by the exciting news. They were people with whom he had had trouble before, lazy, shiftless men and women so foreign to the usual run of Cape Codder who had an inherent respect for law and order. He argued and talked to them for fifteen or twenty minutes but it was a futile effort.

"Your own wife spread the news," a woman shouted at him.

"Yes, and if you won't do the job we'll take the law into our own hands," a man shouted.

Caleb was worried. They would not be quieted. They were too excited, their fever was rising to dangerous high. He went back to the office, gave the trooper instructions to call some responsible men to come down and help in case the crowd should get out of hand.

He suggested Libby's father, Abe Tucker, Martin Chase, Charlie Snow and a number of others. He promised to be back in a few minutes. He left by the rear entrance of the Town Hall, skirted the buildings nearby and gained Main Street beyond the heart of the village.

He broke into a run and was breathless when he reached Miss Nellie's house and found Stryke sitting on the porch in one of Nellie's wooden rockers.

"Better get a few things in a suitcase and come along with me, son," he said as calmly as he could over his labored breathing.

"Then you are arresting me," Stryke said with fatalistic resignation.

Caleb followed him into the house, told him what had happened, warned him of the attitude of the crowd.

"Why should they want to hurt me?" Stryke asked.

"That's the bad part of it, son. They don't want to hurt you nor anybody else when they are in their right minds. They are a little mad right now. I don't think we ought to take any risks. I've telephoned Black. He'll be over just as soon as he can get here. I want you to come along with me so as I can take care of you."

"Where are we going?" Stryke asked as he tossed a change of linen and toilet articles into his bag.

"To my office. There's two troopers there. In case anything does happen we can hold out till Black and his men arrive."

Caleb had been watching the street anxiously and urged Stryke to greater speed when he spied a band of men marching toward them. "We'll go out the back way," he said.

"How come your car is on the back road?" Stryke asked.

"It isn't. I walked. We'll go the back way, might save trouble. Come on." He cut across through Miss Nellie's yard and past the Tucker barn.

"I don't approve of this," Stryke remonstrated. "I'm not afraid . . . not much," he added.

"I am, plenty," Caleb admitted. "We'll circle around and hit the Town Hall from the rear."

"No. We'll walk up South Street. If they see me with you they'll think you've arrested me."

"Then they'll be sure you're guilty. I don't think you are, boy."

"Thanks, Caleb."

"People are funny, son."

"I know, that's why I don't want to run and hide."

"I don't want them to think I've arrested you. That's what they want me to do, because they think you're guilty."

"If they want me brought to justice, the fact that I am with you will mean that I am going to get what they think I deserve and that should quiet any mob tendencies."

"I know it's not the way to do it," Caleb protested.

"It's the only way I'll go," Stryke insisted firmly, striding ahead.

They were halfway across Main Street before anyone in the crowd saw them.

"Here he comes now! Here comes the murderer!" a voice cried.

The crowd turned and looked at the two men. "Caleb's got him," a man shouted jubilantly. "He'll get what he deserves!"

"Death is too good for him," came from the rear of the throng.

"Steady, Caleb," Stryke said as they neared the group. "We'll walk right through them. Don't!" he warned as he saw Caleb's hand go for the gun he carried under his coat.

Stryke's head was up. He showed no sign of the fear which quivered in his muscles. Caleb saw a pulse in the boy's cheek beating steadily. With eyes front they moved on. The crowd hesitated a moment and gradually a path opened before them.

"Once we're inside the door it'll be all right," Caleb thought.

A shout from the street attracted attention, made the crowd surge, closing the path. Caleb and Stryke were surrounded.

Stryke was tall. He could see over the heads of most of the people. His golden yellow hair marked him among all the men.

The band Caleb had seen on the street marching toward Miss Nellie's was running back. The leader brandished a revolver in his hand.

"He's skipped," he shouted, "but we've got the gun!"

"We've got him!" someone called back.

"Open up! Let us through!" Caleb cried to the people who were hemming them in, but his cries were useless.

"Lynch him!"

"No," Caleb shouted. "No."

"He ought to be lynched," a woman screamed.

"No one is safe!" a voice shouted.

The cry was taken up, swept through the people like a swift running fire. Stryke's face had gone white. He tugged at the fighting, straining Caleb.

"It's useless to struggle this way. Don't let them see we are afraid," he tried to whisper in his ear.

A long stick swung from the rear, hit Stryke on the head. His eyes filled with sudden, uncontrolled fury. His suitcase was torn from his hand. He clenched his fists, which were pressed close to his sides by the surging crowd.

The trooper came forward, drew his gun and ordered the crowd to stand back. He was jumped from the rear and robbed of his gun. That complete and utter defiance gave the mob new courage. Eager hands siezed Struke, yanked at him. The crowd opened a little. Caleb pulled his gun.

"Don't shoot!" Stryke cried as he was yanked aside away from Caleb who stood with the unarmed trooper beside him defying the crowd, threatening them with his gun.

"Telling him to shoot, were you?" a crazed voice stormed at Stryke. His fist crashed into the side of Stryke's face.

A hundred hands clutched at Stryke as he struggled to be free. He fell, they kicked him. He rose to his feet, they pummeled him. They dragged him away.

"It's bad," the trooper said. "I wish Black would get here."

"I can't shoot into that crowd and they know it," Caleb groaned.

"Might nick a few in the legs," the trooper suggested. "Give me the gun."

"If there's that kind of work necessary I'll do it myself," Caleb said grimly. "Here come some of the men I sent for."

Caleb's reinforcements came running round the edge of the crowd.

The church bell began to toll. Death was ringing the bell again, and the crazed people, hearing it, were reminded anew of the tragic deaths, and increased their attack on Stryke.

"There's plenty of rope at the church," a wild voice called. "We'll keep Luke working!"

"Hang him with the rope that killed Sidney!" a man bellowed as they milled about the corner like a wild rushing tide.

"We've got to stop them," Caleb cried to the men. "They have at least two guns and we have only one. Come this way and we can head them off at the church, keep them away from the rope. Stay here, Charlie, and send any dependable men who come to the church."

Their feet echoed hollowly as they raced through the Town Hall to head off the mob at the church. The bell continued to toll. Charlie shook his head and peered at the corner, behind which the last of the mob, mostly youngsters, had vanished. He snapped orders to men as they hurried up.

It took two minutes for Nellie to trot from the Town Hall to her house. Libby and Percy had covered the distance in less than a minute. The bell still clanged as they stopped in front of Charlie.

"You'd better stay here, Libby, but they'll need you, Professor. Unless we do something there's going to be a lynching."

"A what?" Libby gasped.

"They've got young Ryder. His grandfather has been murdered and they think he's done 'em all."

"What's that?" a voice asked behind them. It was Abe Tucker, breathless from running.

"Get along to the church and help Caleb, there's no time for chattering," Charlie snapped.

Percy ran through the hall. His thoughts raced faster than his feet. So that was why two people had been killed. He was it all clearly as he slid around the corner and started for the entrance on Webster Road. He could hear Libby and Abe behind him.

The old man was killed this morning before noon, he thought. The murderer feared he had been seen and wanted to eliminate the two people who might have noticed him at Silas Ryder's. They know Stryke was there. Poor devil. All this previous evidence has accumulated against him.

He was through the door. The crowd was pouring over the low fence into the yard moving toward the steps where Caleb and a band of men stood waiting for them. He dashed down the street and across to the steps to take a stand beside Caleb. He saw men looping a length of rope from Sidney's rigging. He stepped forward.

"They're in a bad mood," Caleb warned.

"I know it. They'll resent you and your gun. Let me talk to them," Percy urged.

"If you think it'll do any good, but be careful."

Overhead the last clang of the bell boomed out and sifted into silence. Percy stood on the steps and bellowed, "What are you going to do with that rope?" He pointed toward the man who was coiling the rope.

Their attention was distracted, they looked toward the man who retorted, "Hang the cur!"

"Why?" Percy demanded.

From far off, only a faint sound over the voice of the mob, he heard a siren. Black and his men were coming. He would try to stall for time, he had provided a distraction which he had hoped to do. He saw faces in the mob, faces which were sobered by the thought of hanging. The rope went into the air. Percy was glad when the first throw missed the branch and had to be tossed again.

Percy went toward the ringleaders, saying, "You can't do this!"

"Stand back!" the man with the gun warned. "This gun has killed a couple of folks and can do it again."

He leveled the gun at Percy, who did not hesitate, but advanced slowly toward the man and the gun.

The mob was fascinated by Percy's courage, grew silent as it watched.

"Stand back, I tell you!" the man warned.

"Put up that gun and listen to me," Percy ordered.

"You keep out of this. It ain't no concern of yours," the man warned, but his nerve was not equal to Percy's courage.

"It's the concern of all of us. You can't take the law into your own hands," Percy said quietly.

"Who says we can't?" the man demanded.

"I do. I tell you now that if you do this thing you'll hang for murder yourselves, all of you. I'll have proof against you. But what proof do you have against this man?"

"He killed his grandfather, he killed the acting girl, and he killed Sidney. We found the gun up to Nellie's and it's likely he's killed Nellie, too," the man shouted.

"Nellie Pine is not dead. I know where she is." Percy's voice was steady and clear.

"Where is she?" a hundred voices demanded.

"That I can't tell you now. She is safe, but she is afraid, afraid that the murderer will try to kill her."

"Of course she is," someone agreed.

"Tell her to come back. We'll protect her," a zealot cried. "She has nothing to fear now."

"But she has. Two attempts were made on her life. One less than an hour ago, when I had to defend her and myself with this gun." He pulled the gun from his pocket and showed it to them.

"It was likely him, Ryder," the man muttered.

"It was not. We were miles from here at the . . ." He turned to Libby. "Tell them where I was, Libby."

"At the shooting lodge," she cried in a high voice, "miles from here. Stryke Ryder could not have been there. He wouldn't know where it was. We were followed to Nellie's own cabin and then on to the lodge. We were trailed by someone who knows this country as well as I do. It was probably one of you here in this mob right now, the murderer working under cover, inciting you to this outrage to hide his own trail. If you're so keen about seeing justice done, look among yourselves, for the murderer is there with you, and it is not Stryke Ryder." She was magnificent as she hurled the words at them.

"It's a trick," the man shouted, but his zest was gone.

"It will be more of a trick if you can explain why you wanted to commit this crime," Percy shouted at him. "What are you trying to cover? How did you know where to find that gun if you did find it? Are you the man who killed these people today?"

Percy's accusation had the desired effect. The man dropped the gun and turned back into the crowd.

Percy spread his hands. "Before it's too late, think what you have tried to do. You are not savages. You're Cape Codders. It has been said of you for hundreds of years that you were people who minded your own business, asked no questions and went your own way."

The crowd stirred uneasily. He had stopped them for the moment, but he was afraid some new impulse might drive them on.

"That rope which one of you has hurled over the tree is a symbol of lawlessness. For God's sake think of what you are doing, here in a churchyard, in front of a temple in which you have worshiped. It's unthinkable."

The crowd began to look a little ashamed. The hands which had been mauling Stryke released him. The boy rocked and teetered on his wary legs. He was keeping his head up, but he was dazed, hurt, bleeding.

Percy heard the roar of the motors. Saw a number of motorcycles swing past the old school and come tearing up the short road to the intersection.

They heard the sound too. The crowd frayed at the edges. Their spirit broken, they would have to run for cover, but found themselves surrounded by fearless men in uniform, men with firm, set lips who advanced with drawn guns.

Black looked up, saw the dangling rope. His jaw damped. He came forward.

"Thank God they got here in time," Caleb breathed, and wiped his face free of excessive perspiration.

"Stay where you are, every one of you," Black's voice cut across the guilty throng.

They moved away from Stryke, tried to hide one behind the other as Black faced them, angry yet contemptuous.

Libby ran forward, threw her arms about Stryke and cried, "Oh, Stryke, my darling!"

"I'm all right," he said through swelling lips.

He looked across at Percy. "Thanks, Percy," he said. He swayed. The love in Libby's encircling arms could not hold him. He toppled to the ground.

"I've never had a situation like this to deal with before," Black said.

"May I make a suggestion?" Percy asked as Caleb and a trooper lifted Stryke and carried him across the street.

"Go ahead."

"The murderer is probably in this crowd. He may be the person who incited the riot. Put them all under temporary arrest and take them into the theatre. They are a little ashamed of themselves now and more than a little afraid. You can scare hell out of them. They will talk if they know anything."

"It's an idea." He barked orders to his men.

Old Luke stood on the church steps where he had been watching the scene. He came forward to Black. "The young fellow ain't dead, is he?" he asked.

"No, just fainted."

Luke shot a long stream of tobacco juice into the air. "Then I guess I can go home now."

Black seemed uncertain about him.

"He had nothing to do with it. He's the sexton. He tolls the bell when there's a death," Caleb explained.

CHAPTER FOURTEEN

IN CALEB'S overcrowded office, Black looked across at Stryke and asked, "How are you feeling?"

"I'm still a little shaky in the pins," Stryke answered as Libby and the doctor washed and dressed his cuts and bruises.

"What you need is a good stiff drink," Black said.

"Not a bad idea. I think it would help all of us," Percy agreed and started for the drugstore.

"You came just in time," Stryke said. "I was beginning to get scared. Percy was doing a swell job, but I didn't think he could hold them back much longer."

"He'd broken the spirit of the mob," Caleb said. "I never thought I'd live to see such a thing in this town. What are you going to do with them, Black?"

"You're the Chief of Police in this town, Caleb. It's up to you and Ryder."

"They didn't mean it," Stryke said.

"It's noble of you, son, but them folks weren't fooling none when they threw that rope over the tree. Tomorrow they're going to feel awful ashamed of themselves and it ain't going to be easy for me."

"What started it?" Black asked. "How did it happen?"

"That reminds me. I've a little unfinished business to fix up. You won't be needing me for the next ten minutes, will you?" Caleb said.

"Tell me about this new murder first," Black insisted.

"It's the boy's grandfather. Abbie Glover and I found him."

Caleb had given Black the story of finding Silas, when Percy came back with a bottle and paper cups. He handed one to Caleb, who eyed it for a moment and then polished it off in one long draft.

"I'll be back," he promised Black. He left with a determined set to his shoulders.

"I'll be away a short time myself. I'll take some men up to the scene of the new crime and get them started on their routine work." Black called a couple of men and left.

Percy remembered Miss Nellie and followed Caleb into the hall to tell him of their adventures with Nellie Pine and of her arrival at the Spring house some time after dark.

"I don't know as I ought to let her hide in my house. It seems like blocking justice to hide a witness," he protested.

"You can tell Black about it, but don't tell any one else. I should have told that mob that Nellie knew nothing about the murders, should have told them that she hadn't seen a thinkg all morning because of her splitting headache."

"It might've helped but you couldn't think of everything. You did a pretty good job as it was. You saved the boy's life."

"And you must protect Miss Nellie as long as her life is in danger."

Caleb sighed. "I'll do the best I can. If you had lived in this town longer, you wouldn't have sent her to my house. Phoebe and Nellie haven't spoken for twenty years or more."

"Then they wouldn't think of looking for her in your house, Caleb. That's why I did it."

"I'll have to make some arrangements. I'll have to tell Phoebe and I'll have to see to it that Abbie don't stay with us. I promised her she could. I think I'm going to enjoy telling her that she'll have to get out and I've a few things to say to my wife, too."

"Want another drink?" Percy asked with an understanding grin.

"No. I'm doing all right with the one I had. Just sort of set the wheels in motion, it did. I'd do a lot more than this for Nellie Pine, however. It was right smart of you to find her. I had other ideas. It don't seem possible that she could be in such danger." He shook his head. "It's somebody who knows this country as well as I do. Beats me. I wonder who it is? Well, Phoebe and Abbie are up in the theatre so I may as well go up and get my talkin' over and done with. They ain't agoin' to like what I have to say, either one of them." He winked at Percy.

"Good luck," Percy called as Caleb started up the stairs.

Caleb was back in about ten minutes. "I've fixed things," he said to Percy. "We'll take Nellie in tonight when she comes and I've arranged for Abbie to go back to the house and take care of Eben and Henry, who will most likely stay there until after the funeral."

"Then all we have to do is wait for Black to get back," Percy said.

"That's all, except find the murderer," Caleb agreed.

"I'm afraid the issue has been fogged," Percy said.

"What do you mean?"

"We'll have to start all over. I feel certain that the old man was killed first. We began our investigation at the wrong end."

"There was nothing else we could do, as I see it," Caleb remarked.

"Absolutely. It's unfortunate, however, that we knew about the cover-up murders first. That's why none of it made sense."

"It don't seem too sensible to me right now," Caleb said.

When Black returned from the Ryder place, Stryke was feeling strong enough to face the next ordeal waiting for him. He told both Caleb and Black that he would not press charges against townspeople.

Caleb and Black discussed the matter for a few minutes. Black turned to Stryke and said, "What you do about this fracas you had here is your business, but I don't want you to say anything one way or another until I have finished with them. Peacock has an idea that we might get at the murderer because of what happened to you. It's worth a try. They're going to be uneasy and the more they are afraid, the more chance we have of learning things. Come on."

"It's the third act," Percy said as he walked down to the front of the theatre with Libby and Stryke.

Black faced the restless crowd with his hands behind his back. He rocked back and forth on his trim boots for almost a minute as he looked them over and waited for the rustling and restlessness to subside.

"You know why you're here," he began, "so we won't go into that. You know what you might have done. You were about to commit murder by taking the law into your own hands. I want to know why you wanted to do it." He waited, but no one spoke.

"Did you think it was fun?" he demanded. No answer came from his audience.

"You there." Black pointed an accusing finger. "You were right up front arguing with Mr. Peacock when I arrived. What have you to say for yourself? What's your name? Get up!"

"Jim Shaw."

The man who had brandished the gun during the mob scene rose slowly.

"I guess I was a little out of my head. I don't know just how to explain it," the man faltered. "We've been pretty excited here all afternoon what with two murders and . . ." He gulped, tried to wet his throat. "Well, when they told me that the boy had murdered his grandfather too I began to see red with the rest of them."

"Who told you that?" Black demanded.

"I don't know. I guess six or eight people."

"How did such a story start?"

Caleb rose to his feet. "I think I can shed a little light on that subject."

They all turned in Caleb's direction as he turned slowly and faced the audience. He spoke directly to the man.

"Did you have some notion that the news came more or less from me?"

"Yes."

"I thought so." Caleb turned to face Black. "Abbie Glover and I found the body of Silas Ryder. It seems that Abbie and Silas had some words this morning and he put her out."

"Caleb Spring, you said you wouldn't tell!" Abbie gasped.

"Quiet!" Black roared.

"I went up to the house with her because she expected some trouble with Silas. That's when we found the body. She refused to stay there, asked me if I would leave her at my house. I did. I warned her to say nothing about this new murder, but of course she told my wife. Ask Phoebe Spring to stand up."

Black called on Phoebe, who rose slowly. The air was charged with expectancy. Phoebe was dynamite and the crowd expected Caleb's questions to set off the fuse. They waited eagerly.

"Phoebe Spring, did Abbie Glover tell you about the murder of Silas Ryder?"

"She did," Phoebe admitted. The sound came from between lips so tightly pressed together that it seemed to hiss across the room.

"Did you and Abbie tell anyone else?"

"You know we did. Why do you ask me?" she snapped.

"A matter of record. How many people did you tell?"

"I don't know exactly. I used the telephone, and I told Cora Tucker."

The townspeople who knew about the Phoebe Spring-Cora Tucker feud turned in amazement.

"That's all," Caleb said. He turned to Black as Phoebe slipped back into her chair. "I just wanted you to realize that the news did seem to have authority behind it."

"Are you trying to give me the impression that you believed Ryder guilty of his grandfather's murder?" Black demanded.

"No. I never believed any such thing. But the news came from my house. I found the body, I, Chief of Police. I want you to understand what may have made these people act as they did." Cal sat down.

"A very remarkable man," Percy whispered Stryke. "It took courage to face that wife of his that way."

"Now, Shaw," Black said, "tell me what you did."

"We didn't do anything at first. We were just sort of milling about the Street when somebody suggested that we get Ryder and ask him a few questions."

"Was it your idea?"

"No. I don't know who suggested it, but it seemed like a good notion, so some of us went down to Miss Nellie's, but he wasn't there. We did find a gun, though, under his mattress. It had been fired twice and we figured that one bullet had been used for the Knight girl and the other for Abe Tucker's cow. We were pretty mad by then and started back up the street. Caleb and the boy were going into the Town Hall. It was then things seemed to get out of hand."

"Do you realize that you obstructed officers of the law in the performance of their duties?"

"I never touched Caleb nor the other fellow."

Black swung toward Caleb, who confirmed the statement.

"Whose idea was it to have a lynching?" Black asked severely.

"It was an idea that sort of grew. I don't know," Shaw stated.

"But you were right out in front with the others."

"Yes."

"Now, you as an individual must have had some reason for your actions. Why did you become part of the mob?"

"It's like I told you. I was excited. Two people had been killed and plenty of us thought young Ryder had something to do with both deaths. He didn't have no decent alibi, leastways you didn't find out about it if he did," Shaw accused. "Then when his grandfather was found murdered and we heard that Abbie Glover said they'd had a fight, and Mrs. Verity had seen him coming away from there the second time, it seemed easy to put two and two together. Then Nellie Pine was missing and we thought he'd done away with her, too."

"Who was the leader of the mob? Was it you?"

"No. I wouldn't say as there was a leader."

"But how could people like you be driven to such an act without it being suggested to you?"

"All I can remember is hearing voices in the mob, voices shouting that he killed them all, that death was too good for him, and the first thing I knew we were acting like men who had the right to do what we thought was the right thing to do."

"Are you being a hero, Mr. Shaw?"

"I don't understand you."

"Are you trying to shield other people?"

"No, and I ain't going to carry the weight of this by myself, either."

"Then you had better sit down and think, think hard, because there are no volunteers with information."

By the time Shaw sat down, he was burning with an inner resentment against his fellow villagers.

"Nice bit of psychology that," Percy whispered to Stryke. "Shaw is going to remember a lot of things, or I'm greatly mistaken."

"It isn't fair to make him the goat," Stryke protested.

"And you're being almost too damned noble about it," Percy whispered back. "You should want to see them hang for what they did to you."

"I'll pick a private fight with a couple of the lugs who swung at me when I couldn't hit back. I'll see how good they are then. It's those cracks in the face I got when I couldn't defend myself that got under my skin. I'll settle those scores myself."

"That's better. I was afraid you were turning out to be one of those too-good-to-be-true people."

"Watch for the black eyes," Stryke whispered back as Black looked up from the list of names he had been reading.

"Stryke Ryder," Black called.

Stryke rose to his feet.

"You heard what this man has just said." Stryke nodded. "Do you know who instigated the mob proceedings against you?"

"No. I knew nothing about it until Mr. Spring came for me and warned me I was in danger."

"Did he tell you why?"

"He did."

"When was the last time you saw your grandfather?"

"This morning, when I called on him."

"Did you kill Silas Ryder?"

"No."

"That will be all for now. Sit down, please. Abbie Glover, will you take the floor?"

Abbie rose slowly.

"Miss Glover, it has been stated that you reported a quarrel between Stryke Ryder and his grandfather, Silas Ryder. Is that true?"

"Yes. Stryke Ryder came up to see his grandfather this morning. They quarreled."

"What about?"

"Several things, but mostly this theatrical company. Silas said he'd run the actors out of town, that they were a bad lot."

Abbie's statement caused a stir in the audience. She looked about, rather satisfied with the sensation her news had created. She hesitated a moment, looked toward Caleb, who was watching her closely. "I was listening. That was why I lost my position."

"How did Stryke Ryder react to the threat to have the actors forced to leave town?"

"He was awful mad. He said he'd go, but warned his grandfather to leave the others alone."

"Did Stryke Ryder leave his grandfather's house before you did?"

"Yes. He slammed out."

"Did you see Stryke Ryder at the house again this morning?"

"No."

"Thank you, sit down." Black looked at his list and called, "Mary Verity."

Mary Verity seemed frightened as she rose to face Black.

"Mrs. Verity, it has been stated that you said Stryke Ryder return to the Ryder house. Is that true?"

"Yes. I saw him leave and then later when I went out front, just after the fish man left, I saw him back there. He rang the front doorbell just as I had earlier in the morning, and then he went round the back."

"At what time was that?"

"It was close to noon. I was upset about my dinner and the fish man was late."

"Did you see anyone else at the Ryder house?"

"No."

"Thank you."

Black waited for her to sit down, and called Stryke. After the stir and the craning of necks had subsided he asked, "Did you return to your grandfather's house this morning?"

"I did."

"Did you go to the rear of the house?"

"I did."

"Did you enter the house from the rear?"

"No."

"Why did you return to the house?"

"Because I had decided that I would not let him run me or the members of the theatrical company out of town. I went back there to tell him that I would fight him, that I wouldn't go."

'What did he say to that?"

"I didn't see him. The house was closed. I rang front doorbell and rapped on the rear door, but there was no answer."

"What did you do when you left the house?"

"I returned to the village, along the Webster Road."

Black dismissed Stryke and called Abbie again. "Miss Glover, was Silas Ryder alive when you left the house?"

Abbie's face went white for a moment. "Yes."

"Were there any other visitors at the Ryder house this morning?"

"Only Martin Chase," she looked about, hesitated, "as far as I know," she finished lamely.

"Where was Mr. Henry Ryder?"

"I don't know where he was. He left early, said he was going to New Bedford."

"Was Mr. Eben Ryder at the house while you were there?"

"No. I didn't see Eben until noontime, when I was in the village."

"Did you leave before or after Mr. Chase?"

"After Mr. Chase."

"What time did you leave?"

"I don't know. I was so blistering mad. I had fixed his lunch, but he wouldn't eat it. It was maybe 11:30 or a little later."

"Did you return to the house between the time you left and your visit with Mr. Spring?"

"No."

"Just why did you ask Mr. Spring to go with you?"

"Because I didn't want any trouble with him."

"What made you spread the news that Stryke Ryder was the murderer?"

She considered that, turned defiant eyes toward Stryke. "Because there didn't seem to be anyone else. He quarreled with his grandfather, threatened him, left in a temper, and he didn't have any alibis for the other murders."

A flutter of agreement rustled over the room as eyes swung from her to Stryke.

"You've been with Silas Ryder for a long time, haven't you?"

"Yes."

"Did he have any enemies, anyone who might want to kill him?"

"I don't know of any such person."

"You may sit down."

Black spoke to the audience. "You may return to your homes. I advise you not to leave town, any of you. If you do, I'll have you arrested." As the men and women who had been that hysterical mob rose to their feet and hurried away Black called, "Mr. Chase, I'd like to speak to you."

Abbie and Phoebe exchanged glances and lingered.

"I said you could go home," Black reminded them. He waited until they had left before he turned to Martin.

"What were you doing at Ryder's this morning?"

"Silas sent for me for a business discussion."

"Did it have anything to do with Stryke Ryder?"

"Yes."

"Was Silas Ryder alive when you left him?"

"Good Lord, yes. You heard Abbie say—"

"Miss Glover said that she left after you, and that Mr. Ryder was alive when she left. I'm asking for your testimony, Mr. Chase."

"Are you suspecting me of killing Silas?" Martin demanded.

"I'll want to know more about your visit there, why you went, the time you left, a number of things."

"I don't know what time I left. Why should I know?" Martin growled.

"Don't leave town," Black warned.

Libby, Percy, Stryke and Caleb had been waiting. Black turned to Stryke: "Mr. Ryder, I am going to place you under arrest for the murders committed in this village today. You may seek legal advice, if you wish it."

Libby gasped and clutched at Stryke's arm. "I'm sorry, boy," Caleb said.

Libby was fighting mad; she jumped to her feet and walked toward Black.

CHAPTER FIFTEEN

MARTIN CHASE walked across the front of the room and sat beside Stryke while Libby argued with Black. "The announcement of your arrest came as a surprise, Stryke," he said.

"It's no surprise to me," Stryke retorted. "I've been a marked man all day."

"I can't quite figure Black," Martin said. "He seems to be suspicious of me too. He's not telling us all that's on his mind. . . . Do you still want me to act for you in a legal capacity, that is, if I'm not arrested myself?"

"I'll leave you two alone," Percy suggested as he rose.

"No. Stay, Percy," Stryke insisted and put a hand on Percy's arm and drew him back into his seat. He turned to Martin. "I'll need a lawyer. What should we do?"

"I don't know yet. You'll likely be held without bail. Got any money?" Martin asked.

"No, and I don't know when I'll be able to pay you," Stryke answered honestly.

"I'm not worrying about being paid, if you live," Martin added with something resembling a smile in his dry eyes. "Your credit is good," he added quickly, as if he realized that Stryke had not appreciated his grim wit.

"I have no credit," Stryke denied.

"You have with me."

"Thank you," Stryke said.

"Don't get me wrong. I'm known as a shrewd man. Perhaps I'm acting because of professional information." Again his eyes were lit by that sly twinkle.

"Oh Lord," Stryke moaned. "If there is a will and I'm mentioned in it, I suppose it will make things that much harder for me."

"I'm not giving out any professional secrets but I'll tell you this, boy. Silas admired your spirit. He saw you about in the village, was anxious for you to call on him. He was lonesome, sort of hankered for you, he did, but he was proud and wouldn't make any advances. I'm glad you got to see him before this happened. He told me you had spirit."

"Then why did he act the way he did?" Stryke demanded. "I went to him, offered to be his friend, and he treated me like a dog."

"It was his way. He didn't want to seem soft. Why . . ." Martin looked up and did not finish the sentence. Black and Libby were coming toward them.

"Are you ready, Ryder?" Black asked crisply.

"Yes. May I get a few clothes before I go?"

"Certainly."

"Mr. Chase is going to be my attorney."

Martin squared up to Black. "How is the charge to read?"

"Ryder is being held for murder. There's enough evidence against him to hang three men. I'm taking no chances from now on."

"Then you think Ryder is the murderer?" Martin demanded.

"I'm not telling you what I think." He beckoned to one of his men who stood at the door leading into the hall. "Take Ryder over to the County Jail at Barnstable. Stop off at his house first and let him get anything he needs."

Percy took Stryke's hand and gripped it hard. "I'll be working for you, Stryke," he promised.

"We all will," Libby echoed, and slipped her arm through his as he turned and followed the officer toward the door.

"It's a shame," Martin murmured. "He has so much to live for."

"Such as what?" Black demanded.

"He's one of Silas Ryder's heirs," Martin said, his eyes following Stryke and Libby.

"Did young Ryder know that?" Black asked.

"I don't see how he could. No one but Silas and myself knew about the provisions of the will." He paused for a moment then said thoughtfully, "It's curious, come to think of it." He paused again, gave the impression of weighing things in his mind before he announced, "Abbie Glover and Sidney Stone witnessed Silas's signature. They may have seen something that was incorporated in the document—you know how curious some people are— but I couldn't say for certain. I remember trying to. keep the text covered as much as possible because I knew them so well. It was a short will and either one or both may have seen Stryke's name as a beneficiary."

"What was in the will?" Black demanded.

"I can't tell you that unless you produce a warrant for the document," Martin answered.

"This is murder, Chase. Are you withholding information to help your client?"

"No. I have no right to divulge the contents of that will without a court order and I won't," he stated flatly.

"I'll get the court order," Black assured him.

"When you do I'll turn it over to you," Martin promised. He prepared to leave.

"Before you go I want some information," Black said. "What time were you up there this morning?"

"I don't know exactly. Some time after eleven. Silas called me and said he wanted to see me right away."

"Do you remember when you left him?" Black was impatient.

"It must have been soon after 11:30, because Abbie said lunch was ready and wanted to know if I would stay. The old man bellowed at her, told her to get out, that he didn't want any lunch."

"Then he was alive when you left?"

"Yes, and kicking."

"And Miss Glover was still there?"

"Yes. She was getting ready to leave, asked me to r wait and drive her down, but I was in a hurry."

"Why did you go up to see Silas?" Black asked.

"Business." The word was blunt and barren.

Black called one of his men, told him to get a court order for Martin to produce the will of the late Silas Ryder. That done he turned back to Martin. "If either Sidney Stone or Abbie Glover saw the text of the will when they were signing it, isn't it likely that they talked?" Martin nodded an agreement. "Have you heard any talk in the village about the will?"

"Not a word. I can't even remember a leading question about it."

Black turned to Percy. "Were Stone and young Ryder friendly?"

"Not to my knowledge."

"If Stone had known about the will and mentioned it to Stryke . . ." He didn't finish the thought, shook his head and said, "Too bad the way things keep pointing back to the boy."

"It's ridiculous, Black, all of it," Percy said hotly. "Suppose he did know about the will, suppose Stone had told him, what of it?"

"This. If young Ryder profits by the will, if he got his information from Stone, he would naturally want Stone out of the way after the murder, particularly since Stone could have seen him when he was at his grandfather's this morning."

"Stone did see Ryder up there," Percy assured him. "You're all wrong, Black. You're making Stryke lock the door after the horse was stolen."

"I'm not so sure of that. No one knew that Silas had been murdered when you were in the drugstore and the conversation took place," Black reminded him.

"There were many people in the store, any one of whom might have been afraid of what Sidney had seen."

Black stood looking directly at both men for some time without seeing them. His thoughts were involved with the intricacies of the problem and the fact that Stryke's name bobbed up each time new evidence was brought forward.

He lit a cigarette, looked at the flaming match for a moment, tossed it into the air, still burning, caught it as it came down, tossed it into the air and blew it out as it passed his face.

"That's a good trick," Martin said with admiration. "I'll have to try it."

"You'd better forget tricks and stick to business," Black suggested.

He strode out of the theatre and down the stairs with Percy and Chase trotting to keep up with him. He left by the front door of the Town Hall.

"I'll be handy if you need me," Martin said, as he started across the street toward his office.

Black nodded, threw his cigarette away, rammed his hands in his pockets for a moment. "I'm going up to the Ryder house. Want to come?"

"Thanks. I'd like to be in on the investigation," Percy said honestly.

Black looked at his watch. "We'll walk. I want to see how long it takes . . . for a number of reasons."

"It can't take more than five minutes at a leisurely pace," Percy suggested.

They strode past the post office. It was time for the evening mail. Percy wanted to know Black's reason, but refrained from asking any questions as they went through and past the group of women and girls gathered outside the post office.

They were beyond the center of the village, well into the shadow of the elms along the road, before Percy asked the question.

"Why do you want to check the walking time from Silas Ryder's house?"

"It is only one of the things I want to know about the case. I'd like to fix the time of Silas Ryder's death if possible. With that fact established, I want to know how long it takes to walk from the house to the village."

"Silas must have been killed very close to noon, before and not after," Percy suggested.

"Why?"

"Unless he was killed before noon I can see no reason for the other two murders. I am assuming that the murders are all connected."

"So am I, but I've been wondering if it's a mistake to think that," Black suggested.

"There seems to be no other motive. I've considered all the angles, all the testimony received so far," Percy said. "I am sure that Eve Knight's death was an accident, that she was killed because she happened to wear a shirtwaist like Nellie Pine's. The quarrel between her and Stryke certainly is not cause for a murder, since I heard him myself when he talked to her in front of Spring's house. He was too frank with her about it all to have murder on his mind."

"The same arguments hold with the death of Sidney Stone," Black admitted.

"Exactly. I believe that both of the earlier deaths were protective killings. I also believe that the murderer would have killed them before noon if there had been time."

"What do you mean—time?" Black demanded.

"Exactly that. I think Silas Ryder was killed so close to twelve noon that the killer did not have time to get to the Town Hall to kill Miss Nellie and Sidney."

"Then he was taking a risk by waiting until one."

"Not too great a risk. The whole village knows that Silas Ryder is never disturbed between the hours of twelve and two," Percy stated.

"How did you know that?" Black asked quickly.

Percy's laugh was quick and just a little nervous. "I hear Abbie Glover give Eben Ryder that information this morning."

"The murderer was taking no chances with Miss Nellie. He tried to kill her at her kitchen window. Is that what you're driving at?" Black asked.

"No, I wasn't driving at it, but it is something to consider. While the murderer knew that Silas's body

would not be discovered until after two he probably felt
very uneasy about Miss Nellie."

"Why didn't he try to kill Sidney during the noon
hour?" Black demanded.

"I've been thinking about that, too. I don't think he
considered Sidney as dangerous at the time."

"What do you mean?"

"The murderer either didn't know about Sidney and
the church steeple or didn't consider him dangerous. I
think Sidney sounded his death knell in the drugstore
when he exhibited his binoculars."

Black considered that statement for several moments.
"You were in the drugstore, weren't you, just before one?"

"Yes."

"How did they act? Remember anything that might
give us a clue?"

"No."

"You know the Glover woman is looming as a likely
suspect."

"I wonder." Percy said thoughtfully. Then he added,
"It could be."

"Don't talk riddles. Explain."

"The whole thing is a riddle, so are the people
involved. I've thought about Abbie," Percy said. "She
knew as much of what was going on as anyone, probably
more. It's quite possible she knew about the text of Silas's
will. She had a row with the old man this morning. She is
a busybody. She was in the drugstore, overheard all that
was said. She took Caleb up to the house when Silas's
body was discovered. She helped spread the news about
his death in the village, which caused a near riot."

Black interrupted him. "You keep harping back to the
drugstore. Why?"

"I'm inclined to think that the murderer was there."

"You don't mean Stryke, do you?"

"No.

"Give me the names of the people who were there."

"Stryke Ryder. Abbie Glover. Eben Ryder. Henry Ryder. Sidney Stone. Abe Tucker. Martin Chase. Clyde Perine. The man behind the counter and myself."

"Ten people. One of them is dead and another is on his way to jail. That leaves eight. I'll think about them. Tell me more about Abbie," Black urged.

To make his point clear Percy had to give Black the complete details of his trip with Libby, of finding Miss Nellie and their subsequent adventures. "Why didn't you tell me about this before?" Black demanded with annoyance.

"When did I have either the time or the opportunity?" Percy countered. "I haven't had a free moment all day and I haven't seen you standing about doing nothing. That's why I waited for you up there in the theatre. If you hadn't asked me to come I'd have told you back there in the village. There's so much to think about, do and say that I find myself running about in circles."

"Don't mind me if I seem cranky, I'm dizzy myself. Your story of finding Miss Nellie seems to clear Abbie."

"That's what I thought for a moment. Only I never believe anything is impossible. I know Abbie went up to the house with Caleb, but she might have gone over to that hunting lodge also."

"Do you think she shot at you and blew your tire?" Black asked.

"Do you know that she can't shoot?" Percy countered. "Where was she at the time?"

"I don't know but I'm going to find out." He strode on for a moment and stopped. "Give me a quick summary of the case as you know it."

Percy told Black of the things which had happened at lunch time, of Abbie at the Spring gate, of Miss Nellie's rapid walk down the street, of her shattered kitchen window, Stryke's appearance right after that.

Black interrupted him. "I've been thinking of that, too. Ryder says he returned to the village via the Webster Road. Mrs. Verity saw him. He went through the cut. He

might have killed the cow. He might have seen Miss
Nellie on her way home. After all, the gun was found in
his room. Things do point to him, you know."

"Everything does, but I'm sure he's no murderer."

"What makes you so sure? Now, if I looked at a girl
the way I've seen you looking at Libby Powell, I don't
know that I'd be so keen to help her sweetheart."

Percy felt himself flushing guiltily. He had no idea
that his eyes had been giving him away. Had other people
realized that he had fallen in love with Libby? Did she
know it? Did Stryke?

"She's an unusual girl and I admire her," he said, "but
that has nothing to do with my feeling about Stryke
Ryder's innocence. I'm interested in people. I like to
watch them to see what makes them tick. Stryke Ryder is
coldly intelligent. He has few if any inhibitions. He is a
direct person. He shows his likes and dislikes quickly. He
is blunt. He says what he thinks, and he does think."

"Go on," Black urged.

"If he killed his grandfather in a fit of rage, which is
the only way he might have done it, he would not have
killed the other people. He would have done one of two
things: made a confession at once or have done something
about hiding his trail. None of the facts connected with
the murder of Eve and Sidney show any particular
thought. They indicate fear and fear alone."

Black nodded noncommittally. "I interrupted you. Go
on, tell me all the things which happened this morning."

Percy went on, told him of Eben Ryder's arrival at the
Spring gate while the two women gossiped, referred to
the meeting between Stryke and Eve, and then retold the
scene in the drugstore.

"You're beginning to make me believe in the
drugstore," Black said with a smile.

"I'm positive Sidney brought on his death because of
what he said there," Percy insisted.

"We know that Abbie, Stryke and Chase were at the house," Black mused. "That seems to clear them in my mind."

"No one is cleared in my mind at the moment, not even Stryke. I just don't consider him the murderer."

"Then you're still suspicious of Chase?" Black asked.

"Yes, but not for the same reasons. This morning before we knew about Silas I thought his motive might be one of jealousy."

"And now?"

"How can we tell until we get more facts. The reason for Silas's death is the answer to the problem. What about Tucker?" Percy asked. "You seemed suspicious of him once or twice. He was to have called on Silas this morning but didn't have time. He told me that at lunch."

"What do you think?" Black countered.

"My chips are on Chase. Tucker had nothing to gain. He is buying his place from Silas. Why did you suspect him?" Percy demanded.

"I don't know. Perhaps it was that damned cow of his. He irritated me."

"Abe may be right. The cow may be an important clue."

Black grunted.

"Could be," Percy insisted.

"I'll have to recheck the walking time from the village to this house. We've talked so much that our time is no test. If your idea is right and Stryke is not guilty the murderer has been very elusive Back there in the woods. Didn't you see anyone at all? What did the car look like as it sped around that turn up there in the brush?"

"It looked like any other car." Percy stopped suddenly. "Say, I did see Eben Ryder's fancy car just north of the Park as Libby and I ran toward the village after our tire went."

They were at the Ryder gate. "Eben's car, eh! he said, as he swung up the path toward the front door. "We'll ask these people a few questions." He rapped on the white panel.

CHAPTER SIXTEEN

ABBIE GLOVER was wearing a funereal look as she opened the door. Her voice was softer, her eyes less belligerent than they had been, her whole manner had changed.

"Chastened by death," Percy thought as he watched her step aside for them to enter.

"Is Mr. Eben Ryder here?" Black asked.

"In the dining-room, straight ahead. Would you like some coffee?" she asked.

"I would. How about you, Peacock?"

"I'd love it," Percy agreed, realizing suddenly that he was quite hungry.

"What are you doing here?" Black asked.

"Caleb thought I ought to come back and do for Eben and Henry. It's the least I could do at a time like this," she replied.

"I guess so." Black answered. "Now, we'll have that coffee."

"I'll fix it." Abbie moved ahead of them, along the short hall, to open the dining-room door.

Eben and Henry were idling over some supper. Eben rose to his feet and suggested graciously, "Have some supper? Abbie believes that the inner man must be satisfied regardless of what happens." As Black and Percy sat before the gleaming mahogany, Eben went on as if desirous of filling in time. "She has fed your men. One of them is still in the sitting-room. Too bad the clam pie is all gone. She makes the best clam pie on the Cape."

"She seems to be a woman of many accomplishments," Black replied.

Eben eyed him for a moment before he asked, "Any new developments?"

"No. I'm afraid we will have to be satisfied with what we have for the moment. Do you know anything about your brother's will?" Black asked.

"No, but we can ask Abbie. She knows everything."

"What's that?" Abbie asked as she came through the door with a pot of steaming coffee and a platter of delicious pink ham. She put the coffee and platter on the table and went to the commode, producing linen, doilies and silver.

"Mr. Black was asking us about Silas's will. I told him you would know about it."

Percy was watching her carefully as she placed the doilies and arranged the silver.

"He made a new will about a week ago," she said quietly.

Eben nodded and smiled at Black. Henry scowled.

"Do you know what was in the new will?" Black asked her.

"No. I witnessed it. So did Sidney Stone. He was up here painting that day."

"Didn't you see anything in the will?" Black insisted.

"I saw the name of Stryke Ryder," she said.

"In what connection?"

She stood near the kitchen door, facing them. "I couldn't make it all out, but there were words saying something about the balance and residue of the estate being left to Stryke Ryder."

"Where is the will now?" Black asked.

"With the rest of his papers in that old sea chest in the sitting-room," she answered.

"Are you sure?" Black insisted.

"It was there yesterday."

"How do you know that, Miss Glover?"

"Because I looked," she said defiantly. "When he was out I found a key that opened the lock."

"Then you know all about the will."

"I do now."

"Suppose you get it for us. Do you mind?"

"Tell him," she said as she crossed to the sitting-room and opened the door.

Black instructed his man to let Abbie open the sea chest. In a moment she was back in the room with the will in her hand. Black read it quickly. It was short.

"Mind telling us what it says?" Eben asked anxiously.

"I'll read the bequests. That's what you are interested in, isn't it? 'To my brother Eben Ryder the sum of fifty thousand dollars, to Abbie Glover my housekeeper the sum of twenty thousand dollars. The balance and residue of my estate I leave to my grandson Stryke Ryder. I hereby appoint Martin Chase as my executor without bond.'"

There was silence for a moment before Henry said bitterly, "Well, how do you like that?"

"Frankly, I had hoped for more," Eben said honestly.

"Well, you can be glad you're getting that much," Abbie said.

As they turned toward her, she gave a very good imitation of a woman who would have bitten her tongue off rather than to have said what she did.

"Just what do you mean, Miss Glover?" Black asked quickly.

"We might have been left without a cent," she answered, after a moment's consideration.

"Are you sure that is what you mean?" Black insisted.

"Yes."

"I thought you meant something else," Black said.

Abbie was confused. She looked from one to the other. "You've been talking to Martin Chase," she accused, and turned away.

"Don't go. Sit down," Black insisted.

"I don't want to sit down."

"Just as you like, but do not leave this room."

Abbie's quick temper flared, but she controlled her tongue, clamped her lips into a tight line.

Eben leaned forward. "What did you mean, Abbie?"

"Well, you'll all know sooner or later. Silas threatened to turn everything over to Stryke Ryder," she announced.

"Everything?" Black asked.

"Yes, everything. That's why he called Martin Chase up here."

"We can prove that he was not in his right mind," Henry suggested hopefully to his father.

"Not in a thousand years," Eben said. "And you know it." He turned back to Abbie. "Why was he going to do such a thing?"

Abbie was saved from an immediate reply by the sound of footsteps on the rear porch. A moment later Martin Chase strode in. "I brought the will, if the family is willing you can look at it now," he said.

Black thanked him and explained that they had found a copy.

"Then you don't need me," Chase said, and started to back out.

"We need you," Black replied. "Sit down."

"We certainly do," Henry said angrily. "Why was he going to turn everything over to Stryke?"

Martin looked across at Abbie. "It's a little delicate," he said.

"Don't you fret about me, Martin Chase. I had hoped that with him dead and all, this wouldn't come up, but I suppose you had to tell."

"Tell what, Abbie?" Martin asked innocently. "About him wanting to transfer all his money to Stryke."

"Suppose you tell us all about it, or would you rather Mr. Chase tells us what he knows?" Black said, giving her a choice.

"I'll tell you. I might as well. It all happened this morning, because that Stryke came here. I knew about the will and I thought it was neither fair nor sensible, but what I thought didn't mean anything to Silas. When Stryke came this morning, I listened at the door and Silas caught me at it. He was furious and accused me of snooping. The boy slammed out of the house, they had

been quarreling over the theatre people and the way
Caroline had been treated. You'd have thought it was my
fault that the boy left. He blamed me for it, anyhow,
accused me of listening and told me to get out. We had
had words before, and I didn't pay much attention to it,
but this time he told me to leave the house for good. That
made me mad and I threatened to sue him," she ended.

"That hardly seems reason enough for him to transfer
his money," Black cut in.

"That's because you don't know. I've lived here and
done for Silas Ryder for twenty years or more. The folks
in this town knew what was going on, though they
pretended they didn't. They shut their eyes to it, and
treated me all right, that is what most of them did." She
had been looking at the floor as she spoke and she didn't
look up as she finished.

"You see, Miss Glover's threat of a suit would have
been serious. Under the common law she could have sued
for, and could have claimed, half of the estate," Chase
explained.

"Twenty thousand ain't much, but I could have
managed with it, but when he said he would turn all his
money over to Stryke—"

"What did you do then?" Black asked.

"I told him I wouldn't sue him, but he wouldn't listen
to me. He said he couldn't trust me, that he'd make the
transfer anyhow. He called Martin, asked him to come
right up here."

"Did you and Mr. Ryder mention the will at all during
your talk?"

"Yes. I told him I knew about the paltry little bit he
was leaving me."

"Do you think anyone might have heard you?" Black
asked.

"You came in and went to your room, didn't you,
Henry?" she asked, turning toward him.

"No. I wasn't near the house this morning," Henry
declared.

"I thought I heard you," Abbie insisted.

"If you were here, Henry, you had better admit it now," Eben advised. "It will be harder to explain later."

"How about yourself? You were here," Henry retorted.

"How do you know?" Black asked.

"Because I did come in, heard them squabbling and left," Henry replied.

"But that doesn't answer the question about your father," Black reminded him.

"I saw him under the sitting-room window listening," Henry blurted.

"That's right," Eben admitted. "I was there." He turned to his son. "Where was your car, Henry? Where did you park it?"

"On the East Road beyond the barn. I knew Stryke was coming up here and I wanted to know what had happened," Henry replied churlishly.

"Who told you?" Eben asked.

"I saw him walking up here."

"How did you know, Mr. Ryder?" Black asked Eben.

"I had been to Orleans this morning and was swinging back this way. I saw Suzie Briggs down near the Park and she told me that Stryke was coming up here. I'll admit I was curious and came up to see what was going on."

"And where did you leave your car?" Percy asked.

"In the pine grove on the old cart-track which comes in from the Webster Road," Eben answered.

"Did either of you see Stryke Ryder?" Black asked.

"I saw him leave. That's when I came in through the back and overheard the row."

"And you?" Black turned to Eben.

"I didn't see the boy. I was listening outside the window and was there when Martin came. I'm sorry, but I didn't see Henry, so cannot corroborate his story."

Henry's eyes blazed with angry resentment as he realized that a chance remark of his father's had led him to an admission that he had been in the house.

"Then you both knew the contents of the will," Black said.

"I heard Abbie telling Silas that she knew what was in the will," Eben admitted.

"Now you, Henry," Black said, "did you hear Silas say he would turn over all his money to Stryke?"

"Yes. I heard it."

"Did you know what was in the new will?"

"Yes."

Curious pair, Percy thought. Their reactions are not dependable at all. I didn't believe either of them knew about the new will. Very good actors, both of them, or very bad.

"Suppose we go on from here," Black suggested.

"What happened when you arrived, Chase?"

"The old man was pretty testy and he admitted he was afraid of what Abbie might do."

Abbie sniffed at that, and slid into a chair. Percy watched her, could almost sense her relish of the situation as her eyes widened at each succeeding statement.

"Were you prepared to follow his suggestions and make out the transfer papers?" Black asked.

"I advised him to think it over, to wait until tonight, when we could talk it over."

"Why did you suggest the delay?"

"Because he was mad and wasn't a reasonable being at the time. I suggested that we could doubtless settle with Abbie out of court if she went on with her threat to sue him. There was no question that she was entitled to something. You see, during all the years that Abbie has worked here, he has never had a receipt from her for services rendered. I explained that she could put in a bill against either him or the estate for a considerable amount of money."

"Did you suggest an amount for settlement?"

"Yes. I suggested that he pay her $10,000 back wages at the rate of ten dollars a week for twenty years."

"You mean in addition to the twenty thousand she was to inherit?"

"That was up to him," Martin replied.

"You know very well, Martin Chase, that you suggested he pay me that ten thousand dollars and cut me out of his will entirely. Why don't you tell the truth? Why don't you tell them that you told him a transfer would involve a lot of legal work at this time because of your joint investments?" she demanded.

"Joint investments?" Black asked.

"Yes. Mr. Ryder and I have had several enterprises together. That was one of the reasons for suggesting he think it over until tonight. It would have been necessary to settle our affairs before he could make a complete transfer of his property."

"You suggested that he keep the money that you and him had invested," Abbie said.

"That's right," Chase agreed. "I thought he was foolish to even attempt to turn everything over to this boy."

"You heard everything, didn't you, Miss Glover?" Black asked.

"Yes."

"And you?" he turned to Henry.

"I was not here when Chase came."

"But you knew about the will?"

"Yes."

"And you heard Silas say that he would transfer his money?"

"Yes."

"I heard it all too," Eben admitted.

"Of course you realize that we now have three rather good motives for the murder of Silas Ryder," Black said slowly, and poured himself another cup of coffee.

"I wasn't here, I tell you," Henry insisted.

"I'm not accusing any one of you," Black said as he helped himself to sugar.

"But you might as well," Henry insisted. "That's what you meant."

Black shrugged. "Do you drive a car, Miss Glover?" he asked.

"Yes, I do. Why?"

"Do you have a car?"

"Yes."

"Where do you keep it?"

"In the barn."

"Did you use it today?"

"No. I wanted Martin to take me to the village but he said he couldn't wait."

"Everybody in town knows that Abbie is afraid of getting a scratch on her car," Chase said.

"That's my business," she retorted.

"It's got plenty of scratches on it now," Henry said, with relish. "Have you been in the woods, Abbie?"

"What do you mean?" she demanded.

"It's all scratched up and muddy too," he said. "You were out in your car today. Why don't you admit it?"

"You're a-lying," she cried. "I never touched that car today."

"Suppose we have a look at it," Black suggested. He rose and looked across at Percy, who showed how eager he, too, was to see Abbie's car.

Abbie had gone first to the kitchen. She moved with unexpected agility considering her bulk, When the men followed her, they found her feeling under a shelf near the sink.

"My keys!" she cried. "Henry Ryder, what have you done with my keys?"

"I haven't touched your old keys," he denied.

"They're gone—my car keys are gone," she half cried as she faced Black. "If I get my hands on the person . . ."

What she would do was lost in her bustle and haste as she grabbed a flashlight from the shelf and lashed across the room and out the door.

She reached the barn before they did.

Her car had been hurriedly driven into the barn and abandoned. Beside it lay a huge mass of white material which she used for a cover. She ran the light over the sides of the car and rubbed some ugly scratches with her fingers. She rubbed diligently, futilely. She moaned over the marks. The wheels and tires were splashed with dirt and mud.

"Look at it!" she cried. "It's ruined, that's what it is!" Tears filled her eyes.

"And it is not unlike Mr. Eben's car, is it?" Percy asked quietly, as he looked at the very sporty model, so unlike anything one would expect Abbie Glover to love and cherish.

CHAPTER SEVENTEEN

ABBIE was not interested in Percy's implications. She found the keys dangling in the ignition switch, mumbled something about what she would do to the person who had used the car and was about to reach for them when Black stepped in to prevent her.

"Don't touch this car," he warned.

"It's mine!" she protested.

"It's also evidence," he replied, as he gingerly removed the keys from the switch and dropped them into a handkerchief.

"Evidence!" she repeated. "What kind of evidence?"

"If you didn't use it, why was it taken out?" he asked.

"That's what I'd like to know," she said sharply.

"That's what I'm going to find out. It could have been used for a number of things. The murderer might have taken it to hunt for Miss Nellie. The guilty person does not know yet that Miss Nellie knows nothing to endanger him."

"Then why did she run and hide?" Abbie demanded.

"She used her head," Percy said. "Two attempts were made on her life."

Black was looking over the car, using his flashlight.

"Don't you count my fingerprints on this car," Abbie cried suddenly and unexpectedly. "There'll be plenty on it."

"Let's hope for your sake that there will be theirs," he said.

"Look here, are you saying that I killed Silas Ryder?" she demanded.

"No, I wasn't, but since you bring up the question, did you?"

"Did I what?"

"Kill Silas Ryder and the others," Black stated.

"No, I didn't, and if you were less than half-witted, you'd know I didn't!" she exploded.

"How would I know, Miss Glover?" Black smiled disarmingly.

"Why . . . why . . . why should I?" she finally gasped.

"If Mr. Ryder had lived and settled with you for ten thousand dollars before he turned his money over to Stryke Ryder, you would get ten thousand and that would be all. If he died before he could make the transfer of his money, you would receive twenty thousand, just double the amount."

"I never thought of such a thing!" she declared.

"It seems that someone did," he said icily.

"There were others who stood to lose more than me," she stated. "And you know who they are."

"Don't you try to crawl out from under by throwing suspicion on us," Henry shrilled at her.

"And why not?" she retorted. "You came snooping around today, didn't you? Why? You were supposed to be in New Bedford."

"That's my business!" Henry shouted.

"Henry!" Eben cautioned.

"You keep out of this. I can take care of myself. I always have," Henry said accusingly.

Eben shrugged, walked to the door and stood looking out at the night.

"We'll go back to the house," Black said and stepped forward to join Eben. As the others followed him, he turned to Percy and said, "Would you mind staying here? I want to telephone down to the office for an extra man to watch this car until daylight."

"Go ahead," Percy agreed.

"Do you want me any more?" Martin asked.

"No."

"Then I'll go back," he said.

Percy heard the sputter of Martin's car as it started. He listened until it faded into the stillness of the night.

He was busy tracing the great dipper and the north star, when he heard a rebirth of sound.

A motorcycle roared up from the village, its single beam of light cutting a path through the night. Percy watched the progress of the light and was surprised to see the silhouette of a man crossing the field between him and the road. The trooper turned in, came bearing down on Percy.

"There's someone in that field," Percy said when the motor was cut. He started away. The trooper followed.

They moved quietly toward the house. "There he is," Percy whispered. They cut into the field.

"Who are you and what do you want?" the trooper demanded.

The man was surprised. "I—er—I . . ."

"Perine!" Percy exclaimed. "What are you doing here?"

"Trying to make up my mind what to do, whether to go forward and expose myself to the indignity of questions and suspicions or to let nature take its course," Perine replied.

The trooper had stepped forward as Perine talked, had run his hands over Perine's clothing. "Got a license to carry a gun?" he demanded.

"Yes," Perine replied.

"I feel a bit of a fool," Perine said, "but I'll have to face the music now."

"Whatever it is, I'm afraid you will," Percy agreed.

They entered the house via the kitchen door. Abbie was at the sink washing dishes.

"Oh," she said, after one quick glance. "They're in there." She nodded toward the dining-room. "I've brought Mr. Perine with me," Percy said as he stepped into the room. "He wants to talk to you, Black."

Eben looked up from his chair at the head of the table. "So you've come," he said. "I was wondering about you."

Black was obviously puzzled, so was Henry. "Didn't you tell him about me?" Perine asked Eben.

"No."

"I thought you would," Perine replied.

"Well, what is there about you that I should know?" Black demanded.

"I was here this morning. I thought I'd better tell you myself before someone else told you."

Just beyond the door leading into the kitchen something crashed to the floor. Abbie had been listening again and what she heard had startled her.

CHAPTER EIGHTEEN

BLACK moved toward the door and looked into the kitchen. Perine waited patiently, ignoring Eben's speculative glance. Henry's eyes seemed to be filled with new hope as he considered the possibility of Perine's being involved as a suspect in the murders.

There was a smile in Black's eyes as he said, "Come in, Miss Glover. There's no point straining your ears way out there. Sit down, Perine."

Abbie rounded the door jamb rather sheepishly and slid into a chair. She put her hands on her knees and waited expectantly.

"You heard what Mr. Perine said, Miss Glover. Why did it startle you so?"

"She was probably afraid of being incriminated," Perine answered for her. "You see, I made a little deal with her this afternoon. I bribed her not to mention the fact that she had seen me here this morning. I thought about it, decided it was not fair to put her in a false position and, I'm frank to admit that I knew you would suspect me if she did tell."

"Is this true?" Black demanded of Abbie.

"Yes, sir," she replied meekly.

"You know it is a criminal offense, withholding evidence?"

"It ain't criminal," she refuted. "You didn't ask me."

"I believe I asked you back at the theatre if you had seen anyone other than Stryke Ryder and Martin Chase. You did not tell me about Mr. Perine, nor did you tell me about Henry Ryder."

"I didn't know about Henry for sure," she said defensively. "I only thought I heard him."

"That's beside the point. You'd better watch your step, Miss Glover. Was anyone else here? Abe Tucker for instance?" he demanded.

"You'd better be sure this time," he warned. She sniffed her own private brand of resentment.

"So you came to see the old man." Eben's voice was full of surprise as he spoke to Perine.

"And what do you know about Perine that you should have told me?" Black demanded of Eben.

"He recognized me," Perine said quietly. "It was decent of you not to give me away," he said to Eben.

Black shook his head. "I don't get all this."

"It is very simple. I'm Stryke Ryder's father."

"Land of Goshen. So that's it!" Abbie gasped. Forgetting where she was, ignoring the circumstances, she leaned toward Black and said, "His face has been bothering me ever since he came here. Well, I never!"

"Is your paternity a secret?" Black asked.

"Of course it is. Say, your name wasn't Perine when you married Caroline. It was, let me see . . . Merry, Merry something." Abbie beamed with a lust for gossipy talk.

"Merriweather," Perine obliged.

"What's the idea of the alias?" Black demanded.

"An actor assumes many parts," Perine replied. "Obviously it would not do for me to appear here as Merriweather."

"Why not?"

"It was part of a bargain made many years ago with Silas Ryder," Perine stated.

"Does it have any bearing on the murder?" Black demanded.

"No. It explains my assumed name."

"What was the bargain?" Black asked.

"I sold my name to Silas Ryder soon after I married his daughter. Ours was a summer romance. I was not truly in love with the woman I married. Silas sensed it. He came to me, offered me a large sum of money to desert my wife, to give up my name, to leave the stage for at least ten years."

"You took the money?" Black made no effort to conceal his contempt.

"Yes. I went to California and invested my money in moving pictures. I have been there ever since."

Eben cut in to tell Black the story of Caroline Ryder's elopement.

"And so you recognized Merriweather or Perine and said nothing about it?" Black accused when Eben had finished.

"I wasn't sure until this afternoon, when the crowd started to get out of hand."

"Why were you here at this house, Perine?" Black demanded.

"The old man sent for me this morning."

"At what time?" Black asked eagerly.

"It must have been about 11:30," he said, looking toward Abbie for confirmation.

"It was along about then," she agreed. "Anyhow it was before Martin came."

"Why did Silas Ryder send for you, Perine?"

"Because we were partners."

"What?" Eben gasped.

"Perhaps it would be more explicit to say we were in collusion," Perine explained.

"Just what do you mean by that? In collusion for what reason?"

"How do you come into the picture? Why should Silas send for you? He hated you." Eben was puzzled.

"Because this summer stock company was his idea. His money has been financing it. He had hoped through Stryke to get his daughter back. He was a very strange man. He had no use for me and told me so from the start, but he didn't feel that he could trust anyone else and he had reason to believe that I would do almost anything for money. We had our plans all set. We had located Stryke and his mother. She, however, was ill, so we decided to wait until she had recovered somewhat because we didn't want Stryke to turn us down. He hoped to reach his daughter through her son. He was willing to be patient. As you know, Caroline died. We wired Stryke at once to come here to be our juvenile lead.

"Stryke came here to the house this morning. They quarreled. The old man said he was testing Stryke, told me that he wanted to be sure that Stryke was really a Ryder and not contaminated by too much of my blood. He purposely angered Stryke by threatening to close the company. He was afraid Stryke would go away. He feared he had bested the boy, and that was not what he wanted. He wanted Stryke to stay and fight him. When I left him he said, 'If he hasn't guts enough to fight me, sell him the idea.'"

"Did you talk to Stryke?" Percy asked.

"No. I didn't know what to do about it. What to say to him. When I met him in the drugstore I knew he wanted to talk to me, but I didn't want to discuss the subject with him there. I had to figure out a campaign. I made some excuse and went out. This whole business has been very difficult for me. I had to promise the old man that I would never let Stryke know that I was his father."

"And you have kept that promise?"

"Yes, up to now."

"Why did you come here tonight, Perine?"

"Because Stryke Ryder is innocent."

"How do you know that?"

"Because I saw him here at this house."

"When?"

"About noon."

"Where were you?" Black asked.

"In the cupola, talking to Miss Nellie."

"Did you see him enter the house?"

"No. I was looking through her glasses. I remember saying to her that someone was trying to get in the Ryder house and she said, 'They won't. Everybody in town knows the house is closed from about 11:30 to 2:00.'"

"You watched Stryke through glasses. What did he do?"

"He went round to the back of the house and then walked away."

"Did you see anything else?"

"No, I wasn't interested in anything else. Miss Nellie left. I sat there for a few minutes alone before I went down."

"Silas was killed just before noon," Black stated.

"I don't know about that," Perine replied.

"Did you walk or ride up here this morning?" Black asked.

"I had my car."

Black turned to Eben. "What time did you leave?"

"When Martin left."

"And when did you leave?" Black demanded of Abbie.

"Not more than a minute or two after Martin. He was in such a hurry, he refused point blank to wait for me."

"Then you should have seen Martin Chase when you drove up here," Black said to Perine.

"I don't remember seeing anyone but Miss Abbie," Perine said thoughtfully. "There was no one else here at the time. I didn't stay more than a few minutes. If I passed Mr. Chase on the road I was too preoccupied to notice. I went back to the village and the Town Hall."

"He wouldn't have seen Martin because Martin's car was out on the other road. I remember because he had something to say about my car being all covered up," Abbie recalled. "Martin went out along the back when he left. I remember looking after him and thinking it wouldn't have hurt him none to have waited."

"Then as far as we know, Miss Glover, you were the last person to see Silas Ryder alive."

"I don't know about that. I didn't see him after Martin left. I just lit out."

"You didn't happen to hear a shot before you left, did you?" Percy asked.

"What do you mean?" she gasped.

"Just exactly that."

"Oh, I thought you meant did I shoot him."

"Did you?"

"No, I didn't, and Martin didn't shoot him neither because I was listening up to almost the last minute he was in there. I barely had time to get out into the kitchen before he came out." She suddenly remembered the circumstances of Silas's death. "You know very well he was stabbed to death," she accused. "What are you trying to do?"

"You didn't see Ryder after Chase left?" Black ignored her question.

"No. I went to the door and told him I was going and he said, 'Why don't you go?'"

"You're sure of that?"

"Positive. It hurt my feelings, it did."

"Well, that gives Chase a clean alibi," Black said a little regretfully.

"For the land's sakes! Are you suspecting Martin too?"

"I'm suspecting everybody."

"I don't see why we have to be put to these indignities when you have the murderer in jail," Henry complained.

"Stryke Ryder did not kill him," Perine objected.

"Can you be sure, Mr. Perine?" Black demanded. "How do I know that you are not telling me that Stryke did not enter the house just to protect him?"

"Yes, why is everybody so interested in saving his neck?" Henry demanded.

Eben looked at his offspring with strange, curious eyes. "You'd be surprised, Henry, what a father would do for his son, no matter what the son is like."

"You don't need to rub it in that you don't like me," Henry shouted.

"I'll let you gentlemen quarrel in privacy," Black interrupted. "I have Ryder in jail, but I'm going to be very interested in you, too. Remember a man is innocent until proven guilty. You had better think up some good alibis for this afternoon, all of you." He turned. "Come along, Perine."

CHAPTER NINETEEN

THEY stood in the yard just beyond the house while they lit cigarettes.

"You'll release Stryke now, won't you?" Perine asked.

"I can't. There's too much evidence against him. You know what happened this afternoon."

"Only too well," Perine admitted.

"By the way, where were you while the near-lynching was taking place?"

"I ran away like a coward after Eben recognized me. I had some time for thinking. I didn't know just what to do. Since then I made up my mind. I have a confession here."

"For what?"

"I killed Silas Ryder."

"Why?"

"Does it matter?"

"You'd better give Black your gun," Percy suggested.

Perine obeyed.

Black scratched his head. "I'll be darned."

"I'm glad that it's over," Perine said.

"May I ask Perine a few questions, Black?"

"I'd rather not answer them," Perine said immediately.

"Just as you like," Black said.

"You're a liar, Perine," Percy accused. "A magnificent one, but a liar nevertheless. You did not kill Silas Ryder."

Black swung sharply toward Percy. "What are you driving at, Peacock?"

"The truth," Percy declared, then turned back to Perine. "Why did you kill Ryder?"

"Because he was stronger than I was, because he ruined my life years ago, because he was trying to do the same thing to my son."

"Then you didn't know that he was making Stryke his chief heir, that he had some idea of turning all his money over to Stryke?"

Perine was surprised and showed it.

"Look, Perine, you want to help Stryke, don't you?" Percy pleaded.

"Naturally."

"This confession of yours will only hurt him, will revive a story that might better be forgotten."

"Why don't you make him leave me alone?" Perine cried to Black.

"If he's right, you'd better listen to him now. It won't be so easy later. Suppose you tell us how you committed the murders," Black suggested.

"It would be more to the point if he told us why he secretly believes Stryke is guilty," Percy accused.

"You lie!" Perine shouted. "I don't!"

"That was a bull's-eye," Percy said with satisfaction.

"I insist upon my rights as a citizen," Perine said dramatically. "I demand that you arrest me."

"Go ahead, lock him up," Percy said, "only if I were you I'd make him tell me why he hid the gun in Stryke's room. It's such a nice way for a father to help his son."

"How did you kill Silas?" Black asked.

"Stabbed him."

"What did you use?" Percy asked.

"The dagger he always kept on his desk."

"Wrong," Black said.

"All right, damn you," Perine cried. "I didn't kill any of them, and I was afraid that they could prove Stryke guilty. It's probably the only decent impulse I've had in my life and I've made a fool of myself doing it."

"Far from it, Perine," Percy said and put a friendly arm about the man. "It was a fine thing you did. I'm happy to know a man like you. You were overzealous, that's all. Now tell us why you thought Stryke guilty?"

"Because everything is stacked against the boy, that's why. He's never had a decent break in life and it has been my fault."

They had progressed toward the village. The lights in the Ryder place were growing dim behind them. There had been no conversation since Perine's revealing statement.

It was Perine who broke the silence. "Would you do me a favor, Black?"

"If I can. What is it?"

"Would it be possible to say nothing about my confession?"

"There's no need for my making any official announcement of it."

"Thanks." Perine seemed relieved.

"Don't feel ashamed of it, Perine," Percy said. "It was fine of you to have tried."

"But stupid, as you pointed out, and a little late. I've been thinking about it as we walked along. Stryke would think, and I wouldn't blame him, that I did it to curry favor. Does he have to know I'm his father?"

"Have you forgotten Abbie Glover?" Black asked. "There's only one way to stop that woman's tongue from wagging and that's to cut her throat, but if you don't mind, I'd rather you wouldn't do it tonight. I've had enough murders for one day."

"I suppose I'll have to face it, and him. I don't want him to think that—"

"You don't know your son, do you?"

"No. I wish I did or rather I wish I had. Being with him has given me a great deal to think about this past week. I've found myself wishing . . . But you men are not interested in another man's regrets."

They had reached Main Street. With a quiet "Goodnight" Perine turned and left them.

"Odd development of the case," Percy said as they moved toward the Spring house.

"Is there anything about this case that isn't?" Black countered. "Perine may not be the noble soul he would have us believe."

"I've been considering that point too, have been considering him from every angle. Perine could have killed the old man."

"When?"

"That's your job, to determine the exact time. Perhaps he went back and stabbed Silas."

"All right. Suppose he did. What then?"

"He has been here long enough to know that Miss Nellie would be a dangerous person."

'Why didn't he kill her up there in the tower when he says he was with her?" Black demanded.

"I don't know. Perhaps he decided to follow her home and take a pot shot at her through her window."

"All right. What was his motive for killing Silas?" Black countered. "All the murders hinge on the death of the old man."

"There may be a lot more to the relationship of Perine and the old man than we know. Perhaps the old man threatened to tell something to Stryke, or he may have told him something which infuriated Perine to the point of murder."

"It's a mess. Why couldn't it be a nice clean case?"

"We have plenty of circumstantial evidence. Too much," Percy reminded him. "You have Stryke in jail. I haven't quite believed you about the boy. I have a feeling that you think him guilty."

"And I'll admit I do feel that way about him," Black said. "The boy must have hated the old man. I know I would if I were in his shoes, but I can't see that hatred as the only cause for murder. There would have to be some other reason."

"It's a sexless crime, isn't it?" Percy asked.

"What do you mean sexless?"

"Well, many murders have a sex background, but this one—"

"Aren't you forgetting Abbie?" Black demanded.

"No. If Abbie killed him it was not a sex murder. It was hate, revenge and greed."

"And she had all three motives. He was kicking her out, she was going to lose money by the deal he had cooked up with Chase, and for both reasons she must have hated his guts. It's a nice little set of motives for Miss Abbie. Certainly no one in the town would be more aware of Miss Nellie in the tower than Abbie would have been if she did kill the old man."

"But isn't Abbie the one person who would have aroused no suspicion from Miss Nellie even if she did see her at the house?"

"Aren't you forgetting that Abbie left the house daily about 11:30 and did not return until two or after?" Black reminded him. "You gave me that information yourself. Abbie is the one person whose presence at or near the house at twelve o'clock would have attracted the attention of Miss Nellie. Therefore if Abbie was there after 11:30 she would be worried about Miss Nellie and then later about Sidney after she overheard the conversation about the glasses."

"Right. We'll have to ask Caleb about Abbie. They were together when the body was discovered, Now, how much time did Abbie have between the time Caleb left her at his house and the mob scene? If she has an alibi for all her time from the moment Caleb left her, she is not the murderer." Percy was very emphatic about that point.

"Who did kill them? Any guesses?" Black asked

"No, I wouldn't venture a guess right now."

"You must have some idea," Black persisted.

"I've lots of ideas but there are things I want to know."

"Like what?"

"Well, right after the second session in the theatre Eben Ryder said he was going back to Boston. He didn't go. Why? Where was he?"

Black smiled. "A natural question. Ever hear the old wheeze about giving a calf enough rope That's what I'm doing. With such a crop of good suspects we ought to get something by being a little patient. Every one of them needs an alibi, and needs it badly. Abbie needs one to account for her time between 11:30 and the time you saw her at the Spring gate. Where was she and what was she doing? Also, what was she doing from the time she left the drugstore until Sidney fell?"

"That's true of Eben and Henry too, isn't it?" Percy queried.

"Sure, and Martin Chase, and even you."

"And why would I want to kill Silas Ryder?" Percy demanded.

"Maybe you're a nut. I understand that psychiatrists and people like yourself sometimes go a little batty. How do I know that you didn't do it just to prove how superior you are to a lot of hicks in a little country village?"

"Are you serious?" Percy asked soberly.

"Serious, yes, but I don't mean it. Some such trick would be the solution in a book. You've had a front seat for all of this so far, you know. You are the person who would arouse the least suspicion, except of course for your little affair with Miss Knight."

"You had me worried for a moment. I've often considered a perfect crime, the ways and means of doing one. There is one drawback to a perfect crime, however."

"What?"

"If a crime is so perfect that it escapes detection, how could you get any kick out of it? You would have to give yourself up just to prove how clever you had been."

Black laughed heartily. "I had never thought it from that angle. It would be a burning secret wouldn't it?"

"It's what I call an impossible situation. A man clever enough to think of a perfect crime would want someone else to know how clever he had been."

"Which has nothing to do with this case," Black said.

"Absolutely nothing. Our murderer has been in a frenzy to cover his trail. Can't you imagine the urge the man must have felt between twelve and one, or perhaps I should say between twelve and two? He knew that no one would discover the body until after two, but he didn't want to take any risks. With Miss Nellie and Sidney out of the way, his two danger points, he could feel easier in his mind."

"Boy, we have been asleep!" Black exclaimed "Why?"

"That Verity woman. Her life is in danger. She saw Stryke both times when he went to the house. How do we know that she didn't see the real murderer?"

"We don't, and neither does the murderer," Percy agreed.

"Come on." Black started to trot along the street. "If anything has happened or happens to that woman, I'll never forgive myself for being a blind fool."

Their progress along Main Street was not noticed. There were no pedestrians and oddly enough there were no loungers on the porch of the hotel as they went by.

"Do you know where she lives?" Black asked as they ran down the side of the Town Hall toward his motorcycle.

"On the Webster Road, and it must be the little Cape Cod cottage which faces the field and the Ryder place."

"Want to ride up with me? You can sit on the guard. It won't be very comfortable, but it isn't far," Black said as he swung his leg over the seat and kicked up the rest. Percy was already straddling the guard.

"Hang on!" Black cautioned as the motor broke into a roar and they rushed away.

"I hope we're in time," he said as he ran up the path and pounded on the front door.

For a long time there was not a sound from within the house. He banged again.

"For mercy's sakes, I'm coming. Who is it?" A voice shrilled from inside.

"Black, in charge of the murder case. Is that you, Mrs. Verity?"

"Yes. What do you want at this time of night?"

"I must talk to you."

"Well, wait a minute, until I get somethin on."

"I guess we've been unduly alarmed," Black said sheepishly.

"What are you going to tell her?"

"Why?"

"Unless you want to scare hell out of her, you'd better be very diplomatic."

"And unless she wants to join the others, I still think she'd better be careful," he replied grimly.

Mrs. Verity opened the door and stood facing them, her eyes filled with the panic and fear most people feel toward the law.

"Sorry to bother you at this time of the night," Black apologized. "I've been very busy and I've no idea of the time."

"It's all right," she said. "I'd just fallen off t sleep, seems as if I'd just closed my eyes, but it was about 10:30 the last time I was up. The dog got to barking something awful. I don't know what ailed him unless there was a skunk after the chickens. I looked out the window, but I couldn't see a thing."

"It probably was a skunk," Percy said.

Black gave him a sly, appreciative look.

"Might have been," she agreed, "though I didn't smell a thing, and usually when a dog scare them that way, it's pretty bad for a spell. But goodness sakes! You didn't come here to talk about skunks, did you?"

"In a way, yes," Black replied.   Mrs. Verity blinked. "A human skunk."

Percy did not think that Black was being very diplomatic. Without thinking of the effect it would have on her, Black said, "The murderer."

"Oh!" she gasped. "Oh! What would he be doing here?"

"It's all right," Black said quickly. "There is no danger. We wanted to ask you a few questions."

"I'm not so sure it's all right," she objected. "I've had the queerest feeling ever since, well, ever since they very nearly hanged that poor boy this afternoon. Do you know that I've felt just as if someone was watching me every minute?"

"Perhaps you have been watched," Black suggested.

"But why should I be watched?"

"Because you saw Stryke Ryder over at the Ryder place this morning."

"But everybody knows that. I wish to heaven I had never mentioned it. I've been just about sick thinking that what I said might have cost that boy his life. It was awful."

"Did you see anyone else at the Ryder place, Mrs. Verity?"

"No. I wouldn't have seen the boy if I hadn't been watching for the fish man. I declare he comes later and later all the time."

"I don't want to alarm you, Mrs. Verity, but I wish you would go somewhere so that we could be sure you would be safe for a little while," Black said gently.

"But why should I be in danger? Why can't I be safe here?"

"We don't know. We hope that you are and can be safe here, but we don't want to take chance with a desperate criminal."

"But why should I be bothered?" she insisted nervously.

"The murderer killed two people today because he thought those people might have seen him at the Ryder place. How can he be sure that you didn't see him?"

"But I didn't."

"He doesn't know that."

"Oh, dear. I told Will not to go away this week and leave me all alone. It's just as if I knew something would happen."

"Where is your husband?"

"Down Maine."

"Would you like to join him?"

"How can I go at this time of the night?"

"We'll take care of that," Black promised. "I don't want you to stay here."

"If you say so," she agreed tragically. "Oh, dear! I'll have to pack."

"I'll leave Mr. Peacock here. I'll go back to the village and arrange to have one of our cars come up here for you. Can you be ready in a half hour?"

"Ten minutes. Just make yourself to home, Mr. Peacock." She darted out of the room, pulling the door shut behind her.

Percy heard the roar of Black's motor fade into the stillness of the night. He settled into the barrel rocker to wait. He was tired, the room was restful. An old clock ticked merrily from the mantel.

The hearth was clean and decorated with a paper fan. Some English daisies filled a small bowl at his elbow. The New Bedford paper lay folded beside it. It was a lovely room. He dozed.

A short, nervous laugh wakened him. Mrs. Verity had been seventeen minutes getting ready. She had a small satchel in her hand. "I'll have to draw all the blinds," she said.

"May I help?"

"No, but there is something you can do for me tomorrow. Ask someone to feed my dog while I'm away."

"I'll be very glad to do it myself," he promised. "Is he vicious?"

"He ain't never bit but one person, and that was the milkman who liked to tease him."

"Then I guess he's all right. You know the law in most states allows a dog one bite. Where is he? Why don't you call him in? I can make friends with him tonight."

She went through the dining-room and into the kitchen. He heard her opening doors, then heard her voice. She called and waited, called again.

She came back. "He must have gone off in the brush. He runs with the Ryder dog a lot. He'll be here in the morning. He always is. Sit down, Mr. Peacock. I guess Mr. Black didn't believe me when I said ten minutes."

They sat quietly, waiting, listening for the sound of a car or the roar of Black's motorcycle. Ten minutes had passed when Percy said, "What's that?"

She listened for a moment. "It's the dog. He's out front." She went into the little vestibule and opened the door. "Come in," she said. "What's the matter?" There was a period of silence and then she cried, "Oh, Mr. Peacock. There's something the matter with him. He's whimpering."

In the light from the vestibule Percy saw the mark the dog had made as he dragged himself across a flowerbed on his belly.

The dog had crawled home, had reached his mistress in time to die at her feet. There were tears in Percy's eyes, his voice was soft as he said, "He's dead, Mrs. Verity. Poor fellow!"

"But I don't understand," she cried helplessly.

"Perhaps he died to save you. He stood in the way of the murderer and was put out of the way."

She shuddered. As tears filled her eyes, she said impatiently, "Why doesn't he come?"

CHAPTER TWENTY

AFTER a few minutes they did come, and Mrs. Verity was driven away as soon as she and Percy had told Black about the dog.

When the State car had gone, Black turned to Percy and said, "I saw Henry Ryder crossing the road near the Verity house when I left there. I picked him up with my headlight. Do you think he poisoned her dog?"

"I've about reached the point where I can't think. Sleep is what I need," Percy said, "but Henry makes an interesting prospect. We'll have to check and double check."

"Well, I'm going down to Spring's house to have a chat with Miss Nellie. I'll tuck you in as we pass the Tucker place. No, I'd better not. Tucker's bound to ask me about that damned cow of his. You're on your own."

"I'd like to go with you, if you don't mind," Percy declared, his weariness forgotten.

The lights in the town were out. Only a bulb burned dimly in the drugstore. Crickets chirped and sawed at the edges of the night.

"It's hard to believe that here in this peace and solitude we are shielding a murderer," Black said.

"Is the Cape usually free from crime?" Percy asked.

"There hasn't been anything of major importance on the Cape since the famous kidnaping a few years ago."

"I remember the case. Some queer angles to it."

"Very," Black agreed. "There were people who told me they had never locked their doors up to that time. I'll bet there are a few shotguns on duty tonight."

"It's a great place, the Cape," Percy said enthusiastically. "I like its solidness, its stability and the sense of time that it gives a fellow. Don't misunderstand me. I love the West. It's my home, but it's still a wild and rugged country."

"Indians?" Black asked with a laugh.

"No. But we're still young out there. Except for some old forts and some missions there are very few buildings over a hundred years old. Take this town. It's one of the oldest on the Cape. They had the first school here. Take Main Street. The Tucker house is . . . that is the rear part of it is nearly two hundred years old. I like it here."

"So do I, but I'd like it a lot better if I knew who had killed all these people. Funny thing about Cape people. They mind their own business, don't ask questions, go about their lives and expect you to do the same thing."

"It was grim business today," Percy reminded him.

"But it was their business. Sidney was killed, Nellie's life was in danger, Silas was killed. They thought Stryke did it. In a sense Stryke is a foreigner. He wasn't born here and he doesn't belong, not really. They may take him in, in time, but at the moment he is from the outside."

"I used some of that argument on them this afternoon. Will anything be done about the mob business?"

"I don't know. If Stryke doesn't prefer charges, if Caleb forgets who they were, I don't know that much can be done about it."

"But what about your man?"

"He comes from Truro. He's probably related to some of these folks. I'll bet you ten to one he didn't see a soul doing anything out of the ordinary. Well, here we are at the Spring gate. It's been important today, hasn't it? Coming in?"

"Do you think we ought to get them out of bed?" Percy asked.

"Don't worry about that," a voice called softly from the porch. "I'm here."

They went up the path. The dew on the petunias had brought out their fragrance. The air was sweet and clean.

"Want to go inside?" Caleb asked. "She's here."

Black moved along the porch, sat beside Miss Nellie, and with her covered the events of the morning.

"But there must be some reason for the murderer wanting you out of the way. Are you sure there isn't something important that we should know?" Black insisted.

"I wish to heaven I did, with that poor boy over there in Barnstable in jail. Let me see."

"Think about this morning," Black urged. "What happened when you went to work? Did you see anyone, did you talk to anyone? Did you know that Stryke Ryder was going up to see his grandfather?"

"Now how would I know that?" she scoffed. "I saw Cora Tucker in her flowerbed. I saw Phoebe here in her kitchen window."

Caleb grunted.

"Let me see. I met Sidney at the post office, and yes, I met Martin just as I was going into the Town Hall."

"Was Sidney with you?" Caleb asked, and Percy imagined a smile in Caleb's eyes.

"Why, yes, he was," Miss Nellie agreed. "How did you know?"

"I didn't. I was just wondering. I've told the boys here about the rivalry between Sidney and Martin."

"Caleb Spring!" She laughed girlishly. "You'll be giving them the wrong impression. Goodness me, I never did call Martin! We were supposed to go up Cape tonight to a 'time'. Well, it's too late now. I tried to get him at noon and forgot every word about it."

"I guess he sort of figured you wouldn't be able to go," Caleb said.

"Did you tell Martin about your headache?" Percy asked.

"Yes, I did. I told him I had the blind staggers and couldn't see my hand before my face. That was why I was to telephone him. He said if I couldn't go he'd get some other girl. You know what a one Martin is for just such remarks."

"Are you sure Martin knew you couldn't see?" Black picked up Percy's idea and elaborated on it.

"Yes. Good heavens! Are you thinking that Martin . . . Why, that's incredible! Caleb, you've given these men ideas with your talk. I declare! Martin didn't kill those people any more than the Ryder boy did."

"Someone did it, Miss Pine."

"Yes, someone we know well. Horrible, isn't it?"

There was a sharp creak from within the house, the squeaking of a board under a cautious foot. Caleb rose and went toward the door. There were renewed creakings inside the house, and then the mumble of voices.

Phoebe's at it again, Percy thought.

Caleb's voice sounded annoyed, Phoebe's in reply was full of irritation and smoldering anger. Miss Nellie said something vague about the rain's having helped the flowers. She talked quickly about her petunias and the lateness of some of her roses. It was nervous and embarrassed talk, but it did cover the argument going on within the house, and it cloaked their discomfiture.

When a door slammed inside they showed their relief. Miss Nellie's voice trailed away, drowned by the strum of the night noises.

"Tell me about your trip back to the Town Hall just before one," Black suggested.

"Let me think. So much has happened since, that I don't rightly remember what went before. I don't know as I saw much of anything. I was mad all over again as I went down the street. That broken window annoyed me. It's a good thing I didn't know then what I know now. I was rehearsing in my mind the things I was going to say to Caleb."

"What about me?" Caleb asked, as he returned and slumped into a rocker which creaked under his weight.

"I was just trying to recall what happened before one o'clock," she explained. "I was going over in my mind the things I was going to say to you."

"You did all right. I didn't know you had rehearsed your anger," he chided.

"Did you see anyone, speak to anyone?" Black asked.

"Not until I saw Caleb, then I guess I said plenty."

"Then Caleb is the only person who knew difinitely that you had gone into the tower," Black remarked.

"Now you look here," she said crisply. "It's all right to try and find this murderer, but it isn't all right to say things about Caleb."

Black laughed quickly.

"I mean it," she insisted. "First you try to prove something about Martin Chase, and now you are suggesting that Caleb—

"I'm just trying to get at facts, clues," Black explained.

"Well, as a matter of fact, I did have something on my mind besides Caleb. I thought of Martin because I saw his feet on the windowsill, as usual. I was going to stop in the booth and call him before he went out, but Stryke Ryder was in the booth."

"Did Stryke see you?" Percy asked quickly.

"Not unless he has eyes in the back of his head."

"You could have used my telephone," Caleb suggested.

"And have you twitting me for a week about running after a man!" she chuckled.

"When you left Caleb's office, what did you do?"

"I started back to work."

"Any of the actors about as you went up?"

"No," she said slowly, "not unless you call Mr. Perine an actor. He was speaking to Eben Ryder just outside the theatre door." She leaned forward, looked across at Black. "I don't know what you have found, or where your suspicions are taking you, whether they are leading you anywhere away from that poor boy, but . . ." She stopped, leaned back.

"But what?" Black asked eagerly.

"I feel terrible about this, honestly I do . . . but Eben had just come down the stairs and had crossed to speak to

Mr. Perine." She leaned forward again. "When was the Knight girl killed, Mr. Black?"

"We are not sure, but it must have been about one o'clock."

"Oh, dear," Miss Nellie sighed. "I had hoped that my information would not involve Eben."

"Did he seem surprised when he saw you?" Percy asked.

"Come to think of it, he did. 'Why, Nellie,' he said and took out his watch to look at it, 'you're late. I'll have to report you to the town fathers.'"

"Tell us all about your movements from then on," Black urged.

"Eben had reminded me that I was late to my work. I was. No one has ever checked my comings and goings since I've been the fire lookout. That may be why I've tried to be conscientious about my work. Anyhow, I hurried up the next five flights of stairs. I was puffing when I reached the sixth floor and paused for a moment to catch my breath before climbing the ladder. I was through being mad at Caleb by then. I got a sniff of smoke and saw a pile of rubbish smouldering over in a corner. It gave me a bad turn, I can tell you that." She turned indignantly to Caleb. "The fire extinguisher wasn't there. I thought I could stamp it out but there was too much of it ready to burst into flames at any minute so I headed for the iron ladder."

"Why did you do that?" Black asked. "I should have thought you would return to Caleb's office and send in the alarm from there."

She gave him a pitying look before she said, "Mr. Black, there were six long flights of steps between me and Caleb and only that short ladder between me and a telephone. They say I'm quick, but electricity and the telephone is faster. I've been taught to use my head when fire is concerned. That's why I scampered up that ladder like a monkey. You can imagine how I felt when I saw her. She was dead. So was the telephone when I tried to use it."

"It must have been a shock to you," Percy suggested.

"I didn't stop to think about that. With the telephone out of order I grabbed my old coat and hurried back to smother the fire, if I could, but it was too much for me by then, old paper and pieces of carton had begun to burn. I did what I could and started down. As things turned out it would have been quicker for me to have gone down in the first place but I didn't know about the telephone then."

"I see your point," Black said.

"I don't know how I got down those steps without breaking my neck, the way I went, but I did. I ran to the firehouse and turned in the alarm."

"Why didn't you tell Caleb when you reached the main floor?" Black asked.

Miss Nellie was impatient and showed it. "Because I was out of breath. It takes time to run into a man's office and talk, not that I object to talk when there's plenty of time and nothing else to do, like now."

"Why did you hide?" Black asked.

"I don't know exactly, but the wail of that siren did something to me, made me realize that the shot through my kitchen window was not an accident, that, but for the grace of God, I might have been that poor murdered girl. I'm not one to tempt Providence too far. I knew death had missed me twice. I decided to run away and hide."

"And you were very wise to have done so," Black agreed. "Tell me something else. Why didn't you tell Peacock about Eben on the stairs?"

"I didn't think of it. There was nothing suspicious about his actions then to make me keep hin in mind. It was only now looking back that i seemed in any way important."

"How did Perine act when he was in the cupola with you just before noon?"

"Like a man with a problem on his mind."

"Why do you suppose Eve Knight went to the cupola?" Black asked.

"She often came. We were friends. I rather imagine she came for sympathetic understanding. I've heard about the scene between her and Stryke."

"One more question, Miss Nellie. Did you see anyone or anything during that hurried flight of yours which might be of some help to us?"

"I wasn't looking one way or another. I went as 'tight' as I could, with one thought and one thought only in my mind—to get away."

While Nellie talked, Percy had been looking through the branches of a lilac which grew at the end of the porch. He had been counting the clusters of seed pods which were outlined clearly by the street lamp. He had counted twenty-five, when Black said, "It's too bad that you can give us nothing definite which would lead us to the killer. I had hoped, and the killer obviously feared, that you possessed information which would point to him."

"I don't know a thing," Miss Nellie said emphatically, and yawned.

Percy yawned too, and very nearly threw his jaw out of joint by his sudden reaction as the lilac bough dipped and swayed violently.

He jumped to his feet, ran along the porch so unexpectedly that Miss Nellie gave a startled squeak.

"Damn!" he cried when he reached the porch end. The lilac and vines were so closely matted against the porch that he could neither get through nor see through. He ran back.

Caleb and Black were on their feet.

"Someone was listening," he cried as he went down the steps and around the end of the porch.

There was no one in sight, but Caleb's guinea hens at the foot of his lot started to chatter.

"We're a little late," Caleb said.

"Do you think it was the—?" Miss Nellie did not finish.

"No question about it," Black replied. "I'm sorry he got away but glad that he heard enough to realize that Miss Nellie was not a menace to him."

"Do you mean I can go home?" she asked eagerly.

"No, I wouldn't go home tonight, but I think you'll be safe from now on," Black assured her.

"He's awful worried. His conscience must be bothering him," Miss Nellie said.

"I'd say he was more worried about his future," Caleb corrected.

"To think he was right here within a few feet of us!" Miss Nellie breathed with horror. "Maybe pointing a gun at me! Oh, dear!"

"Now don't go and faint on us, Nellie," Caleb warned.

"I'm not the fainting kind, Caleb Spring," she answered tartly.

"I'm glad to know that," Percy said, unable to resist the impulse to tease her.

"Well, I guess we'd better sleep on our problems," Black said. "Goodnight and thank you, Miss Nellie." He moved toward the gate.

Percy joined him and asked, "Where are you going to sleep, Black? I could put you up."

"Who said anything about sleep?"

"You did."

"Pure rhetoric. There are a lot of things for me to do yet. I haven't checked the fingerprints, the gun or anything like that. There hasn't been time. Things have happened too rapidly."

"I'm coming with you, if you don't mind. I've always wanted to be in on the ground floor of a murder, and if you can take it, so can I."

"Let's go." Black yawned, stretched and started down the street.

CHAPTER TWENTY-ONE

"THE more we learn, the more certain I am that Stryke Ryder is innocent," Percy stated as they went down the street.

"So am I," Black agreed. "As a matter of fact, I knew he was innocent."

"But—" Percy started to expostulate.

"I'm more interested in good hot coffee than anything else right at this moment, and there isn't a Chinaman's chance of getting it," Black said disconsolately as he looked at the darkened houses.

"Do you mean that about Stryke?" Percy demanded.

"Yes."

"Then I think I know how we can get some good hot coffee. Come on, let's get to Caleb's office." As they quickened their pace he asked, "Why were you sure about Stryke and why did you arrest him?"

"Stryke Ryder could not have fired the shot which blew your tire this afternoon. The mob had him in hand then."

"Right! How stupid of me to have forgotten it. I should have used it as an argument against you."

"I'm glad you didn't. The murderer might have heard you, and that would have spoiled my plan."

"The old theory—enough rope. You see I was right. Our murderer was snooping about Caleb's house. Now, who knew that Miss Nellie was to be at Caleb's house?"

"No one but us."

"Which proves that I'm just about as half-witted as that Glover woman suggested this afternoon. I should have had one of my men follow us."

"But how could the murderer even think that we were going to interview Miss Nellie?" Percy demanded.

"He probably used his head."

"We mustn't lose sight of the fact that I told everybody in town that I had seen Miss Nellie, that I knew where she was," Percy reminded him. "I am the one who has been grossly stupid, a perfect dumb-bell, as a matter of fact."

"You're not that perfect," joshed Black.

"Seriously, Black, I've been very stupid. We've been followed all evening. I should have considered that possibility. After all, I pride myself on knowing something about the way the human mind works."

"Bosh!"

"But it isn't bosh. Don't you see? Henry Ryder may have followed us when we went up to see Mrs. Verity."

"If he did, it explodes the theory that he went there to get at her. No, we might have interrupted Henry Ryder in whatever he was attempting to do at the Verity house but I don't believe he followed us."

"You're saying that because you are thinking that he could not have followed us on foot when we were on your motorcycle. But Henry might have been somewhere near the Town Hall. From the road he could have watched us, could have seen us turn in at her place. Henry will bear some careful investigation."

"Yes, and I want to know what Eben Ryder was doing in the Town Hall just about one o'clock this afternoon," Black said grimly.

"There are a lot of things I want to know. You probably have the same questions in mind," Percy suggested. "Alibis for the murder periods."

"Yes. Just what periods interest you?" Black asked.

"I'd like to know where all our suspects were from 11:45 to their appearance in the drugstore. Then there is the period from approximately one o'clock until the time Sidney saw the body in the cupola. It's very important."

"It certainly is. We'll get at that tomorrow." They turned into the Town Hall. As Black opened the office door, he said, "Now let me see you produce that coffee."

A trooper dozed in front of Caleb's desk. "It's a shame to wake him up," Percy said as he went to the telephone.

The desk was an old-fashioned one, had a roll top. The telephone sat on the top.

"Give me Libby Powell," Percy said to the operator.

The trooper opened his eyes, yawned and stood up. "We've got company," he said, pointing toward an old wooden settle under the big window which opened on the Webster Road.

Delano Crowell, the young lad who had seen Stryke going into the churchyard just before Sidney fell to his death, was stretched out on the bench. He snored lustily.

Percy heard the bell ringing at the end of the line and was growing impatient when a sleepy voice finally answered. He asked for Libby.

"But tell her it is Percy Peacock. Say I have news about Stryke," he said, after a moment's wait. He put his hand over the mouthpiece and explained, "I guess it was her mother. Libby's in bed."

A moment later he said, "What's some good news worth? Black, one of his men and myself would like some coffee and a sandwich if you . . . Black knows Stryke is innocent. . . . No we don't know who did it . . . Sure, he'll probably release him tomorrow. . . . You're an angel from heaven. 'Bye."

Black had waited for him to finish. "What does the kid want?" he asked the trooper.

"He wouldn't tell me, said he'd tell you. He just coiled up there on the bench and dropped off to sleep. It's great to be young."

"You were doing all right in the chair," Black reminded him. "How about the reports?"

"They're all here. There were a lot of reporters in. I told them you had gone for the night, that there was nothing new to tell."

"Did you give them the statement I left?"

"Yeah. They figured it would make a swell story."

Black had picked up several reports and had looked through them quickly.

"This will interest you, Peacock. The gun found in Stryke Ryder's room belongs to Silas Ryder. It was the gun which killed both Eve Knight and the cow."

"Then Abe was right after all and there is some connection between the two."

"This case is just screwy enough to have a dead cow in it. A nice clue, isn't it? Who ever heard of a cow mixed up in a murder before?"

"Cows get into history. Remember, a cow is supposed to have been responsible for the Chicago fire."

"What burns me is the way that Tucker man is going to say 'I told you so.' He'll brag about it until he dies." He turned back to the reports.

"Want me to wake up the kid?" the trooper asked. "He sure can make a lot of noise."

"In a minute. I was afraid of this." He let the papers fall to the desk. "Perine's fingerprints were found up in the cupola, on the trapdoor, on the table and on the glasses. There are a number of other unidentified prints on the door, rail and ledge in front of the windows, but none match up with those we have."

"What about the gun?"

"No sign of Stryke's prints, just those of that fellow Shaw who found the gun under Stryke's mattress and carried it back to the village."

"Any prints on Abbie's car?" Percy asked eagerly.

"A lot of Abbie's and plenty of blurred marks which indicate that the person who used it wore gloves. Eben is the type of man who would wear gloves, isn't he?"

Percy nodded agreement to that and asked, "What about the bullet in Nellie's kitchen wall?"

"From a rifle. Our murderer was evidently equipped with an arsenal."

"Strange," Percy said. "I can understand the man using Silas's revolver, but the rifle puzzles me."

"I have more than that on my mind," Black replied. He turned to the trooper. "Wake up the kid."

The boy was very sleepy. It took him some time to realize where he was. He stretched his stiffened muscles, yawned, ran his hands through his hair and finally, wide awake, walked across the room to the desk, and stood behind it facing Black. He leaned his elbow on the top and began to talk.

"It may not be important and I don't want anybody to know what I'm going to tell you," he said.

"It will be an official secret," Black assured him.

"I mean it. My folks don't know I came." He lowered his voice. "I sneaked down here, so I don't want you to give me away."

"All right, we won't," Black promised.

"It's about something I saw just about one o'clock. I was coming down the Webster Road in my flivver, when bang! my old exhaust gave an awful pop. At that moment . . ."

They saw the boy's eyes widen as his voice stopped. The next instant there was a crack, the sound of tearing, shattering metal, and the boy had fallen behind the desk with a thump.

"Phew! That was close to me!" Black said as he jumped toward the desk.

The trooper darted across the room and into the hall, pulling his gun as he left.

The boy was slumped on the floor. He was shivering. His face was dead white.

"Are you all right?" Black asked anxiously as the two men crouched beside the boy.

"I will be in a minute. I feel kind of sick at my stomach. I guess it scared me."

"That sounds like an understatement," Percy said nervously.

"No, it ain't, neither. It scared hell out of me. I ain't never looked into the muzzle of a gun before, ain't never seen one come up over the edge of a window to be pointed right at me."

"It was a good thing you had presence of mind enough to duck," Black said and patted the lad on the shoulder.

"Ain't you going to see if you can catch him?" Delano asked. "I thought you'd run after him."

"The trooper has gone. We were more interested in you."

"He got the stove pipe," Delano said. "I could hear it rip right through that old stove pipe."

"Now suppose you tell us what you saw," Black suggested.

"I saw the gun coming, figured it was for me, and ducked."

"I mean the thing you saw about one."

"Oh, I didn't think she'd do a thing like that!" Delano said.

"Who?"

"Abbie Glover."

"Why should she?" Black asked. He tried to keep his voice on a normal key, but it was excited, curious.

"Because when that exhaust of mine popped like I told you before, she was coming along behind the Town Hall. She just about jumped a mile into the air, she did."

"Are you sure it was Abbie Glover?" Black asked. The boy was nervous but he laughed. "Sure."

"Is that what you were going to tell me when the gun came through the window?"

"Yeah. About Abbie jumping and Martin Chase coming along by the church at about the same time."

The trooper stormed in. "Missed him," he growled. "This damned building is a rat hole. This door leads out into the main hall. I thought it would be quicker to go out the back door but it was locked. By the time I got around to the window there wasn't a soul in sight. Nothing but a dog barking up the road a bit."

"Why didn't you go up the road?" Black demanded.

"I did. Ever try to look for a needle in a haystack?"

Black curbed his annoyance and turned back to Delano. "Why didn't you tell me this when we were in the theatre this afternoon?"

While waiting for the boy's answer Percy quietly took the receiver off the hook and asked the operator for the Silas Ryder house.

"I didn't think of it then," Delano replied. "But tonight at home we were talking about the murders and I remembered it and told my folks. I told them you ought to know, but they told me to mind my own business and keep out of it."

Percy replaced the receiver. "I had forgotten that the Ryder line was dead. Don't you think it would be a good idea to have your man run up there? If Abbie is out of the house, then the case ought to be closed."

Black nodded and the trooper was on his way. "Gosh," the boy said. "I didn't think she'd try to kill me."

"Let's check on all our suspects. You get the hotel and ask for Perine, and I'll go into the booth and call Martin Chase," Percy suggested.

Black's hand was on the receiver as Percy started for the door.

Almost as soon as the bell started to ring at the other end of the line, Martin Chase answered Percy's call.

Percy did not know exactly what to say. His idea when he suggested making the calls was to find one of the suspects away from home.

"Well, what do you want?" Martin asked when Percy explained who he was.

"I've had a long talk with Black tonight. He is convinced that Stryke is innocent. You don't have to worry about defending him or anything," Percy ended lamely.

"Well, you didn't have to wake me out of a sound sleep to tell me that. The morning would have done just as well."

The receiver slammed down.

Black had not been so successful. He had had difficulty rousing the night porter at the hotel. Five minutes later he was still waiting for a connection with Perine when the porter returned to say that Perine was not in his room.

"What you calling them people for?" Delano asked. "I told you about Abbie Glover because I thought maybe she had killed the girl. You see, I saw her cross the road behind me and go toward the church and—"

The trooper came back, eyes twinkling. "If it was the old dame, she traveled on something faster than my bike. She was home and how. Boy! Has that woman got a tongue. She sure did let me have it for rousing the house. The father and the boy both heard the racket and came out."

"How were they dressed, all of them?" Black asked.

"Well, the father and boy were in pajamas and she wore something that looked like a tent. They had been asleep all right by the look of them."

"How about Chase?" Black asked Percy.

"Answered his telephone immediately."

"Where does he live, do you know?" Black asked.

"He lives on South Street, that's the road which runs parallel to Main Street. Martin's house is directly behind the store where he has his office,' Delano explained.

"So it's Perine," Black said.

"Had me fooled, too," Percy admitted.

"He's probably trying to make a get-away. I'll send out an alarm."

Black called headquarters at South Yarmouth and told them to watch all cars going off the Cape, to telphone ahead and stop everything going over the bridges. He described Perine very minutely. "Do you mean that he's the murderer and it ain't Abbie at all?" Delano gasped.

"Something like that," Black said.

"Beats me," Percy said. "I can't believe it. Why didn't he kill Miss Nellie when he was in the tower with her?"

"Maybe if we're nice to him, he'll tell us," Black said acidly.

"Here we are," Libby called cheerily as she came through the door. She had a basket over her arm, which she put on the desk. "You men are in luck. We had fried chicken tonight, but we were all too excited to eat. Why, Delano Crowell, what are you doing here?"

"Helping solve the case," he answered importantly.

"Did you see anyone on the street?" Percy asked.

"No. Why?"

"I thought you might have seen the person we suspect."

"The case is solved," Black said.

"Really? Is it a secret?" She had put some cups on the top of the desk and was filling them with coffee.

"Looks like Perine," Black explained.

"Perine! Why should he? What makes you think so?" she asked.

"It's too long a story. How about a piece of that chicken?"

She laughed and handed him a piece, with a bread-and-butter sandwich. She passed the basket to the others.

"I can't believe it. May I go over and get Stryke, please? May I?" she begged.

"And may I have some coffee?" a voice asked from the window.

It was Clyde Perine, peering in through the open window. He was smiling.

"Well, I'll be—"

"Come in," Black said.

Perine left the window.

Delano took his drumstick and slid behind the desk.

"Come into my parlor, said the spider to the fly," Libby muttered.

CHAPTER TWENTY-TWO

BLACK had his hand on his gun as Perine walked into the room. "You fooled me once tonight," he said. "Sit down."

"Fooled you?" Perine repeated. "Oh yes, of course."

"Sit down. Frisk him," Black snapped at his man. Perine was puzzled.

"Thought you could do it again, eh?" Black said.

"I don't understand," Perine protested. "I was walking and—"

"Save it. You are under arrest."

"There's no gun," the trooper said, having finished with Perine.

"Certainly not," Perine agreed.

"Get your kit, prepare some wax. I want an impression of his hands, both of them. We're taking no chances from now on," Black ordered.

"May I ask why you are doing this?" Perine demanded.

"Yes. You tried to kill this kid a few minutes ago because you were afraid he had seen you near the church this afternoon."

"That's utterly ridiculous," Perine gasped.

"Then why weren't you in bed where you belonged? Where have you been all night? You knew Miss Nellie was in town. You have been following us."

"There is some terrible mistake," Perine said. "It is true, I haven't been in bed. I've been walking, walking and thinking about my actions for the future, trying to decide the best thing to do."

"You'll have plenty of time to think in jail," Black assured him.

The wax was ready and molded over Perine's hands. He talked as they worked, tried to explain his actions, protested his innocence; but nothing he said could change Black's mind.

While waiting for the wax to cool they drank their coffee and nibbled at the chicken. When the wax was removed Perine reminded them that he had asked for coffee.

Libby gave him a cup, which he drank before Black and the trooper took him to the local jail for the night.

Libby was very happy about the turn events had taken as she dropped Percy at the Tucker gate.

"Stryke will be free tomorrow. I'll marry him at once if he still wants me."

"He'll want you, Libby. He'd be a fool not to." She put her hand over his where it rested on the door of the car. "Percy," she said softly.

"Yes, Libby."

"We'll never speak of this again, but I . . ." Her voice trailed away. The crickets filled the gap in her speech, gave them both time to consider what she had left unsaid.

"You knew," he said finally as he bent forward and kissed her hand.

"I sensed it. You've been wonderful working for Stryke this way. You're a grand person, Percy."

"You're pretty swell yourself."

"I don't think I have been much of a person but I will be from now on. I've learned a lot today about men and women, about the things that count and the things that are unimportant. Nothing seems worthwhile now but love, companionship and understanding. This morning I thought a career was what I wanted. I was wrong. Stryke's freedom, our life together, acting or just making a home is what I want. You understand, don't you?"

"I think I do."

"I'm sure you do."

She smiled at him. Her eyes were moist. The car slid away into the night, making just enough noise to still the sharp cry of the crickets for a moment.

He watched her go. He shrugged. That was over. He was glad that no more had been said. He hated the old line in plays and novels about a love that was not quite love. He had been in love with her, not violently but rather appreciatively, he admitted, as he turned toward the house. He stopped beside some tall spikes of delphinium to wonder about himself. Was he so analytically minded that he would never fall completely in love? Would he always be a rational lover?

The crickets seemed to mock him, seemed to say, "Your time will come."

He took a last look down the road. Libby's car had turned off the road. She would go home to dream of Stryke while he would think about the case. He sighed as he tiptoed into the house.

"Damn," he muttered as he bumped into the hall hat rack.

Without turning on the light, he undressed and slid onto the bed.

He was very tired, too weary to sleep. As he lay with his hands behind his neck the procession and succession of events marched before his eyes again, from the moment Miss Nellie had trotted down the street until Perine has asked for coffee through the office window.

It was all clear in his mind, but he was bothered by forgotten bits of conversation, casual remarks dropped here and there, little things he had heard, small items which he wanted to fit into the pattern as a whole.

He reviewed the line of suspects. Stryke was definitely out.

He was not so sure about Eben and Henry. He found he rather admired Eben. Eben made no pretenses about being anything other than what he was. The people in the town considered him a playboy and a ne'er-do-well. He was probably both. It was obvious that he enjoyed life.

There was a graciousness about the man which made him attractive. There might be more stable citizens but few who had his natural charm. Money must mean a great deal to Eben, it was the breath of the life he lived.

Percy had no way of knowing how much Eben had expected to inherit from his brother but he felt certain that fifty thousand dollars would be very important to him. Since he loved and needed money, the fifty thousand certainly had been worth saving and hence became a reasonable motive. Yes, it was conceivable and quite possible that Eben had taken steps to prevent the loss of the money.

Eben was familiar with all the important facts. He knew about Abbie's car, knew that it was almost identical with his own. Would Eben drive her car out to the woods to take suspicion from himself?

Percy tried to recall how much time had passed after the shot had been fired at Delano before the trooper started out to check on Abbie and the other members of the Silas Ryder household. It might have been possible for either Eben or Henry to run across the fields and get home before the trooper arrived. Abbie certainly could not have made the run and got into a nightgown to fool the trooper. The men, however, could have managed it.

It would have been easy for Henry. Percy did not like Henry, whom he considered too sour, but he found himself trying to be fair to the young man. He ignored his prejudices as he considered the possibility of Henry's guilt. What had Henry been doing near the Verity house? Perhaps he had been out all evening, had been lurking near Caleb's office. He was a very likely suspect.

So was Martin Chase on the surface of things as they now stood. But what was the motive? Outside of being Silas's partner, which information Chase had offered himself, there seemed to be no logical reason why Martin should want the old man out of the way. He had told a straight story, which Abbie had corroborated. What would Martin gain by Silas's death? The executor's fees did not seem a sufficient lure to make him commit murder. He had said a transfer of property to Stryke would have complicated the partnership arrangements. That was reasonable, and not a seeming cause for murder. But what was he doing near the church about one o'clock?

Percy went back to consideration of Perine—to wonder why he was not convinced of Perine's guilt. Perine was the only person without an alibi after the shot had been fired at Delano. He was the one person who could have done all the things which had been done, the one person who had admitted that he had no alibi for the time when the mob had been lynch-minded.

"The trouble with you, Percy, is that you are a romantic. You want Stryke and his father to patch up their differences and be friends," he mumbled to himself before he drifted into sleep.

Mrs. Tucker wakened him at the usual hour, 6:45, so that he could be ready for breakfast at a quarter after seven. At first the idea of such an early breakfast had been a shock to Percy. He mentioned the fact that he thought it rather early. Mrs. Tucker had been pleasant but firm. That was their breakfast hour. He could room with them and eat at the hotel if he wished or he could room and board at the hotel. She had, she informed him, just so much work to do and three meals a day at regular hours were all that she could manage. He had suggested that he would go without the morning meal if he preferred sleep. It had been left that way.

This was the one morning that he would have liked to sleep. He was still tired, but the memory of the events of the previous day gnawed at his consciousness. He had to get up, to know what was going on.

Breakfast in the Tucker house was a lusty affair. Orange juice, stewed fruit, oatmeal, ham and eggs and griddle cakes. There were doughnuts, too, and pie if you wanted it.

Percy was amazed at how much food he wanted; he was drinking his second cup of coffee and eating his third set of cakes. Tucker was preoccupied. Mrs. Tucker watched him anxiously. "Eat your eggs, Abe," she urged.

"Don't want any eggs," he said with finality.

"I'll fix you an eggnog."

"No," he said, but she did not listen. She came back in a moment, a whiskey bottle in her hand. "Abe Tucker, did you drink all this yesterday?"

"What if I did?" he demanded. "I don't want any now. Sit down."

With a sigh she obeyed him but her eyes went from him to the bottle as if she could not quite understand the emptiness of one and the indifference of the other.

Tucker was working on a doughnut, picking it apart, dropping bits of it into his coffee and dishing it up with his spoon. He looked up and grinned. "You didn't get in until late, did you?"

"No. I hope I didn't disturb you."

Mrs. Tucker leaned back, her eyes still filled with speculation. She moved her head slowly. Percy was not quite sure whether it was in wonderment or if she were telling him mutely that she had not been disturbed.

"You didn't disturb me none," Tucker said and swallowed half a coffee-soaked doughnut.

Mrs. Tucker sniffed. "Nothing could have disturbed us last night, we were both restless. Abe, I don't believe you settled down until Mr. Peacock came in. No wonder," she said, with a glance toward the bottle. "What ailed you?"

"Nothing."

"I heard you up in your room two or three times. Was your leg bothering you?"

"No, just restless thinking about things, wondering what was going on." He turned to Percy. "What does go on? Do you think this Perine man is guilty? Has anyone given a thought to my cow?"

Percy considered the questions for a moment before he replied, "Your cow seems to be more and more important."

"I'll say it is, ninety dollars' worth of importance somebody's got to pay me," Abe blustered.

"We know that the bullet that killed your cow was fired from the same gun which killed Eve Knight."

"Who owned the gun?" Mrs. Tucker asked.

"Silas Ryder."

"Silas Ryder didn't kill my cow," Abe vowed.

"Don't talk nonsense, Abe," Mrs. Tucker cautioned wearily.

"It ain't nonsense, Mother. If that gun was taken from the Ryder house, it proves one thing to my way of thinking."

"And what is that?" Percy asked.

"A Ryder is the murderer. There ain't never been a Ryder who had any use for animals. I wouldn't go so far as to say they were afraid of cows and such things but they never did cotton to horses or livestock unless they had a hired hand to take care of them. That's why Silas was willing to sell this place to me. There wasn't a Ryder that would run it as a farm."

"It might be one way of gettin' out of doing a lot of hard and dirty work," Mrs. Tucker said thoughtfully. "I wish I had thought of it years ago."

"How many times a year do you do the milking?" he demanded testily.

"More than is necessary," she retorted. "Who fed the calf this morning?" She sighed heavily. "Maybe we won't get the place now. You should have gone up there yesterday," she accused.

"How could I go when he was dead?" Tucker growled.

"Why didn't you go in the morning when you were supposed to go?" With that thrust she rose and went into the kitchen.

Abe looked after her and shook his head. "She's tired. We've worked hard to get this place and now . . ." He was lost in thought for a moment. "Murder certainly does complicate things."

"Yes," Percy agreed.

Abe took another doughnut, broke it in half, dipped it into his coffee, and said, "I understand you have five or six people under suspicion."

"The police have," Percy corrected.

"Well, it's the same thing the way you was glued to Black all day and all night. When does Black figure Silas was killed?"

"After considering all the possibilities, it seems almost certain that he was killed a little before noon. How much before we don't know."

"Well, I guess I can rub one of your suspects off the list for you. I heard you've been suspecting Martin Chase. Abbie told us that. Now, I happen to know that Martin was in his office yesterday. I saw his feet on the windowsill while I was waiting at the post office. The mail was late, as you remember."

"We certainly do," Mrs. Tucker remarked as she came in for more dishes to be carried to the kitchen. "You just about ruined our dinner. I was so sure you were up at the barn when I had everything ready, but you didn't answer, and I could have sworn that I saw you go into the barn just about noon while I was frying the clams."

"Must have been someone going along the road, Mother, you often make that mistake." He turned to Percy. "I'll tell you what I think." He reached for another doughnut.

"There's too much thinking been going on. Better keep your ideas to yourself, Abe," Mrs. Tucker advised as she turned away.

"It was a Ryder," Abe stated. "Either Eben, Henry or this here Stryke, I don't know which," Tucker insisted. "You'll see that I'm right." He pushed his chair away from the table. "I've got work to do. You tell Black what I said."

"Don't you do any such thing," Mrs. Tucker counter-advised. She turned on Abe. "Are you crazy? Do you want

Black and Mr. Peacock to think that you're a fool
altogether? The idea naming three people as suspects
that way when they have arrested the murderer!"

"Who told you?" Abe demanded.

"Never mind."

"Who told you?" he insisted and grabbed her wrist. "It
wasn't Mary Verity, because they sent her away."

She yanked her hand out of his grasp, rubbed her
wrist where his fingers had been and said, "Phoebe
Spring told me this morning, she asked me not to
mention it."

"Why didn't you tell us before?" Abe growled.

"Because I wanted you to get done with your food so I
could go about my work." She retreated into her kitchen.

"Well, I'll be blowed! Don't women beat all tarnation?
That Perine man! Beats me! But I still think I'm right
and it was a Ryder."

The telephone rang. He went to answer it. "For you,"
he said, and went out through the kitchen.

It was Black. "Come over to Caleb's office right away,"
he said.

Percy left the Tucker house via the kitchen. He
walked up to the barn to see if his car had been returned
by the local garage man. It was there ready for use. He
heard a movement inside the barn and blinked as he
stepped inside the door.

Abe's cow, trussed open, was hanging from a rafter.
"I'm going to butcher her," he said. "The meat's good,
maybe a little tough but it'll be tasty. If you want your car
take it now as I'll have to keep the doors shut to keep the
animals out."

Percy walked back to get a better view of the cow.
She had been slit open. A large galvanized wash tub was
full of blood. "It's a gory mess," he said.

"I can remember when we used to do all our own
butchering," Abe replied. He glanced rather fondly at the
carcass. "I may have to sell her for pet food," he said
sorrowfully. "I've cut off a few chunks and sprinkled them

with arsenic in case the rats come. Rats and skunks will be a botheration until I get rid of her."

"What do you do about the skunks?" Percy asked.

"Shoot 'em, always shoot skunks."

"I thought there was some law about skunks."

"There is. You can't trap 'em any more the way we used to, but you can shoot 'em if they are on your property and are destroying things. That's why I keep my rifle out here. I get one every so often near the hen coop. I nearly got one last night but he got away before I could get a shot at him."

"Isn't it rather dangerous using a rifle here in the village? Why not a shot gun?"

"A shot gun spoils the pelts. I sell 'em."

"I'll see you later," Percy promised and walked back toward the house.

The Spring house showed signs of life. A wisp of smoke curled from the chimney. On the other side of the Tucker place Nellie Pine's house seemed cold and forlorn.

On his way to the village Percy laughed to himself. He was trotting at about the same pace that characterized Miss Nellie as she went to her work. Incredible that Miss Nellie should have been in so much danger and utterly remarkable that she was still alive. He was glad that death had missed her.

He had other ideas. They crystallized with the quick pounding of his feet. He forgot the quiet beauty of the village, which had always impressed him before. His mind was on the murder and he felt sure he knew the answer to the riddle. He smiled again as he looked up at Martin Chase's window and saw feet on the sill. What if those were not feet at all but the soles of the riding boots in their long trees? He had been suspecting Martin Chase. He had many things he wanted to discuss with Black.

Caleb was in the office. His eyes smiled a warm greeting.

"There's no sign of powder in the wax casts we took of Perine," Black announced bluntly.

"I didn't think there would be," Percy tried to keep superiority out of his voice.

"And why not?" Black demanded, then said: "There was time for him to have washed his hand, you know."

"Yes, but did he?"

"You look to me like the cat who ate the gold fish," Caleb accused.

"I've an idea. Want to try it out?" Percy asked.

"What is it?" Black was slightly caustic.

"I'd like to get all the principals together this morning. Are you willing?"

"Tell me more about it," Black hedged.

Percy talked for ten minutes. Both Black and Caleb were skeptical at first, but as Percy went on their doubts gave way to possible conviction as Percy urged, "We must have them all here."

"It's a risky business," Caleb objected mildly.

"What do you want me to do?" Black asked, his mind made up.

"You go to the post office and check that angle. I'll get Libby and the Crowell boy. Caleb, you know your job. Be sure to bring Miss Nellie with you. We'll meet at the theatre at eleven o'clock. Agreed?"

"I don't like it too much," Black mused. "It's screwy."

"But it's worth a try," Percy insisted. "We didn't have any perspective on the case yesterday. We were too interested in the obvious. What can, we lose?"

"If it doesn't work I'll lose my job," Black said solemnly. "That's what I can lose."

"Okay. Let's call it off," Percy said. "I think this plan would save time because of its surprise value."

"But you can't be sure the plan will work," Caleb doubted. "Who is going to believe this stuff?"

"You are forgetting the state of the murderer's mind. I'm sure he is temporarily insane. I'm basing my whole idea on that. He is worried, completely frightened. He doesn't know how much we know. He wants to protect himself. He's more worried than a witch. He is covering his emotions outwardly with that craftiness so often displayed by the insane but inwardly he is seething with fear and apprehension. Caleb, if you fail to find the things I believe you will find, then we can call it off and no harm done."

"Can we trust Perine to do the trick properly?" Caleb asked.

"Get Stryke here as soon as you can. Don't let anyone know that he has been released from jail if you can help it. Bring Perine to the theatre and leave the rest to me."

"No reporters in on this," Black stated emphatically.

"No one but the people involved," Percy agreed.

"Let's go!" Black banished the last of his doubts as he squared his shoulders and prepared for action.

CHAPTER TWENTY-THREE

THE suspects began to assemble a little before eleven.
The theatre was dimly lit by a few of the overhead
lamps. The footlights were out, the curtain was open, but
the stage itself was a dark mysterious cavern yawning at
the few people scattered in the auditorium.

Abe, Mrs. Tucker and Nellie Pine were already there.
Delano Crowell crouched in one of the seats in the last
row, completely hidden from sight. At five minutes of
eleven Henry, Eben and Abbie arrived. Perine came from
backstage just before Martin Chase entered. At eleven
sharp Caleb closed the doors and moved down front with
Black.

"What's the matter with the lights?" Caleb demanded.
"Are you trying to cut down expenses?" Perine jumped to
his feet.

"The lights are all right," Black said. "The footlights
made too much of a glare yesterday. Sit down, Perine!"

With a grunt Caleb took a seat on the aisle. Martin
Chase sat next to him. Perine sat down, leaving an empty
seat between him and Martin.

Percy moved over and sat beside Perine. "I hope this
is the last act," he whispered.

"I hope so," Perine replied nervously. "I'd like to see it
ended. Stryke was wonderful about me."

"He would be," Percy replied.

"We're all here," Black announced, after counting off
the audience.

"What is the purpose of this meeting?" Martin asked.

"We can call it an alibi meeting for want of a better
name. All of you, including the Professor here, need
alibis."

Abe Tucker chuckled.

"Me?" Percy demanded in surprise.

"Yes, you. Unless someone can give me more definite information you are the only person known to have been in Nellie Pine's house after the two murders. You may have left the gun on that visit."

"Ridiculous!" Percy snorted. "I was on the Tucker front porch when the rifle shot shattered Miss Nellie's window."

"He's telling the truth," Mrs. Tucker said indignantly.

"Am I to understand, Peacock, that you have a tight alibi for the one-o'clock period?"

"You know very well that I haven't," Percy replied crisply.

Black shrugged. Percy watched the audience. Black's attack on him had been a surprise and had released the tension which had been electric as they waited. They all sat back, a little less worried than they had been a moment before.

"Perine, Peacock, none of you have proper alibis for the murder periods," Black stated. "That's why we are here. It will pay you, all of you, to remember where you were from 11:50 until a few minutes after twelve, and from one o'clock until the fire siren sounded."

Libby came in and hurried down to sit near Percy.

Black waited for her to be seated. "As I was saying before Miss Powell came in, you need alibis. How about you, Miss Glover? Where were you at the times mentioned?"

"I don't know as I can prove anything," she said as she rose. "I didn't know as I'd have to have proof. When I left the house yesterday I was upset. I didn't know just what to do. We'd had quarrels before and I'd always gone back. This time, what with the talk about money and all, it seemed different. I went down the road toward the Park. I had been crying. My eyes were red. A body has their pride and I didn't want no one to see me in that condition, so I went to the bandstand and sat there until I had a hold of myself. Then I washed my face at the spigot and went along Main Street until I came to Phoebe Spring's gate. I stopped and talked to her for a spell, then I went across to see Miss Abernathy. She wasn't home so I went to the drugstore and had some lunch. When I left the drugstore I went across to Miss Abernathy's again, but she was still out. I had it in my mind to ask her if I could board with her in case I had to get out from up the road. I looked at her flowers and went out through her back yard. I was almost to the Webster Road when that Crowell boy nearly scared the life out of me with that old car of his. After that I don't remember much of what did happen as there was so much excitement with the siren blowing an' all."

"What time did you leave the Ryder house?"

"I don't know. I wasn't wearing no watch. I just told you what I did and I don't know at what time I was doing it," she answered with a return of her crisp shrillness.

"Sit down! Now how about you, Henry Ryder?"

Henry rose and said sulkily: "I don't know where I was or what time it was either. When I left the house I was mad at what I had heard. I drove up toward Webster, took a back road and returned along the Wood Road. By that time it was between twelve and one. I drove into the village and stopped in at the drugstore. I was telling my father about what had happened at the house until a few minutes before the siren blew."

"That part of what he says is true," Eben said, getting up. "We have a joint alibi for that period."

"Then Henry was not with you in the Town Hall just before one?" Black asked.

Eben was surprised.

"You were seen on the steps of the hall just outside the theatre about one. You were coming down, I think," Black said crisply.

"Oh. That! As a matter of fact, I was on my way up to see Nellie when Perine called to me from the theatre. I went to him."

"Both you and Perine neglected to tell me that you had seen Nellie about one o'clock," Black accused. "Why didn't you speak up?"

"I don't know why Perine kept quiet, but I saw no point in involving myself. Perine saw me on the stairs. I spoke to him. He returned to the theatre, I left the building. Perhaps we both realized that neither of us could explain those few minutes or provide a suitable alibi for the interval of time."

"You still haven't told me where you were from the time you left the window outside Silas's room until you were seen in front of the Spring house about noon or a little after."

"I drove over to the Chatwich depot."

"Can you prove it?"

"No. There wasn't anyone there, not even the express man. I went up to look at my cranberry bog and then came back to the village and stopped to speak to Abbie."

"None of you have established alibis," Black warned.

"We've told you what we did," Abbie complained.

"Which isn't enough. How about you, Mr. Chase?"

Martin smiled. "Well, if you think I need an alibi I guess I have it. Like Abbie, I was a bit upset by what I had heard. I went back to my office and sat down to think. Someone likely saw my feet up there on the window ledge. That's the way I do my thinking. It was quite a problem the old man had presented to me. Of course, there was no reason why Silas Ryder shouldn't transfer his money if he wanted to do it that way but there were a lot of legal angles to be considered. I guess I sat there from twenty minutes of twelve until I went down to the drugstore."

"Then you can't prove you were in your office?" Black stated.

"No. Not unless someone saw me," Chase replied.

"I saw him about noon," Abe volunteered. "I saw his head once as he bent forward."

"Are you sure, Mr. Tucker?"

"Yes, I told you I saw him," Abe replied with annoyance.

"Very well. Now how about the period about one o'clock, Mr. Chase?"

"Let me see. I went over to the post office to see about some mail. I hadn't been in at noon. Then I went into the hardware store to get some screw eyes. Harry wasn't there. I figured he'd gone over to the grocery store or something so I just waited for five or ten minutes. I was in the store when the siren went off."

"That's very interesting, Mr. Chase. It's too bad you can't prove your points."

"I guess Harry will remember I was in the store about one if you want to ask him."

"And I still say it is not enough. We are interested in the ten minutes when you were alone. They are important."

"But look here," Chase remonstrated as he ran a finger between his collar and his throat. "You don't think that I—"

"I think you are acting like a man who feels a noose about his neck," Black said sharply.

"What are you saying?" Martin demanded angrily.

"That you killed Silas Ryder, Eve Knight and Sidney Stone."

A gasp of horror rippled through the room. "You're crazy! I just gave you my alibis," Martin shouted, beside himself.

"Suppose you repeat them. I'm willing to listen. Where were you at 11:50 yesterday morning?"

"In my office, checking papers for Silas."

"With your feet on the window?"

"Yes. I had a file in my lap."

"Miss Nellie, when did you call Martin yesterday morning?"

"It was exactly noon or a few seconds before," she answered crisply.

"Can you prove it?"

"I don't see how," she said.

"I can prove it," Perine said. "I was in the cupola when she made the telephone call."

Black turned to Martin. "You have heard what these people have said. If you were in your officde why didn't you answer your phone?"

"It didn't ring. She must have called the wrong number," he suggested lamely.

"Martin Chase, I called you. You were expecting a call from me."

"It didn't ring, I tell you," he cried desperately. He was confused and more than a little worried. "Maybe it rang up at the house," he suggested hopefully. "Sometimes I forget to throw the switch."

"Miss Powell, what time did you see Mr. Chase on South Street?" Black asked.

"I thought I saw him between twelve and ten past. I couldn't be sure," she said.

"You didn't see me, Libby," he cried and stepped forward. "I wasn't there."

"Then why didn't you answer your telephone?" Black's repetition of the question was sinister.

"Oh!" Martin cried in exasperation as would brush the whole absurd business aside in that way.

Black saw only the fear lurking in the depth of Martin's eyes as he went on: "You haunted the mails since yesterday. You were angry with the postmaster because he refused to give you the Ryder mail. We have checked that mail. You knew some negotiable bonds were due. You wanted to get them, didn't you?"

Martin gloomed at Black. His eyes betrayed him. Black had made a bull's eye with the bonds. He followed his advantage. "You knew when Silas suggested turning over his property to Stryke that it would include those bonds. Now, I'm willing to admit that half of them might possibly belong to you, but you saw a good chance to get them all. Silas's sudden plan was a surprise to you. There would be explanations about your business that you would have to make. I don't believe you were ready to make those explanations."

"I tried to get his mail yesterday to protect my own interests. Half of those bonds belong to me," Martin declared.

"I realized you had your interests very much at heart," Black replied grimly. "You thought fast, you worked fast. You came back to your office, propped those riding boots of yours on the windowsill and went back to kill Silas."

"No!" Martin shouted desperately. "I didn't. I didn't."

"Delano Crowell," Black called.

Delano, who had remained in the rear of the theatre out of sight came forward, stood aloof from the group. Caleb, two troopers who had slipped in, Black and Percy were alert ready for an unexpected turn of events, to protect the boy's life if necessary.

"Delano, you saw Abbie Glover at the rear of the Town Hall about one o'clock yesterday. What else did you see?"

"I saw Martin Chase over by the church," Delano stated flatly.

"You went there, Chase, to cut Sidney's ropes," Black said.

"It's all a ridiculous theory. Remember I am lawyer," Martin threatened.

"Perhaps we have made a mistake," Percy suggested.

"I'll say you have and I'll make you pay for this." Martin pointed an accusing finger at Black. He would have said more but he was startled by an unexpected voice which floated through the room.

It was an old voice, not quite real, saying, "It's not theory that you killed me, came with your usual profession of friendship and stabbed me."

"Land of Goshen," Abbie screamed and jumped to her feet. "That's Silas Ryder's voice!"

CHAPTER TWENTY-FOUR

THE voice had been unexpected, and Abbie's exclamation had caused a thrill to ripple through the room.

"It's nothing but theatrical trickery," Martin shouted and slumped back into his seat.

"No, it ain't neither," Abbie cried. "Look!" She rose in her chair once more and pointed toward the yawning cavern of the stage.

In an eerie half-light a figure moved along the stage, coming up from the back, groping. It was the form of Silas Ryder, tall, thin, stoop-shouldered, uncertain in its outline, but unmistakably Silas Ryder. He faltered forward rather helplessly, trying to get himself out of the fog of light which surrounded him. He stretched out an arm, lifted his head. His eyes seemed to burn as he peered out at the few people in the audience. With a wavering finger pointed toward them he walked forward. Someone sobbed. The shadowy form stopped, seemed bewildered, "Don't be afraid, Martin," the voice advised. "You've nothing to fear."

Martin's jaw dropped open in an unbelieving gape.

The shadowy form seemed to be trying desperately hard to see beyond the shimmering light. He turned his head. The bony finger no longer pointed at Martin. The arm shifted, swung across the aisle and the voice quavered, "There is my murderer. It's . . ." The figure crumpled, seemed to dissolve within the circle of light.

A shot rang out. Abbie screamed.

Caleb had been ready for action. He leaped across the aisle and struck the gun as it barked fire. The bullet went wild, cracked against the arch over the stage. Bits of powdered plaster fell like a curtain over the fading light.

There was a sobbing moan of incredulous agony. As Abe Tucker struggled with Caleb and Black, Mrs. Tucker slid from her chair in a faint. The house lights flashed on. Abbie was fanning herself with a handkerchief. The others were on their feet looking dubiously at the struggle, not quite believing what they had just seen. The troopers joined Caleb and Black. Abe was subdued. Libby and Perine were reviving Mrs. Tucker.

"I never in all my life," Miss Nellie gasped in complete amazement. "Abe Tucker! He tried to kill me." Her hand fluttered toward her throat. "I wouldn't have believed it."

Abe was quiet. Caleb held his gun. Martin, not quite understanding it all, was wiping his brow.

"We've got the goods on you, Tucker," Black said.

Abe growled a denial.

Mrs. Tucker rose slowly, helped by Libby. "Please," she begged. "He hasn't been himself for weeks, what with worrying about one thing and another." Tears glistened in her eyes, rolled down her cheeks as she looked at her husband. "Oh, Abe," she sobbed. She turned to Black. "Don't hurt him."

"We won't hurt him, Mrs. Tucker," Percy promised her.

"Not if he tells us all about it," Black added.

"I don't talk," Abe muttered, a crafty look in his eyes. "You can't prove nothing."

Percy faced Abe. "That shot you fired just now was an admission of guilt, Abe."

"Why don't you confess?" Black urged.

"If he knows so much let him tell you," Abe replied. He seemed to retreat behind an invisible curtain, which made him an entirely different person.

"Let's have it, Peacock," Black said.

Percy saw Mrs. Tucker's tightly drawn lips, the agony in her eyes, the expectancy on the faces of the others, and wished for a moment that he had had no part in the affair.

"He can't," Abe challenged.

"Since you won't confess, Abe," Percy began, "I'll have to tell you how we were able to determine that you were the culprit."

"Don't give us the credit," Caleb said. "You were the one who figured it out."

"I happened to have access to certain information," Percy said. "You would have arrived at the ultimate conclusion by eliminating each of us as a suspect, for we were all under some shadow of suspicion yesterday, that is all of us except Abe. The death of the cow eliminated him. No one had seen him at the Ryder place. I knew that he was to have gone but he told us at dinner that he hadn't had time to get up there. I believed him then.

"As you know, we were confused by the murders at first because Eve Knight's death, in spite of the evidence against Stryke, did not make sense. It seemed to be an aimless and purposeless murder without any real underlying cause. Sidney's death an hour later seemed just as senseless. Why had two people been killed? Why had a cow been shot? There was no answers to the questions, but the fact that an earlier attempt had been made against the life of Miss Nellie gave us an idea about the crimes without answering the question. We realized that the murders were an attempt to hide some previous action, but what it was we could not guess.

"It seemed imperative to find Miss Nellie. Caleb had the same idea, but Miss Powell and I were luckier. Miss Nellie, however, could give us no information but she was still in danger because the murderer did not know that she was harmless. When the body of Silas Ryder was found we knew why the other people had been killed. We then realized that we had discovered the second and third murders first and were forced to start at the beginning.

"There were a number of people who might have wished Silas Ryder out of the way. Motives and emotions became involved. We found many reasons and, we thought, some clues, but each time we believed ourselves to be on the right track a new development blocked us.

"We worked late into the night, found it necessary to send Mrs. Verity, under police protection, to a safer place. Delano Crowell just missed being murdered in Caleb Spring's office."

There was a general stir of excitement as this information was given.

"We checked our suspects. Mr. Perine became involved and was arrested but I was not convinced of his guilt. As a matter of fact at that time I thought Martin Chase was guilty."

"You almost made me believe I was," Martin said with a grim smile.

"This morning, because of a series of simple things, I arrived at the truth. As you know I have been living at the Tucker home. At breakfast we talked about the murders. In our conversation Abe asked me if I thought Perine was guilty. I thought nothing of the question at the moment. I was stupid, not at all like the quick minds in books, I neglected to realize another obvious point. Abe knew that Mrs. Verity had been sent away although her going was as secret as we could make it. A little later when Abe was suggesting that a Ryder was probably guilty Mrs. Tucker informed us that the murderer had been arrested.

"Abe knew that it was Perine who had been arrested last night although Mrs. Tucker mentioned no names. It was later at the Tucker barn that I began to realize the facts. Abe's rifle stood in a corner. He told me he kept it there to kill skunks.

"Then I remembered two facts that I had learned yesterday. Mrs. Tucker thought she saw Abe in the barn just before noon, just before the shot broke Miss Nellie's window. Libby Powell thought she saw Martin Chase on South Street about noon. At a distance the two men are not unlike."

Eyes turned to check the similarity of the two men. There were silent nods of agreement.

"Libby had seen Abe after he had fired the shot at Miss Nellie and was on his way to the post office. I also recalled that Libby and I stood in the Tucker barn just before we started our search for Miss Nellie and agreed that the shot could have been fired from Tucker's barn without anyone being able to see the culprit. Black's men traced the probable course of the bullet and agreed that the line of fire was from the barn.

"Abe told me that he had had a restless night last night. He didn't settle down until he heard me come in. He knew all the things we had done during the night while the rest of the village was asleep. It was you, Abe, who listened at the end of Caleb's porch while we talked to Miss Nellie. You didn't realize it, but there was a dead honeysuckle blossom caught on the sight of your rifle, and there is no honeysuckle on your place.

"Do you remember Caleb's guinea hens last night, Abe? They were quiet until you made a run for it. You startled them and they chattered. You know as well as I do that guinea fowl do not make a noise unless they are disturbed by something strange."

Again there were nods of agreement and surprise in their eyes that he should know so simple a fact.

"Abe did go to see Silas yesterday about buying the place. Instead of finding a man ready to make a sale Abe found Silas possessed with a new idea, that of turning his property over to Stryke. I assume that they quarreled over the sale and in his anger Abe killed Silas.

"After that he was terrified by what he had done. It was not a carefully planned crime as we had supposed, but one of violence due probably to temporary insanity."

Abe looked up at Percy and in his eyes there was something resembling relief as though for the first time he began to understand what had happened.

"Naturally Abe was terrified by what he had done. He went home. Then he began to wonder and worry. He felt the urge to protect himself. He remembered Miss Nellie and was afraid that she might have seen him at the

Ryder house. He fired the shot at her from the barn and then went to the post office to establish an alibi. By giving Martin Chase an alibi he proved one for himself. His plans miscarried. Miss Nellie had not died. Abe had to protect himself before Silas's body was found. At the drugstore he heard Sidney talking about his binoculars. Sidney was a new problem. Abe did not know that Eve Knight had a waist similar to the one worn by Miss Nellie. He thought he saw Miss Nellie go into the Town Hall. He went up to the cupola and shot the woman he believed to be Miss Nellie. While there he ripped out the telephone cord and either purposely or accidentally dropped a match in the pile of rubbish up there.

"Why he killed the cow I don't know unless he hoped, in that way, to divert suspicion from himself."

Abbie, her mouth open, turned to stare unbelievingly at Abe.

"While the town was in an uproar over the fire and the discovery of Miss Knight's body, Abe cut Sidney's rope. Perhaps you remember he left this room when we were all here. We thought he was going to look at his cow. It was then, I believe, that he cut the rope."

Abe gave Percy an incredulous stare.

"His next problem was to find Miss Nellie. He probably overheard Libby and me when we were at the barn to get my car. He followed us. He was too smart to use his own car. He went back to get Ryders' and took Abbie's car because it would throw suspicion on Abbie."

Abbie snorted indignation.

"It was Abe who after racing back to the village waited for us and shot one of my tires. I didn't know about Miss Glover's car at the time and thought I had seen Eben Ryder driving away from the ball ground.

"Abe probably felt reasonably safe after our return because nothing was done about him. He must have worried about Mrs. Verity. We think he went up there and was scared off by her dog. We also believe he returned to her house with some of his cow meat and poisoned her dog.

"He knew Mrs. Verity had been sent away. He watched us, listening outside of Caleb's office. He tried to kill Delano Crowell but failed.

"From some safe place he continued to watch us until Perine was put in the local jail. That's all." Percy turned to Black.

Black said, "You're under arrest, Tucker. Is there anything you want to say?"

"He's said it all," Abe replied.

"Then you're admitting your guilt."

Abe looked about helplessly, sought the eyes of his wife. She nodded slightly. Abe nodded. "Why did you kill Silas Ryder?" Black asked.

"Like he said," Abe spoke slowly. "I went up there with money. Money Mr. Peacock advanced to me. It was to be a first payment on the place. Silas told me the sale would have to wait; that he was turning everything over to Stryke. We argued. I told him he wasn't being fair; that he was going back on his word. That made him mad. He said he didn't give a damn what I thought. You all know how he was. That made me mad. We got to saying things to one another and I asked him why he was so suddenly interested in his grandson when he had let his daughter die in poverty. He hit me right across the mouth and said he'd see to it that I never got the place. I didn't know what I was doing. My mouth stung. I've worked hard to get that place, so has my wife, and to see it slipping away from us for no good reason did something to me inside. I guess I grabbed that whale-bone knife and stuck it into him. Anyhow the next minute I knew I had killed him."

Mrs. Tucker sobbed softly.

"And when did you cut Sidney's rope?" Black asked.

"Like he said."

"Why did you kill the cow, Abe?" Percy asked.

"She was an ugly brute and she started after me when I went up along the side of the post office to get into the

Town Hall from the back way. She was always ugly when she had a calf. I had two or three reasons for killing her. I figured the Ryders would be suspected of having killed the cow, too. I was just trying to protect myself. That's why I put the revolver under the mattress in Nellie's house when I saw how they were suspecting Stryke."

Percy turned and saw Abbie Glover sitting beside Mrs. Tucker, a protective arm about the woman's shaking shoulders.

"We'll have to take you over to Barnstable, Abe," Black said.

Abe looked at Caleb and asked wistfully, "You going to take me, Caleb?"

"Why yes, I might as well," Caleb agreed. They started down the aisle. Mrs. Tucker turned and buried her face against Abbie.

Stryke came down from the stage. He still wore the makeup which he had used to appear as Silas.

"He's the spitting image of his grandfather," Miss Nellie breathed. "I wouldn't have believed it possible. Look at him!"

They looked and turned away. Libby was in Stryke's arms.

Martin Chase rose from his chair and shook his head. He crossed to Mrs. Tucker and said, "Cora, I'll defend him if you want me to."

She nodded, unable to speak. Martin came back to Percy. "You gave me a bad turn, Peacock."

"We had to do it," Percy explained. "It was necessary to shock and surprise Abe before he would talk. The ghost trick was a little corny, but it worked."

Mrs. Tucker had conquered her tears. She came forward and asked, "What will they do to him?"

"Peacock says he was insane, says something snapped in his brain due to worry, strain and overwork," Black replied.

"Will they be good to him?" she begged.

"Yes."

"Come, Cora," Abbie urged, "let me take you home."

"I'm sorry, Mrs. Tucker," Percy said. "You won't want to see me about your place. I'll arrange to move somewhere else."

"You had to do the right thing. I'll have your dinner ready for you as usual, but it will be a little late today," she warned.

Miss Nellie stepped forward. "You'll not be bothering your head about a meal today, Cora Tucker. Young man, it won't hurt you to eat at the hotel until tomorrow morning, will it?"

"Certainly not," Percy agreed.

"Then that's settled." Miss Nellie and Abbie took Mrs. Tucker between them and started up the aisle.

"It was smart work, Peacock," Black said. "Thanks a lot."

"I, too, am grateful," Eben said.

"Forget it, please," Percy said shyly. He turned to Perine, who was rather wistfully watching Stryke and Libby and asked, "When do we start rehearsing again?"

"Is he as good an actor as he is a detective?" Black asked, with a wink and a nod of his head toward Percy.

Perine smiled. "He's not a bad actor. He's very intelligent, reads his lines well." His eyes crinkled in merriment.

"What about rehearsals?" Percy demanded.

"Under the circumstances I think we ought to wait until after the funeral," Perine said with a glance toward Stryke and Libby.

"Right," Percy agreed. "That's the thing to do and all I wanted to know. I'm going to buy a few sandwiches and go down to the beach." He turned away.

"Hey, Percy!" Stryke called and ran toward him. "We're going to be married next week and we both want you to be the best man. How about it?"

"It's a date," Percy promised, and went on his way.

THE END

Resurrected Press Books in *The Chief Inspector Pointer Mystery* <u>Series</u>

Death of John Tait
Murder at the Nook
Mystery at the Rectory
Scarecrow
The Case of the Two Pearl Necklaces
The Charteris Mystery
The Eames-Erskine Case
The Footsteps that Stopped
The Clifford Affair
The Cluny Problem
The Craig Poisoning Mystery
The Net Around Joan Ingilby
The Tall House Mystery
The Wedding-Chest Mystery
The Westwood Mystery
Tragedy at Beechcroft

MYSTERIES BY ANNE AUSTIN

Murder at Bridge

When an afternoon bridge party attended by some of Hamilton's leading citizens ends with the hostess being murdered in her boudoir, Special Investigator Dundee of the District Attorney's office is called in. But one of the attendees is guilty? There are plenty of suspects: the victim's former lover, her current suitor, the retired judge who is being blackmailed, the victim's maid who had been horribly disfigured accidentally by the murdered woman, or any of the women who's husbands had flirted with the victim. Or was she murdered by an outsider whose motive had nothing to do with the town of Hamilton. Find the answer in... **Murder at Bridge**

One Drop of Blood

When Dr. Koenig, head of Mayfield Sanitarium is murdered, the District Attorney's Special Investigator, "Bonnie" Dundee must go undercover to find the killer. Were any of the inmates of the asylum insane enough to have committed the crime? Or, was it one of the staff, motivated by jealousy? And what was is the secret in the murdered man's past. Find the answer in... **One Drop of Blood**

- The Problem of Cell 13 by Jacques Futrelle
- The Conundrum of the Golf Links by Percy James Brebner
- The Silkworms of Florence by Clifford Ashdown
- The Gateway of the Monster by William Hope Hodgson
- The Affair at the Semiramis Hotel by A. E. W. Mason
- The Affair of the Avalanche Bicycle & Tyre Co., LTD by Arthur Morrison

RESURRECTED PRESS CLASSIC MYSTERY CATALOGUE

Journeys into Mystery
Travel and Mystery in a More Elegant Time

The Edwardian Detectives
Literary Sleuths of the Edwardian Era

Gems of Mystery
Lost Jewels from a More Elegant Age

E. C. Bentley
Trent's Last Case: The Woman in Black

Ernest Bramah
Max Carrados Resurrected:
The Detective Stories of Max Carrados

Agatha Christie
The Secret Adversary
The Mysterious Affair at Styles

Octavus Roy Cohen
Midnight

Freeman Wills Croft
The Ponson Case
The Pit Prop Syndicate

J. S. Fletcher
The Herapath Property
The Rayner-Slade Amalgamation
The Chestermarke Instinct
The Paradise Mystery
Dead Men's Money

The Middle of Things
Ravensdene Court
Scarhaven Keep
The Orange-Yellow Diamond
The Middle Temple Murder
The Tallyrand Maxim
The Borough Treasurer
In the Mayor's Parlour
The Saftey Pin

R. Austin Freeman
*The Mystery of 31 New Inn from the Dr. Thorndyke
Series*
*John Thorndyke's Cases from the Dr. Thorndyke
Series*
The Red Thumb Mark from The Dr. Thorndyke Series
The Eye of Osiris from The Dr. Thorndyke Series
A Silent Witness from the Dr. John Thorndyke Series
The Cat's Eye from the Dr. John Thorndyke Series
*Helen Vardon's Confession: A Dr. John Thorndyke
Story*
As a Thief in the Night: A Dr. John Thorndyke Story
*Mr. Pottermack's Oversight: A Dr. John Thorndyke
Story*
*Dr. Thorndyke Intervenes: A Dr. John Thorndyke
Story*
The Singing Bone: The Adventures of Dr. Thorndyke
The Stoneware Monkey: A Dr. John Thorndyke Story
*The Great Portrait Mystery, and Other Stories: A
Collection of Dr. John Thorndyke and Other Stories*
The Penrose Mystery: A Dr. John Thorndyke Story
The Uttermost Farthing: A Savant's Vendetta

Arthur Griffiths
The Passenger From Calais
The Rome Express

Fergus Hume
The Mystery of a Hansom Cab
The Green Mummy
The Silent House
The Secret Passage

Edgar Jepson
The Loudwater Mystery

A. E. W. Mason
At the Villa Rose

A. A. Milne
The Red House Mystery
Baroness Emma Orczy
The Old Man in the Corner

Edgar Allan Poe
The Detective Stories of Edgar Allan Poe

Arthur J. Rees
The Hampstead Mystery
The Shrieking Pit
The Hand In The Dark
The Moon Rock
The Mystery of the Downs

Mary Roberts Rinehart
Sight Unseen and The Confession

Dorothy L. Sayers
Whose Body?

Sir William Magnay
The Hunt Ball Mystery

Mabel and Paul Thorne
The Sheridan Road Mystery

Louis Tracy
The Strange Case of Mortimer Fenley
The Albert Gate Mystery
The Bartlett Mystery
The Postmaster's Daughter
The House of Peril
The Sandling Case: What Would You Have Done?
Charles Edmonds Walk
The Paternoster Ruby

John R. Watson
The Mystery of the Downs
The Hampstead Mystery

Edgar Wallace
The Daffodil Mystery
The Crimson Circle

Carolyn Wells
Vicky Van
The Man Who Fell Through the Earth
In the Onyx Lobby
Raspberry Jam
The Clue
The Room with the Tassels
The Vanishing of Betty Varian
The Mystery Girl
The White Alley
The Curved Blades
Anybody but Anne
The Bride of a Moment
Faulkner's Folly
The Diamond Pin
The Gold Bag
The Mystery of the Sycamore
The Come Backy

Raoul Whitfield
Death in a Bowl

And much more!
Visit ResurrectedPress.com
for our complete catalogue

About Resurrected Press

A division of Intrepid Ink, LLC, Resurrected Press is dedicated to bringing high quality, vintage books back into publication. See our entire catalogue and find out more at www.ResurrectedPress.com.

About Intrepid Ink, LLC

Intrepid Ink, LLC provides full publishing services to authors of fiction and non-fiction books, eBooks and websites. From editing to formatting, from publishing to marketing, Intrepid Ink gets your creative works into the hands of the people who want to read them. Find out more at www.IntrepidInk.com.

www.ingramcontent.com/pod-product-compliance
Lightning Source LLC
Chambersburg PA
CBHW070855250626
47159CB00003B/1073